FINAL DOWN

The Waiting Series Next Generation

by USA TODAY bestselling author
GINGER SCOTT

Final Down

The Waiting Series Next Generation
Book 3

Ginger Scott

For Arizona.

Chapter One

Wyatt

Twenty-eight doesn't feel old. Not until I get dragged by a bunch of footballers ten years younger than me. Then? Then it feels ancient.

"Arm sore, captain?" Reed catches me rotating my shoulder on the sideline after showing the Coolidge quarterbacks how to throw the cross route.

"I'm fine, old man. You keep your arthritis cream to yourself. I don't need it yet," I tease. Honestly, though? I could maybe use a little.

Spring ball at the high school is always a shit show. We get a lot of the hopefuls out, guys who probably shouldn't be in the game of football but always wanted to try, or their parents want them to play. We play touch in the spring, then seven-on-seven in the summer with flag rules, but tackles happen. Only the solid guys come out for that. We travel, so it's not worth the expense for guys who aren't serious about the game. It's where guys get the early college looks, too. It's what got me my offers.

"Hey, Coach Stone? Does this look broken?" Brady, a sophomore who should *not* come out for summer or fall, holds up his elbow. He's got a good raspberry. It's not even bleeding anymore.

I pat his helmet and smile.

"I think you'll be fine, Brady. Maybe check out the summer track program, though. You're fast as hell." He's decently fast. He's better at running than he is at throwing and catching. And at a buck-twenty, maybe, he's not built to take a tackle. I wouldn't feel right encouraging him to be out here.

"Yeah, I was thinking about it."

I'm glad to hear him say that.

"Well, if you do, I'll come to your meets."

"Okay." He nods and smiles.

I keep my promises to the kids. There are a few players I've encouraged to go other directions for safety reasons or their own mental health, and I always support their new paths. Kai, a guy who had one hell of a foot but was jittery under the pressure of Friday night lights, found a good home guarding the net for our soccer team. I've been to all his starts since he was a freshman. He's a senior now and looking to play in college.

"You're good with them—the young ones." Reed squints from the sun. It's hot out today.

"Thanks. Hey, maybe I'll get the head coaching gig when this old fossil retires," I jest.

He glowers at me, then snags a full cup of cold water from the bench and tosses it at my face.

"Ah, fuck. Okay, yeah. I deserved that." I wipe the droplets from my eyes and smooth back my hair before pushing my hat back on my head.

The spring guys are running laps, so Reed and I start to pick up. I've been coaching with him for five years now, since the combine came and went when I was twenty-three. I really thought I had it. We all did. But it wasn't my year. I'm not sure I would have been ready right out of college, anyhow. I have zero regrets, even though Peyton always asks if I do. I understand where she's coming from, but my life's work is making sure she never feels an ounce of guilt for anything. I made my choices then, and I'd make them again. Spending the year with her—every follow-up surgery, the work she put in—it was inspiring to the human spirit. Ain't no game of football that would give me that. And now that we're trying to have kids—man, I'm a lucky has-been, and I'm good with that.

But the competition? Yeah, I miss it a little. It's what makes coaching so satisfying. And I feel like I have a lot to teach. Hell, sometimes I learn more out here than the young guys do. The things I've added to my football IQ over the last five years sure would have served me well in college. Maybe it would have helped my combine showing too. Who knows?

"Well, I'll be damned. They'll really let anyone on campus, won't they?" Reed says.

I follow his gaze to the gate by the track. I haven't seen Bryce Hampton since he got drafted. I probably should have stayed in touch, but it was awkward, especially since he got the call and I didn't. And then he washed out in two years, and that felt *extremely* awkward.

"I guess that former Coolidge High QB title carries a lot of weight," Reed says, pulling his hat off and swinging an arm around Bryce.

Bryce rubs Reed's balding head, and I laugh, having done it myself a few times. Once today. Reed sneers at us both, then pushes his hat back on. He shaves what hair he's got up there, which is a good look on him, but it's harsh in the sun. At fifty-two, I'm glad he's not so proud that he doesn't take care of himself. Mostly. He still drinks too much beer, considering he has a family history of heart problems. His dad is still kicking, though, which is the point he always brings up when Nolan warns him off the red meat.

"Bryce, good to see ya, man," I say, pulling him in for a hug. His beard is thick, but it's patchy in places. Mine is better. I'll always be trying to one-up this dude.

"You're actually the reason I'm out here. You got a minute?" he says, glancing at Reed in a way that makes me feel as though he wants to chat with me alone.

"You know what? I'll get these little shits to finish picking up the field, then head in. Stop by the office before you leave, though. I want to catch up and hear all about what you're doing now."

Reed shakes Bryce's hand.

"For sure. I'll see you in a few minutes," Bryce says.

He drops his hands into the pockets of his slacks. He's wearing a deep gray polo and sunglasses that look expensive as shit.

"You look more like a golfer every day," I tease, leading him over to the bench. I offer him a paper cup of water, and he chuckles as he takes it.

"I'm probably a better golfer than NFL quarterback, so that's for the best," he says, tipping the cup back and gulping the water down.

"What's up?"

I take a seat on one end of the bench as he sits on the other, pulling his sunglasses off and tucking them in his collar. Leaning forward and balancing his elbows on his knees, his gaze swings in my direction. He breathes out a short laugh, his mouth pulled into a tight smile that I can't read.

"You talk to Jason lately?" he asks.

My chest tightens a little, and I shake my head.

"Not this week, but I mean, yeah. We've talked."

Bryce nods slowly, and I start to feel a little uneasy.

"What . . . Bryce, what's this about?"

He leans back, stretching an arm out along the back of the metal bench as he squints into the sun.

"You played that semi-league a few months back, with the Rattlers?"

I nod, then utter, "Yes." How does he know that? Is he stalking me? It's a minor, minor, minor league. I did it for fun, to hang out with Whiskey and see if I still had it. We won the league, and that meant five grand, which mostly went to taxes.

"Portland noticed," he says.

I stare at him until he turns his head my way and repeats his words slowly.

"Portland. They noticed." His eyebrows lift.

I tuck my chin and gurgle a belly laugh.

"Yeah, they're all up on the Tyler, Texas news, I'm sure. I bet they've got a whole list of QBs staring down thirty."

"Not a list. A name," he says, and I realize he's fucking serious.

"Bryce, I'm . . . I can't hang with that anymore."

Can I?

He stands up and pulls a card out of his wallet, handing it to me. It's the same firm Jason's at. He's an agent now. He's dead serious. This conversation is really happening.

"Think about it. Give me a call in a couple of days."

He slides his sunglasses on and turns halfway, gazing out on the field as he nods at distant memories.

"Those were some pretty great games, weren't they?"

"Which ones?" I ask, feeling the sharp edges of his card press into the pads of my finger and thumb.

His head swivels back to me, his lip tipping up on one side with a faint laugh.

"All of them, Wyatt. All of them."

He holds up a hand, and I do too.

"Call me," he says.

I think I answer, "I will." I'm not sure if that was out loud, though. And I'm not sure I told the truth if it was. Will I? Do I even want to entertain this?

I glance to my right, where Reed is pointing toward the storage shed, directing the gangly group of freshmen to stack the pads neatly. I chuckle silently as I watch—they're too short to stack them. Reed knows it, too. He's fucking with them.

I stand up and stuff Bryce's card into the pocket of my joggers and rotate my arm a few more times. It's not sore. It's just . . . out of practice. Especially for throwing so many passes in a row. I wave to Reed as he looks my way, gesturing that I'll wheel in the cart full of balls. He gives me a thumbs up, then holds out an arm to sling over Bryce as he walks up beside him. I pick up a few stray balls and drop them into the basket, but keep one in my hand, rotating it with a short toss in the air repeatedly, until Bryce and Reed turn the corner and are out of sight.

Portland noticed, huh?

I had a good summer. It was a lot of fun. Mostly, it was a nice excuse for Peyt and I to get away with Tasha and Whiskey. Since they got married and had twins, double dates have been hard to manage, and getaways are impossible. But with the rental house in Texas and the summer off, it was a nice chance to escape and pretend we were young again.

And the lights. The night games under the lights felt . . .

I walk down the field, stop at the ten-yard line, and toss the ball in my hand a few more times before scanning the landscape for witnesses. Joey, the seventy-year-old guy who works in maintenance, is swapping out a trash bag by the bleachers, but he's not looking up.

I dig the toe of my shoe into the turf, testing how well my sneakers grip. These things are orthopedic, so not great. But they'll do.

With my eyes focused on the way the ball fits in my hand, I tune out the world around me and mentally put myself there—in the game. It's a clean snap and I fall back a few yards, checking the pocket, spotting my receivers, nodding to Keaton Jones as he pivots at the sideline and sprints to the fifty. The defense is rushing, so I have to spin and run wide right to buy more time. There are three seconds left. This is it—game on the line. One final play.

I sling the ball with all I've got and fall back a few steps, imagining the blow I'd take if this were real. The ball spins tight, cutting through the air, on track to hit Keaton mid-stride. Nobody's guarding him. It's a clear shot to the end zone.

My ball crashes into the middle of the cart, knocking it sideways and spilling the fifteen balls inside it in all different directions. My gaze pops up a tick to Joey, whistling with his fingers in his mouth.

"You still got it, Coach!" He waves, and I wave back.

I rotate my arm a few more times, expecting to feel something. And I do. I feel . . . good. Better than good. I jog to my mess and pick the balls up, tossing them in one at a time, but I keep one out and tuck it in under my bicep as I push the rest into the shed. I hold on to it as I hike across the parking lot to my truck, and I keep it nestled safely in my grasp as I stare out at the high school field of my old rival, where I now coach.

Portland noticed.

Chapter Two

Peyton

I should have followed my gut. Wyatt has a thing for red, and the red satin slip I was set to buy at the boutique made me feel sexy. But then my bestie got in my ear, talking up the value of the lacy black and gold bodice and panty set with cut-outs in all the naughty places. She insisted that spicing things up for the scheduled sexcapades might do the trick and turn that second line on the pee stick blue.

I've been trying to snap the last hook in place in the dead center of my spine for the last forty minutes, and all it's done is make me sweaty and given my bicep a cramp. The slip would have been so easy, and Wyatt would have looked at me with heat in his eyes. Because . . . *red*. Instead, he's going to have to help me finish dressing up just so I can lure him to take this stuff off.

The clank of keys on the counter downstairs jolts me from my last attempt. I laugh out a breath and flop on my back, the cool of the comforter against my skin a refreshing embrace.

"I'm upstairs!" I holler. I lift my chin and look down at my body, at the place where my skin puckers from the emergency surgery to remove a clot in my leg four years ago, then the way my belly sticks out between the lace panties and the hard ridge of the bodice. I don't exercise the way I used to. I can't. This is a disaster.

"Hey, sorry I'm late. I had an interesting practice, and—" Wyatt's hard stop as he stands in the now open doorway to our bedroom makes me bite my lip and hold my breath.

"Is that *good* shocked or *did you fall and can't get up* shocked?" I really can't tell from his speechless stare. And my low opinion of myself is leaning toward the latter.

"Uh, I'm pretty sure this is a *I suddenly love black and gold* stare," he says, pulling his Coolidge High T-shirt up over his head in one smooth motion as he moves toward the bed. In under a second, he's slipped his hands under my knees and pulled me to the edge of the bed. The movement knocks my breath away a little and I giggle, feeling a bit like a teenager, embarrassed for being so bold.

"Are you sure? I feel silly," I say, the sudden chill of cool air against my exposed pussy reminding me that these panties are crotchless. I cover my face with both palms, and my cheeks are hot. I should not have listened to Tasha.

Wyatt's hand covers mine, peeling my fingers away, his subtle grin pulling up one side of his mouth, his five o'clock shadow looking all sorts of inviting.

"You should definitely not feel silly, Peyt. You should feel a lot of things, which I'm about to make sure you do, but silly is not one of them. You are fucking . . ." He bites his lower lip and shakes his head as the dimple dents his right cheek. How can a man be both sexy and adorable at once?

"You better finish that sentence, Wyatt Stone. I'm fucking what?" Okay, the warmth is creeping into my body now. Maybe this outfit will do. And maybe my belly isn't quite as pudgy as I imagine. And maybe—

"Ahhh," I sigh out as Wyatt's thumb gently strokes between my legs. My knees part at his touch.

"I figured you were done listening to me talk," he hums, pushing my legs farther apart as he drops to his knees and brings his mouth to my skin. "Do you want me to talk? Or would you rather I . . ."

His tongue flicks against my tingling skin, and goose bumps rush down my legs. The sensation is enough to make me want to press my thighs into him and hold him hostage against me. He must sense my muscles twitching because his hands rush along the insides of my thighs, holding me apart for him to feast. And feast he does.

"Oh shit, Wy!" I arch my back as his tongue assaults me in the best way, wasting no time diving inside as his mouth covers the rest of me, suckling me in.

I bite my knuckles to stifle my cries, knowing full well that my mother is still working with the horses outside and could be passing between the guest house and their home any second now. Sure, we're married. Five years in. And yeah, my parents know we have sex and blah, blah, blah. The thought of one of them *hearing* us still makes my cheeks go beet red.

"Come here," Wyatt commands, slipping a hand under the arch of my back and holding my lower body tight as he buries his face between my thighs.

I lift on my palms, no longer worried about the missing hook on the back of the bodice. I move my right hand into Wyatt's hair, gripping the long waves and holding him to me as the first wave of pleasure threatens to knock me back again. He flicks his tongue against my pulsing pussy, forcing me to take every single incredible second that passes until I'm soaking wet and exhausted.

"I hope you saved some of that for my cock," Wyatt says,

running his forearm along his mouth to wipe away my wetness as he stands and tugs down his joggers and boxers.

"I hope *you* saved the important stuff for making a baby," I say, unable to help myself from reminding both of us of the mission at hand.

Wyatt's eyes flicker as his gaze hits mine, and my heart patters like a drum break. I don't want to make sex feel like a job, but I can't help constantly dwelling on the end goal. It's *all* I think about. I want a baby more than I wanted to walk after my accident. Wyatt hates that it's been a struggle for us, and he worries about how anxious it makes me.

His gaze drifts down the center of my chest as his hand wraps around his shaft. I fall back on my elbows, forcing myself to stay in the heat of the moment, to not drift back to the self-conscious thoughts about how my clothes fit, or rather *don't* fit.

"I like this." He doesn't bring his gaze up to mine. Instead, his heated stare locks on the small cutouts on either side of the bodice that expose my pebbled nipples.

"Oh, this part?" I hum, lying on my back and circling my hard tips with my thumbs. I pinch myself on either side, pulling my tits up and letting myself enjoy the rush of pleasure.

"Yeah, I like that part," Wyatt says, swatting my hands out of the way. He quickly tugs on my right nipple with his thumb and index finger, coaxing my back to arch again.

The tip of Wyatt's cock brushes against my pussy as he pinches my nipple again, and I whimper loudly. I don't even care who hears me. I've let myself get lost. I'm fully in this, not for the results but for the instant gratification. For the intimacy. For having this man who has only grown more chiseled, more worn, rougher, and rugged. Wyatt has me drunk with need, and I deserve to be. Right now, I'm nothing more than a woman who wants to *feel.* And when Wyatt slides inside of me with a hard thrust, I . . . feel . . . everything.

"Wy!" I cry out as he rocks his hips, sliding out of me completely before driving in again.

"I need to touch you," he growls, ripping the bodice open. The fragile hooks that I spent an hour trying to connect tear apart as he pulls the bodice down so he can cup my full breasts in both of his palms. His body leans into me, his hips thrusting as he swells inside of me, and I fall over the edge again just as my insides warm with his cum.

My fingertips trace the ridges along his muscular back, his skin sticky with perspiration as he pumps into me until he's empty and exhausted. His heavy body pins me to the bed, and I wrap my legs around him to hold him to me for a few extra moments. I love it when he lingers inside of me, and yeah, partly because my mind wanders to the possibility of this being the moment our baby is made. But it's also the familiar fullness he gives me, the perfect fit of our bodies together. The years have only made our bodies match one another more.

Wyatt lifts himself up, resting on his forearms as he presses his lips to the center of my chest. He kisses his way to my right breast, sucking on my nipple one last time and leaving it with a soft bite before blowing it cool.

My hands move to his jaw, cupping his cheeks as my thumbs feel along the rough stubble that carves around his chin. He lifts his head enough to meet my eyes, then turns his mouth into my palm, kissing my wrist.

"I may have ruined that top part," he says with a playful wince. "Sorry."

"It's okay. It didn't really fit anyway."

His eyes squint as his head tilts a hint.

"Don't do that." He pulls his lips in tight and shakes his head slightly.

"What?" I know what—but it's embarrassing to be called out for not loving your own body. Maybe embarrassing isn't the right word. Maybe it's painful. And I know his reprimand comes from a place of love, but it still causes a hard stop in my chest to hear it.

Wyatt crawls up my body until my shoulders and head are caged between his arms. He drops his forehead to mine, and my eyes flutter shut.

"You're beautiful," he says, and I force a smile on my face because it's not his fault I don't completely believe it for myself.

"Thank you," I mutter, lifting my chin enough to press my lips to his.

Our chaste kiss lingers for a few seconds before my phone begins buzzing on the nightstand. I blink my eyes open as Wyatt pulls away, shifting to sit next to me. He grabs my phone and lets out a heavy sigh, turning it to flash Tasha's photo my way.

"Hey, at least she didn't call five minutes earlier. She's getting better," I joke, taking the phone from him and answering her call.

"Hey, Tash."

I barely have time to get her name out before the words start rushing out of her. I smack Wyatt's bare ass as he gets out of bed, and he rolls his shoulders and neck before shooting me a tempting glare.

"Don't start the engine when you can't drive," he teases, his lips puckering for an air kiss as he makes his way toward our bathroom.

"Are you even listening to me?"

I roll to my side and move my phone to my other ear.

"Yeah, sorry. I was just talking to Wyatt."

I brace myself for her usual interrogation and jokes about interrupting us during sex. She thinks her timing is funny.

"So, he told you, then? I mean, this is wild, right? Portland? I couldn't believe it when Bryce called Whisk, but I mean, it is what he's wanted. He's been working so hard. And he's not that old for a lineman. He has a lot of good years left, and he's probably in better shape now than he was in college, and—"

"Wait, Portland . . . as in . . . for football? Tash, that's amazing!"

I may have missed more of her early conversation than I admit to. Is Whiskey getting his shot with the new expansion team? He's wanted this for so long, and I could tell when he and Wyatt played in that summer league in Texas how much football was still a part of him. Honestly, it was incredible seeing the two of them on the field again together. I think it meant a lot to Wyatt, too. He says he has no regrets, but I see the way he lingers on the field after practices. He reminds me of my dad when he finally left the game. It's a bit like grieving.

"Yeah, didn't Wyatt tell you where? Maybe he's getting to that."

I sit up and snag a T-shirt from the floor, slipping it on so I don't feel like a total hooker walking around the house.

"No, he didn't tell me about that. He just got home, though, so—"

"Oh, shoot! Okay, well, pretend I didn't say anything. He probably wants to tell you himself. So, act surprised. Really sell it."

"Ohhhh-kayyyy." My mouth twists into a wry smile because it doesn't seem like that big of a deal. I mean, yeah, we both love Whiskey, and I'm sure he's excited to tell me about his friend's big break. But I don't know that he cares if Tasha beat him to it.

"We have so much to plan! Do you want to fly out together? We could get a vacation rental again, like Texas. Oh, my God, this is so exciting! The boys are back! NFL wives . . . together!"

My mouth freezes, along with the words caught in my throat. My lips hang open as I work backward from my friend's last ramblings, unable to catch up in time to respond before she hits me with, "Yeah, call me later. I want to hear all about what Bryce said to Wyatt. I guess the Portland coach was really impressed. Okay, love you!"

My hand falls to my side along with my phone. The shutters are opened to show off the sky across the room, and I stare at the pink clouds that peek through the top few slats. I can't even blink.

The shower shuts off, and I turn my head just enough to see Wyatt's form step from the shower as he wraps a towel around his waist. I'm finding it hard to breathe, my mind racing in two polar-opposite directions—wanting to hold on to blissful hope that my husband and I just made a baby, and preparing myself for his big news. I didn't even know he was trying to make a comeback, that he wanted to give it another shot. And if he leaves, what does that mean for us? For our not-quite-yet-real family? What if we miss our chance?

"What did my favorite friend of yours want?" He steps around me, stopping in front of me as he runs his hands through his wet hair.

"She, uh," I let out a short laugh, blinking my gaze to meet his. "She said Portland is giving Whiskey a tryout."

His hands drop to the back of his neck, threading together as his eyes lock on mine. He's never been able to lie to me. It's one of the things I love most about *us*. And right now, his eyes are telling me everything—Tasha's right. Portland wants him, too.

His hands fall to his sides as his chin drops a tick. He chews at the inside of his cheek, his forehead etched with worry lines.

"You already know. And before you question anything, I was going to tell you. I got a little— He waves a hand between us as he chuckles.

"Distracted," I answer for him.

"Ha, yeah. Just a little." His gaze drops to the floor, and he lifts his shoulders.

"Do you want this?" My voice sounds more panicked than it should. It's not fair. I can't mask it, though.

He shrugs again.

"I don't know. Honestly? Right now, I wish Bryce had never shown up, and that I never agreed to play in that summer league with Whisk. But it's too late to undo any of that, so I guess . . ."

"You guess . . ."

His eyes snap back to mine, and for the first time since we were kids and he was trying to find his way as the new kid in town, Wyatt Stone looks lost.

He moves toward me, stepping between my knees and wrapping his arms around my head, hugging me with my cheek against his stomach. His head falls forward enough for him to press his lips to the crown of my hair, and long, weighted breaths fill his lungs and stay there.

"Tell me what to do, Peyt? Cuz I don't know. I just don't know."

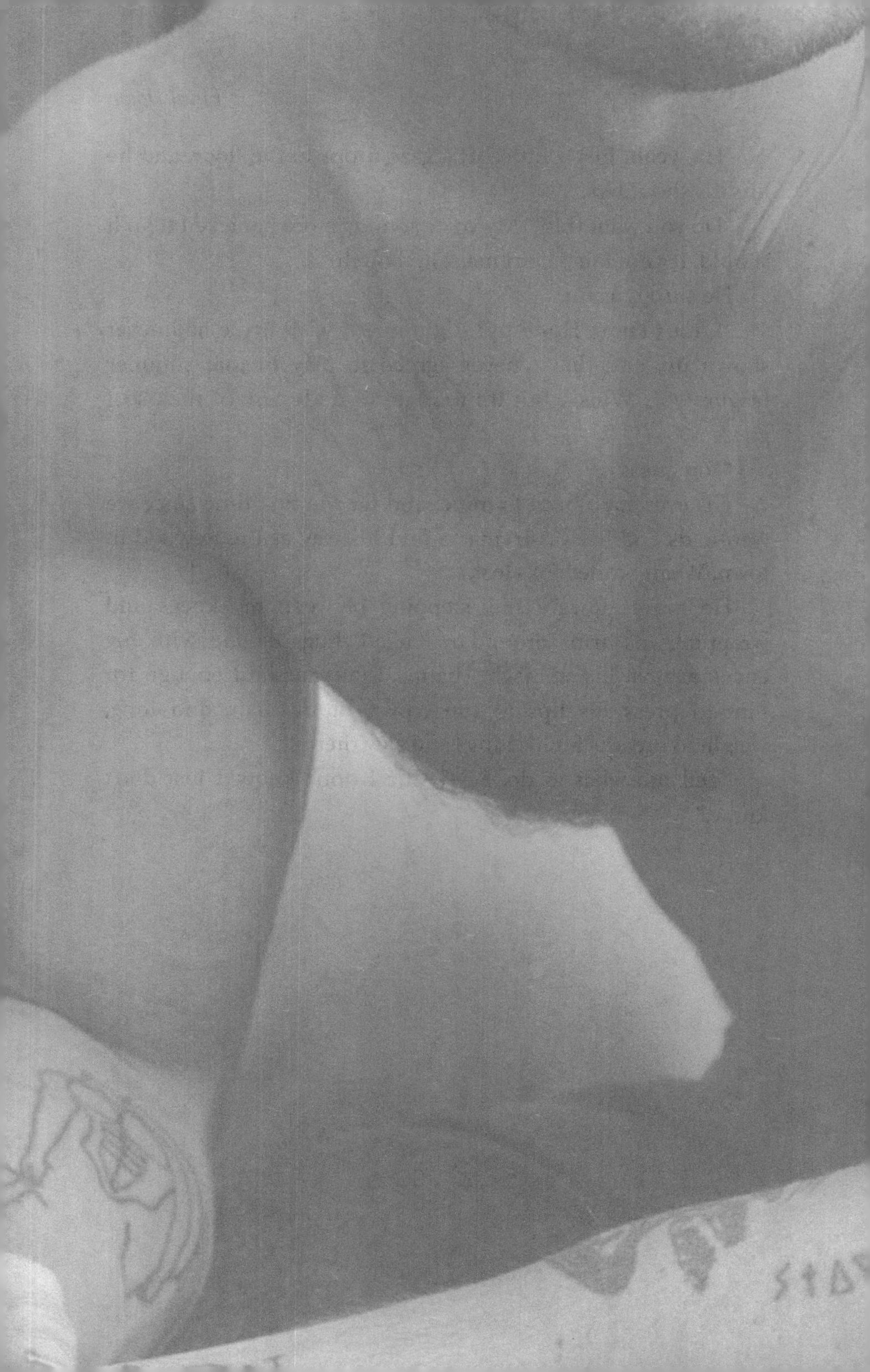

Chapter Three

Wyatt

It's times like these when I really miss my dad. I didn't inherit his decision-making skills. He was decisive, confident, somehow always right, yet never an asshole about it.

That's one of my favorite qualities about Peyton. It's a piece of my father that I see alive in her, like a gift he sent me—someone who knows what they want out of life. But she can't help me with this. And really, even if my father were here, he wouldn't be able to make the choice for me, either. He'd guide me, but ultimately, the path I drive in this life comes down to me.

It's not just *my* life, though, and that's what's got me stuck.

"You're making eggs. You do that when you're working out aggression." Peyton's bicep flexes as she whisks the seven yolks I watched her drop into the mixing bowl. I was planning on grabbing an apple on my way out this morning, but she was awake well before me and insisted on making breakfast.

She quirks a brow as she glances at me over her shoulder, arm still flexed, whisk . . . *whisking*.

"You know what gives me aggression?"

I shake my head, but I have a feeling it's me. Right now. That's what.

"People pointing out when I have aggression when all I'm doing is making some goddamn eggs." Her slow, single blink is the cherry on top. Yeah. Zero aggression.

"Sorry," I sigh, dropping my face into my palms and rubbing my tired eyes.

We talked through the scenarios for hours last night. I found out about Whiskey getting the shot on my way home from practice. Having my best friend with me nudges me in the direction of wanting to give this a try. I also have a lingering worry that Whiskey's opportunity hinges on me to a certain degree. Like, if I don't show up, his invite gets revoked. It feels arrogant to think that, but Peyton voiced the same worry last night.

"He's going to want an answer today. You know that, right? If not a definitive one, at least a promising update so he knows you're taking this seriously." A plate slides in front of me as I uncover my eyes. I snag Peyton's hand in mine before she flits back to the stove, where she is definitely not aggravated.

She drops her chin to her chest as her hand relaxes in my hold. I massage her fingers with both of my hands and hold her gaze hostage. It softens, probably because my eyes look something like those of a drowning puppy. I can feel how puffy and red they are without needing a mirror to confirm it.

"Babe, I told you I'm behind you, no matter what," she says, sliding a hand through my hair, then down my jawline.

I close my eyes and shift my cheek against her palm until my lips find her wrist. I kiss it and let out the small bit of air left in my lungs.

"I don't deserve you, you know that?"

She bends down as she tips my chin up and kisses me.

"Wyatt, you're the only man who does. And that's a fact."

She holds my stare for a beat, then squeezes my cheeks in her grip before leaving me to tend to the massive omelet she's making.

The two of us eat in silence. Not a tense one, but a heavy one, regardless. There's nothing more to say until I decide. We'd just be kicking around the same ideas, talking in circles, predicting and worrying, hoping and hedging.

Peyton said she supports me almost immediately when we started to talk last night. Still, it's that flash that passed behind her eyes after Tasha called that sticks with me—the worry of what our lives would look like if I took this chance, and more pointedly, what it means for a future family. *Our* future family.

I finish my breakfast and carry my dish to the sink, rinsing it off and smirking when I hear the little sigh Peyton lets out behind me about a second before she swoops in and shuts the water off.

"The point of the dishwasher is that it washes these for us. Don't wash to wash."

She's already putting my plate and hers in the dishwasher before she's done griping. She stands up, flipping her hair from her face and blowing up at the strands that sometimes stick to her cheeks in the morning, and I help her push them out of the way before holding her face in my hands. She catches my smirk and rolls her eyes.

"You do that just to watch me get all huffy, don't you?"

I glance up and to the right, my mouth tugging up on one side.

"Maybe."

She pushes my chest gently but easily gives in to the kiss I pull her in for.

"I'm off to pick your dad's brain. He's always in his office early. And I'm sure he already knows all about this."

I'm a little surprised he hasn't called, to be honest. But then again, if anyone understands the weight of this decision—whether to put my body through the grind or not—it's Reed.

"You may as well plan to sit with Grampa for about an hour later, too. You know he has opinions."

I meet her smirk and let out a soft laugh.

"First, that chat will be more than an hour, and somehow devolve into your grandmother pulling out the highlight DVDs from your dad's high school days. Then I'll be on the floor again, figuring out how to get the damn DVD player to connect to his television, and probably end up hurting myself, which . . . I guess . . . results in not having to make a choice." I flash my hands in the air between us, like a headline. "Promising quarterback taken out of the game by ancient technology."

Peyton laughs hard enough that her head kicks back, and for a moment, my lungs fill. I love that sound. Her eyes dazzle when she rights her head again and meets my gaze. And for a tiny moment, I believe everything she's said since finding out—that no matter what, she and I? We'll be all right.

I'm not sure what to make of the fact Reed isn't in his office when I pull into my usual parking spot, but rather is throwing balls from the caddy through the targets on the field. For a man in his fifties, he's still got one hell of an arm.

I kill my truck's engine and fold my arms over the steering wheel to watch him for a minute. I've seen his highlights enough to know his movements by heart. It's been thirty-plus years of throwing, and I don't know that he's lost a step. At least, not when the defenders are invisible figments of his imagination.

He's lost in his past, I think, and it's kind of fun to watch. He pulls a ball from the caddy and steps back a few yards before pretending to take a snap. His feet seem so light on the turf as he falls back before spinning to his right and rushing toward the sideline. My mouth inches up at the corners as I anticipate his moves, his arm dropping to that signature three-quarter slot as he slings the ball practically side-armed and into the target net about twenty yards away. He fakes a jump-shot, then claps his hands like he's still in the game, under the lights, hearing the crowd.

I step out of my truck and push my fingers into my mouth to let out a whistle. When Reed jerks his head around and spots me, I clap above my head. He laughs me off and pinches the bridge of his nose, probably a little embarrassed that he got caught—*by me.*

My truck beeps as I press the fob to lock it, and I jog to the field to help Reed pick up the balls.

"Let me guess, you heard Portland was looking for a quarterback?" I joke, figuring he knows all about my invitation. He chuckles.

"Little competition is good for everyone, right? You don't mind going up against me for the gig, do you?" The weight of his palm as it slaps my back would be enough to take me out of the running if I thought he was serious. Of course, he's not. But I have a feeling this little exercise he's in the middle of is part of a bigger point he plans on making.

"Who told you?" I squint as the sun hits my eyes over his shoulder.

"You mean first? Because Bryce couldn't help himself yesterday. I don't think we made it all the way to my office before he blabbed about it. And then, well, ya know . . . Whiskey called. And that wife of his. And Jason and I met up for a beer last night, so you could say I've gotten most of the angles covered. I mean, except yours, of course. And my daughter's. You two have been remarkably mum about the news, which makes me wonder—"

"Well, keep wondering," I laugh out. He joins me, getting it. I'm lucky to have Reed in my life. He's not my father, but I know they would have been like brothers. There is so much about them that's the same. And Reed sees me in ways that only a man who's been in my shoes can.

We push the caddy to the sideline, then take a seat on the middle bench, both of us leaning forward and resting our elbows on our knees as we knead our hands.

"What's Peyton think?" He swivels his head to meet my gaze.

I shrug.

"She says she supports me no matter what."

Reed shakes with a short laugh.

"Well, shit. That's not helpful at all, is it?"

I shake my head.

"No, sir. Not in the least."

I sit up straight and grip the bench on either side of me, shifting my focus to the golden light coloring the tips of the ripe spinach and kale fields on the other side of the fence. There aren't many farms left in Coolidge, but I hope this one stays. I can't imagine sitting here one day and seeing rooftops or a block wall around a shopping center. It won't hit the same.

"You probably came out here early thinking I'd be able to get your head straight." The way he says it hits my chest with a thud. Something about his tone tells me Reed's not going to be able to give me any answers, either.

"How did you decide? I mean, when you went in the draft, and when you left the game. All of it." I squint one eye as I look at him. His eyes meet mine as he softly chuckles.

"Nolan." He shrugs, as if it's that simple. It's not. It can't be.

"Nah, there had to be something else."

He shakes his head as he gets to his feet. He takes a ball from the cart and tosses it up a few times before throwing it to me. I catch it against my chest, still baffled. *More* baffled, in fact.

"Deep down, when the time is right, it will hit you," he says, moving back a few steps with his hands held out. I stand and throw the ball back to him.

"And when is that right time? Is it soon? Because I don't think Bryce has the cache to buy me loads of time."

Reed slings the ball back to me with a laugh.

"You know now; it's just your head can't get out of your own damn way. My guess is, sometime around dinner, you'll figure this out."

I throw the ball back, pretty sure my father-in-law smoked a little weed this morning. He's making zero sense.

"All I can tell you, Wyatt, is that nothing in my life was ever really my own choice. I know that looking back. Everything that happened to me was either the game's call or Nolan's. I was simply a man good at throwing a ball and fairly decent at being a husband and a parent. But I'll tell you one thing." He jogs back a few steps and tosses me the ball again. "If I weren't fifty-two and in need of a knee replacement, I'd absolutely leap at the chance to have that feeling in my chest again."

I slap the ball with my opposite hand and clutch it at my chest as I nod in question.

"And what feeling is that?"

Reed's head falls back as his grin spreads.

"Game day, on a pro-level, is like nothing else. On any field. But on a *home* field? It's downright euphoric. Running out to the huddle, being the guy. You know? *The guy.* It's like starring in your own damn movie, the way it all happens in slow motion, and the way you get to write and direct the script. For three hours on the gridiron, there's nothing but you and the game. All the other noise in life takes a rest. And sure, that stuff doesn't go away. It's waiting for you when you take the pads off. It's there when you hang up the cleats. But for a few hours every week in the fall and winter, I got to be a superhero. I don't know if I'd be the man I am right now without having gone through it. Who knows, maybe I would be a better man. But I wouldn't be *this* man."

He flattens his palm on his chest, and my own heart beats harder. I'm imagining it all, the feeling he described, the way the crowd sounds, the faces of young kids wearing my jersey. The glory is awfully tempting.

"It comes with sacrifice; I won't lie to you. It takes a toll on the body, sure, but you're also going to miss things off the field. First words, first steps, dance recitals, Little League games . . ."

My heart cracks at his examples. I don't want to miss those things. My dad did sometimes, and I remember all the big moments I wish he had been there for—and he wasn't a professional athlete. He was a firefighter.

"Hey, Coach Stone?"

Brady's voice pulls me out of my spiral, and I'm grateful to see my favorite skinny sophomore right now.

"Hey, man. What's up?" I toss the ball to him, and he fumbles it. Reed and I exchange a glance, in complete agreement that this kid does not belong on the fall roster.

"Uh, I was hoping to talk for a minute. I . . ." He drops the ball again. It rolls my direction, so I hold up a hand and pick it up myself.

"Sure, what can I do for you?" I toss the ball to Reed and take a seat on the bench. Brady joins me while my father-in-law goes back to reliving his glory days. Brady is completely uninterested in watching him show off, which sort of amuses me.

"I wanted to find out how to turn in my spring jersey? I think . . . if it's okay with you, I mean . . . I'd like to try track and field?" He's vibrating with nerves, and I feel bad that he seems to be afraid of disappointing me. If anything, his decision gives me relief.

"Absolutely, Brady. I think you might just be a stand-out on the track. Your times out here are solid."

Brady's proud and hopeful expression flashes up from his lap to meet my gaze.

"Really?" His face puzzles, but the smile is itching to be set free.

"Oh, yeah. You are always in the top ten for time. And if you don't have to hold on to a ball when you run, imagine how fast you're going to be." It's not so much the ball as the defender running at him that slows him down. The ball, however, is also problematic for this kid.

His grin inches higher.

"Yeah, that's what I was thinking. Anyway, I spoke with Coach Skye, and she said I could work out with them as they finish up the season, then maybe pick it up again for the summer. You think . . . maybe you'd come to a meet?"

I give Brady a half smirk. I did promise him I would.

"Wouldn't miss it," I say, reaching out a hand to shake on the deal. His long, thin fingers wrap around my palm, and his fist pumps with a decent shake. Not bad for a kid with zero body fat.

"Just drop the jersey off when—"

Brady is already pulling it out of his backpack, so I snap my mouth shut.

"Got it. Well, you're all set, then," I say. It's strange, but the same warmth that coats my chest when one of our quarterbacks finally gets something I've been teaching him is settling inside me now. Maybe I just like the idea of guiding someone.

Brady nods again, somehow seeming taller. I bet he's been carrying the weight of forcing himself into football ever since he started spring ball. I wonder if his uncle pushed him into it.

He was a player here after Reed graduated, and was kind of a superstar on the high school level.

I watch the kid head back up the hill toward the library, every step a little longer, his bounce higher. I want to feel like that. I'm just not sure which path comes with the light, puffy clouds, and which one has the gray, gloomy kind.

"You know, if you're in Portland, you won't be making many of those meets," Reed breaks in behind me.

My shoulders sag, but only briefly before I turn to face him.

"Oh, not true. Track is in spring. After the Super Bowl. I can make 'em all."

It's partly a joke. Mostly a comeback to my father-in-law's usual quick wit. But it's also the first time I've spoken as if this new future is a possibility. And that has both of us a bit stalled for conversation. It also puts a bit of a smug grin on Reed's face.

Deep down, when the time is right, it will hit you.

I've known all along.

Chapter Four

Peyton

My entire life, my mom has read me as clearly as an oversized eye chart. And the older I get, the easier it has become for me to read her right back.

She hasn't come out and directly asked what Wyatt's decision is, which is good since I have no clue myself, but she is dancing around the topic with expert finesse. I'm not sure why she's kid-gloving the topic with me.

"It's been forever since we've taken a family trip anywhere," she says, letting the spoken thought linger in the air as she tugs on the cinch to make sure Otis is set for our morning rider.

"Okay, I give. Are you itching for a family cruise or something?" I know what she's itching for—information. I'm simply curious what route she's taking this time to get at it. A vacation is an interesting tactic.

"Oh! A cruise is a great idea. You know, Aunt Sarah went on one of those Alaskan ones last fall. She said it was breathtaking. She saw whales!" The way her eyebrows shoot up at the word *whales* when our gazes meet sends me over the edge, and I can't contain the laughter any longer. I bury my face against my forearm as I lean against Otis's side. My eyes are watering, I'm so amused.

"What?"

I lift my head in time to catch the forced quizzical expression she's putting on. This time, I snort, I laugh so hard.

"Peyton, I'm not sure what you think is so funny about whales, but—"

"Mom, stop. Please, just . . ."

I hold out an open palm to buy time to catch my breath, dropping my gaze to the dirt as I suck in a deep breath to calm the itch in my chest. With my outburst under control, I lift my chin and meet my mom's eyes. She seems to have given up on her bad acting, her sheepish expression rather guilty looking.

"I want to make sure you're doing okay with it all," she finally admits.

"I know, but really? All the *fall* questions—first asking if we want to look at places of our own starting in August? Then . . . whaling? And what was that bit in the barn about how we should take the Cardinals up on the season ticket offer and go to some games? You *hate* stadium crowds. You may as well come out and ask whether Wyatt will be around this fall. Or, and I know this is a ground-breaking idea, you could ask if he's made up his mind yet. Maybe try direct?"

My mom's mouth quirks up on one side with a guilty grin.

"Okay, so maybe I was a little passive aggressive—"

"Passive. Like a snail," I correct.

She purses her lips and holds Otis's reins against her hip.

"Okay, point taken. I was being sensitive. I remember what it's like." Her gaze softens, and in that small, quiet moment, I finally get why she's been careful with me. She's not worried about Wyatt playing again. She's worried about me, and the element this adds to our family plan.

"I think he really wants this," I admit. My eyes tear up with the emotional release of finally speaking it out loud.

"It's okay if you don't," my mom says. She always has the right words. How does she do that?

I laugh through my tears, sniffling and blinking away the moisture before I get in too deep and full-on cry.

"I'm not sad, Mom. I swear," I spill out. She moves to stand next to me, her palm warm at the center of my back. I swivel into her and wrap my arms around her, blotting my cheeks dry over her shoulder.

"I understand," she says, using that word again. And it's true. I know she does. She's been here. Year after year. It's why I fought this life so hard, because I watched my mom cry these same tears out here in the arena when my dad signed a new contract or got traded to a new team.

"Is it okay to both want and *not* want this?" I laugh out as I break our embrace.

"Abso-fucking-lutely," my mom affirms, and my shoulders drop, feeling the release with her permission. It's silly, but there's something powerful in being told it's okay to feel wildly different from moment to moment.

The slam of a car door in the distance draws our attention to the circular driveway by the barn. Our morning client is in recovery from a spinal injury, and today is his first time with a horse, which is why we pulled out Otis. He's a gentle soul, and when I share how significant he was in giving me emotional strength, it has a way of reigniting dimmed fires. I think Otis can do the same for Macon, a young college guy whose world changed when a drunk driver side-swiped his bike as he was on his way to his morning class about six months ago.

"It's going to happen for you, Peyt. When the time is right. You're going to make an incredible mom."

I quiver from my mom's words, but steel myself, not willing to turn the tears on again.

"Thanks, Mom," I simply say.

It takes Macon several minutes to make his way to us, his steps aided by the walker he's going to need to rely on for a little while longer. The urge to move toward him and help twitches in my muscles, but Mom and I stay put. Knowing how independent a person wants to be during their sessions with us is something I've made sure we include in the onboarding for new clients. I know how important it was to me that I took steps on my own, and having people hover, wanting to help, is both frustrating and enabling. It's easy to get in a habit of leaning on others, and that's not to say having people there to lean on isn't just as important. It is. But doing something on my own was equally vital, if not more. And for Macon, getting from point A to point B is a challenge he wants to conquer every time he faces it. He's already making the trip to us faster than the first time we met, when we showed him what the arena looks like and walked him through our program. Like before, his mom waits in the driver's seat of her sedan. I give her a wave, and she smiles as she waves back.

Macon's neck tendons strain with his final few steps, but when he reaches us, the exhausted smile on his face is a good sign that the effort was worth it.

"Let me guess, time's up! I need to head back to the car?" he jokes, his breathing hard.

Macon's a handsome guy, only twenty-one. He probably envisioned spending his free time at football games or in bars, flirting with girls on campus—not hanging out with two old married women and a horse. But here we are. It's good that he can be funny. That will help him in unexpected ways. Humor always did for me.

"Well, I fed Otis extra carrots this morning, so after fifteen minutes on this gassy boy, you may find you can make the trip out of here in half the time," my mom teases. *Sort of.* Otis does have his fair share of stomach distress.

"Noted," Macon says.

I take his walker for him as he shifts his balance and grips the straps on Otis's saddle. My mom goes through the introductions to Otis, familiarizing the two of them with one another, and I look on as I park his walker by the gate. I love watching the magic happen, and it always does. I didn't always get it when I was a kid. I knew my mom taught people to ride, but I didn't fully grasp the reason. I was too busy living in my own head back then, a spoiled girl who grew up on a ranch and had so much privilege that she didn't appreciate.

My sister, Ellie, is in that phase right now—*the world is unfair, we're all embarrassing, and everything we do as a family is stupid.* It's knowing how my mind worked at thirteen that has me eyeing her extra close lately. Like I am now. I've noticed she hasn't ridden her bike by us yet this morning on her way to school. I'm sure my mom has noticed, too. *Nothing* gets by our mom. But thirteen is hard. It's been a while since my mom was thirteen. And I'm starting to wonder if there's something more to my sister's abrasive attitude beyond the obvious hormones drowning her emotions.

"Hey, you okay if I check on her?" I holler to my mom.

Our eyes meet for a breath, and my mom chews at the inside of her cheek for a second before nodding toward the house.

"I'll be right back, Macon," I say, knowing he couldn't care less if I'm around or not. Otis is the star of the show. They've bonded. It happens in a blink.

My body aches today, more than normal. I've battled spasticity throughout my recovery, and some days are better than others. The way my muscles decide to spasm and tighten randomly is one of those inconveniences I doubt I'll ever fully be able to handle, but I've made huge mental strides with it. There are times, however, when I still think everything should work the way it used to. Peak performance at all times, minus the normal aches and pains. But what is normal anyway? That's what my mom's always preached. And if you ask me, the fact I can walk on my hands, tumble, and ride the horses when I need to escape for a little while is pretty peak.

I expect to hear my sister's latest musical obsession blaring from upstairs, but when I enter the house, it's incredibly quiet. She's taken to faking sick a lot lately, something I never really did, and that's what has my internal worry alarms set to sensitive. I know my mom's are, too, even though she hasn't said so.

I tiptoe my way down the hallway when I reach the top of the stairs, my ears primed for clues. I press my ear to Ellie's door, listening for signs that she's awake, and am relieved when I hear water running in her bathroom sink. I rap on the door and move my hand to the knob.

"Ellie? Can I come in?"

She doesn't answer, but the sink faucet shuts off, so I knock again.

"Elle? You okay?" I move to the knob and give it a twist, half expecting it to be locked. It's not, and the door opens a few inches.

"One second! I'll be right out!" Her voice is quivering, and I know my sister well enough to read her tone. She's panicking.

"Elle, I'm coming in," I say, pushing the door wide open. She bumps the door to her bathroom closed with her hip just as I enter. She's definitely into something. I just hope it isn't dangerous.

"You're going to be late. I'm working with Mom this morning, and I noticed you hadn't left yet. Want me to give you a ride today?" I inch my way closer to her bathroom, the door open just enough that I catch a glimpse of her reflection in the mirror.

"I'm not going to school," she gurgles out. I push the bathroom door open as she drops her face into her palms, her shoulders shaking with sobs.

"Ellie, what's wrong?" I run my palm along her shoulders. She's built differently than me, her shoulders thinner, arms slender, waist tiny. She's a size four, and I eat a size four for lunch. But we have the same hair—an unruly combination of my mom's dark brown and my dad's natural waves that don't really do either curly or straight well, no matter how many products we use. I can tell by the droplets of water on the sink and the wet strands matted to her cheeks that this is what Ellie's been battling this morning.

"Let me see," I say, my voice gentle as I coax her hands from her face and urge her to look at me.

It takes my mind a few seconds to compute the visual. At first, I'm not sure if the spiked hairs jutting in all directions are where they're supposed to be, so I blink rapidly, trying to understand what my sister did. Then she drops her gaze to the scissors on the counter, and her eyes flit to the trash can by her right leg.

"Oh, Ellie ..." There are long bits of hair piled in the plastic bag lining the small silver can. It looks a bit like one of the nests tucked into the eave of the house.

My sister's head falls back as her hands drop to her sides, her shoulders bobbing up and down as tears run down her cheeks. She's fallen victim to the age-old pitfall that strikes most women at some point in their lives—Ellie tried to cut her own bangs.

"I'm sure it's not as bad as you think. Here," I say, taking her comb in my hand and finger-feathering the rest of her hair out of her face. I comb the portion intended to be bangs down along her forehead, the length maybe two inches, and that's only because it's wet. It's as bad as she thinks, but like hell am I going to say that.

My sister's eyes flutter as she fights off another round of tears, and her lips pucker as she blows out a wobbly breath.

"Be honest," she says.

Ooof. I can't do that.

"It's a little short," I go with. She laughs out once, but it's more of a sob than a chuckle.

"We just need to kind of figure out the look. Here, let me try a few things. Is that all right?" I meet her stare, and she nods.

Her panic wrangled, at least for the moment, I pull open the drawer and take out my old flat iron and a few of the hair bands my sister's collected. I shake out the headband from the back of the drawer, the yellow and blue floral-print one I gave her when I left for college. She used to wear it all the time, and it may be ready for its comeback.

"So, what prompted this makeover attempt?" I don't make eye contact, instead focusing on plugging in the iron and lining up the products and tools I'm going to need. There's likely a boy or some popular girls or some trend at school involved. I just hope it isn't a bully.

"Rachel cut her hair last weekend, and it's this really cute short style that barely reaches her shoulders, and she has these bangs that like, I don't know, sort of sweep over her forehead, and, well . . . Kaden told Jace he thought Rachel looked cute, and . . ."

I smirk to myself as my sister's ramble goes on, unraveling the reasons behind a lot of her behavior over the last few months. I lock away that his name is Kaden, a fact I'll share with Mom later so we can do our own investigating of this boy who has set off Ellie's first real bout of angst. Plus, her best friend, Rachel, getting his attention might mean my sister is in for a first heartbreak sooner rather than later. I don't like that for her, but it's both inevitable and necessary.

"Okay, well, first thing you need to learn is that you and Rachel are two totally different people—personalities, interests, and . . . *hair.*"

I gather Ellie's thick hair into my hand and hold it at the base of her neck. With everything pulled back, the unusually short bangs almost have a modern look. If I can get her on board, I think we can work with it.

"I hate my hair," my sister mutters. My heart deflates a little.

"I've been there," I hum, not dwelling on the negative feelings longer than necessary. I validate her, but we're moving past this. She doesn't see it now because she's thirteen, but in a few years, Ellie is going to look like she belongs on a runway. Her large eyes and high cheekbones are going to fill out and come out of the awkward baby-bird stage to become something interesting and beautiful.

"Do you trust me?" I snag a hairpin from the counter and clamp it between my closed lips while I hold the flat iron in a ready position to swoop down her hair.

Ellie's eyes flit to mine in the reflection and despite looking nervous, she gives me a tiny nod.

It takes me about ten minutes to get her hair completely ironed out and straight. I do my best to dry the bangs she cut, too, and give them enough lift to curve into her forehead rather than stab out into the universe like those pointing things they put over storefronts to keep birds from nesting. I turn her to face me, mostly so she can't watch me work with her hawk-like eyes.

I want to surprise her with how beautiful she is, and a few small accents with some blush and a little eyeliner might make her believe Rachel's new haircut isn't all that. The final piece is my old headband, and I slide it in place with the short bangs lined up along her hairline. I hand her the deep red lipstick, something I'm sure our mom would say is a little too old for her, but is just what she needs, and then spin her to take in her reflection. Her eyes flash wide, just for a second, and then her mouth ticks up on the corners.

"What do you think?" I ask. I know how I feel—I outdid myself, and also, cosmetology school really was an option for me. But what's important is what Ellie sees in the mirror, and how it makes her feel about herself.

"I look like I should drive to school," she whispers, a mischievous grin playing at her lips. Her eyes flit to mine briefly, and I laugh.

"Don't push it. I'm already going to have to sneak you out with that lipstick. Go ahead and put some on, then we have got to go. I'll sign you in late and tell them it was a family emergency."

Ellie flings herself into me, her long skinny arms wrapping around me as her cheek pushes into my white T-shirt. I'm sure she'll smudge me with blush, but this hug from my sister is worth every bit of laundry.

"Thanks, Peyt," she says, her long lashes dabbing at her cheeks. I could cry at this visual, and she's only my sister. I wonder how my mom handles watching us grow up. Also, I put her through a lot of hell. I owe her one of these hugs.

"Anytime, Elle. Now, get to it," I say, kissing the top of her head, then leaving her to finish getting ready.

I wait by my Jeep, flashing my mom a thumbs-up when she holds out her palms, likely curious what the hang-up was. I'll fill her in later. For now, I need my sister to hustle.

Ellie skips out of the house a minute later, and while my mom's double-take signals that she noticed the change in her look, she doesn't say a word as I usher my sister into the passenger side. She's at school ten minutes later, and after I finish signing her in, I spend a few minutes watching the long lines of kindergarteners weave along the walkways as they head in and out of recess. One day, one of those spunky kids is going to be mine.

I leave my longing behind me, heading to the parking lot, and promptly driving from the elementary school to Coolidge High, where Wyatt's truck sits next to my father's. The two of them are on the field, arms crossed as they talk, their focus on the end zone and the ball caddy that I have a feeling is there for them more than their players. My dad loves reliving his past. And right now, Wyatt needs to build something of his own to relive.

This nudge is going to take a little more than a flat-iron and some makeup. But I'm up to the task.

Chapter Five

Wyatt

I hope when I'm in my fifties, I can move half as well as my father-in-law. I was mostly kidding when I slapped the ball in my hand and told him to go out for a pass. When he took off in a slow jog, I figured I'd drop one in for an easy catch, and that would be the end of it. But now it's been thirty minutes, and his legs don't seem tired at all. If anything, that fucker is getting faster—and my throws are going deeper.

Reed crosses the end zone as I drop back and sling the ball thirty yards to hit him in the chest. He palms the ball over his head as he runs toward the field goal, leaping to dunk it over the bar. The ball barely clears it, and I laugh out hard, a bit relieved that he's finally not great at something—jumping.

Peyton's whistle from the sidelines sells the move, and Reed picks up the ball then jogs over with a proud grin on his face. He may as well have hurdled the goal post himself based on the wide-ass toothy smile he's sporting.

"You still got it, Daddy," Peyton says, hugging her dad sideways.

His T-shirt is soaked with sweat, and his cheeks and forehead are red. Thirty minutes going hard is a lot for him, so I snag the half-filled gallon of water I left on the bench and hand it to him. He wastes no time peeling the cap off and chugging about half of it down.

"I'd better hit the showers, too. I'm supposed to talk to the state athletic board in an hour about easing up sponsorship rules for high school sports. If I show up like this, I doubt they'll let me in the room."

He hands me back my gallon, then leans into Peyton, kissing her cheek and giving me a wink before heading up the hill to the locker room.

"He's gonna need two showers after that. Your dad put me through it this morning. I think he's in better shape now than when he won his last Super Bowl."

I ignore the invisible weight that showed up on my shoulders the second Peyton arrived. It's only grown heavier now that we're alone. I knew we'd have to have this conversation, that I would have to tell her I want to try to do this thing. I just figured I'd be able to work up to it in my head, maybe couple it with a nice dinner—and a foot rub.

"How mad do you think he's gonna be when you break his Super Bowl passing record?" Peyton says, instantly drawing my eyes to her.

I blink, a little dumbfounded and not quite certain I heard her right. She simply tilts her head to the side, pursing her lips as she gazes at me with a knowing smirk.

"I haven't decided yet. Not completely anyhow," I say, though I'm ninety percent there. Maybe ninety-eight percent. I don't want to make this decision on my own, though. It's not just me in this life. We're a team for everything, forever, from the moment I met her until I die. And that includes the act of entering into pro football contracts.

"You know, I had you pegged as a quarterback the second

you walked into Jack's." Her lips pucker slightly into that sassy smile she puts on when she's feeling confident.

"You did, huh?" I hold her gaze, tilting my head to match hers.

Peyton's never told me this, and a part of me wonders if she's making it up. I don't care if she is. I like it when she looks at me like I've got something special. And right now? She's eying me as if I'm some famous movie star she used to keep pictures of pinned to her wall. Five years of marriage, she still acts like, of the two of us, I'm not the lucky one.

My gaze drops to the ground, and I kick at a worn spot on the turf. That's part of Reed's sponsorship discussion today—he wants to replace the turf for Coolidge High and Vista. But he's tired of footing the entire bill himself.

"Come here," I say, moving to the bench.

I sit down and hold my arms out, inviting Peyton to sit on my lap. She loops her hands together behind my neck and sits on my left thigh. She's the epitome of a country girl, her cut-off denim shorts that, now that I look closer, were once a pair of my jeans. She's still wearing her work boots from the arena, and her hair is pulled up into one of those messy buns she wears when the temperature starts to climb. There's a pink smudge on the center of her T-shirt, and I nod at it.

"It's a long story, but basically, Ellie has the coolest big sister in the world. That's me, by the way. I'm the cool big sister." She waggles her head with play bravado, and I chuckle before kissing the tip of her nose.

"You're the coolest lots of things."

She shrugs, pulling her mouth into a tight smile.

"I know."

I hold her gaze for a few quiet seconds, long enough that her cheeks blush. I love that I can still make that happen.

"And why are you here now?" I lead.

Her mouth closes into a soft smile.

"You want this," she says.

I squeeze her and nip at her ear.

"I mean, I always want this, but—"

She laughingly pushes my chest, her palm flat over my heart, arm stiff, holding me away enough to meet her gaze. I know what she means. I want to go for it, take Bryce's offer, see where it goes.

I nod.

"I know I shouldn't, but yeah . . . I do."

Peyton shakes her head.

"Uh uh. Don't do that. There's no reason you shouldn't," she scolds.

I pull my mouth in tight, still feeling guilty despite her insistence.

"The timing isn't ideal," I say.

Peyton's soft laugh makes her wiggle in my lap, which also isn't ideal—not *here* anyhow.

"Wyatt, the ideal timing was about six years ago. But there's nothing we can do about that."

She's right. But also, maybe not completely, because I'm not sure how I would have handled leaving her right after saying our *I do's*. It would have been hard then, as newlyweds, to navigate setting up our new life together in two different places. If she had moved to another city with me, she wouldn't have been as happy. At least, I don't think so. I've seen the strength being home, having her family around, has given her throughout her recovery. And the Arizona weather doesn't hurt when rain and cold are hard on her nerves and joints.

Peyton moves from my lap, walking backward a few steps on the turf until she's standing on the hashmark in front of me. She pulls the tie from her hair and gathers it into a tighter ponytail before tucking her T-shirt into her shorts—aka my former pants. I'm about to tease her and ask what she's up to when she smirks and launches into a back flip that ends with her feet flat on the ground and in nearly the same place they started.

"Ha! It's so cool you can still do that," I say, watching her with wonder as she winks and holds up a finger.

Turning around, she leans forward until she's in a handstand, and she walks toward the center of the field on her palms. Her legs wobble in the air, the right one always struggling a little more than the left to help her find her balance. She possesses greater strength and muscle control than most normal humans, but it's still not up to her standards. It probably won't ever be completely. But it doesn't stop her from trying.

She bends back until her feet land on the ground again, and she rubs her temples while squeezing her eyes shut tight.

"Head rush?" I ask.

"Ohhhhh yeah." She laughs, taking slow shuffled steps back in my direction. I open my arms and pull her back to my lap the second she's close enough, and it takes her a few seconds to get her focus right. When she does, there's nothing clearer than the warm, golden brown of her eyes locked on mine.

"If I could do it again, be on a squad, fly through the air? I would do it in a heartbeat, Wyatt. I wouldn't even flinch. I'm not scared of falling. I'm not afraid of someone slipping. And in my head, I can still do all of it. But in reality, I can't. And there isn't really a place for that. ESPN isn't streaming women approaching thirty hitting the mat to tumble."

She laughs softly at her joke, but there's a touch of melancholy in the sound, the way it trails off, and her mouth fights to keep her slight smile in place. She never got to finish her senior year of competition, and that's something she'll never get back.

This opportunity I'm being given is as much hers as it is mine, at least vicariously.

"I guess we're going to Portland?" My stomach drops like it does on those thrill rides Peyton likes so much.

Peyton's smirk widens, and her forehead lands on mine as her cool hands press into my cheeks.

"We're going to Portland."

The words are out there now. Peyton's called it, and when she decides for us, it sticks. I just hope like hell I don't disappoint her. I was never nervous about the game before, but this is different. I'm not coming at this from the top. Hell, I'm not even coming at it from the same field as the other guys. I'm coming out of the woods, under-prepared and unsure of myself. If I'm going to make the most out of this—for *us*—I need to get my ass in shape.

"I guess I gotta call Bryce back, huh?"

She nods, then presses her lips to mine.

"I'm so proud of you," she says against my mouth.

I chuckle.

"I haven't done anything yet," I say, sucking her top lip in and holding on to it for a beat. I don't want to fail her. She deserves for me to be the man she thinks I can be. It's a high standard; one set by a goddamned legend. But I know Reed's story. He didn't exactly start from the top, and he didn't always stay there.

"You've done a lot more than you think, Wyatt Stone. A lot more," she says, holding my stare for several quiet seconds. Her focus shifts from my left eye to my right, and I sense the weight in her words, the meaning behind them. She thinks I sacrificed for her. But I would do it again in a heartbeat. This life with Peyton? I wouldn't change a thing.

Chapter Six

Peyton

"This is weird."

I'm glad Wyatt said that out loud because I've been thinking it for days now, ever since we found out Bryce would be picking us up at the airport and essentially escorting us everywhere for the next four days. I'm not sure how the universe worked out this life for all of us, but the fact Bryce is always here for these pivotal moments in our lives seems like some sort of omen. I'm just not sure whether it's good or bad yet. It's a sign of change to come. It always is.

"There he is!"

Bryce is holding up a whiteboard that reads "Wyatt Stone" in black marker. Bryce's exuberance, coupled with the sheer size of him, Wyatt, and Whiskey, has drawn a lot of attention our way. A young woman sitting in the arrivals area has her phone out, and she's clearly filming us.

I wonder if she recognizes Wyatt. Is he recognizable? He will be, if this works out.

My first boyfriend and my husband hug, and I shake my head, still not used to the sight.

"Fucking weird," Tasha breathes out at my side.

I chuckle and turn my head her way, widening my eyes and mouthing, "Right?"

"Hey, what gives? No sign for me?" Whiskey interrupts, breaking up Bryce and Wyatt's embrace.

"Bro, I can't hold up a sign that says Whiskey. People will think I'm an alcoholic," Bryce laughs out, bracing himself for Whiskey's incoming body. In seconds, he's lifted Bryce off his feet with a bullish hug.

"Yet, that's not weird at all," I mutter to Tasha.

She sighs to my right.

"Sadly, no. It's not."

Whiskey finally drops his old friend, and Bryce takes my carry-on bag from my shoulder, a chivalrous move that catches Wyatt's eye. His brows pinch, but I shake my head. Bryce isn't coming on to me. Those days are long gone. But every time we see him, he's extra everything with me, like he's making amends for being such a shithead sixteen-year-old.

"Do you have a lot of luggage?" Bryce asks over his shoulder.

Wyatt and Whiskey both groan, and Tasha punches each of them in their biceps.

"The ladies may have planned for a month," Wyatt says, and I slap his other bicep as we follow behind Bryce toward baggage claim.

He rubs the spot, then smirks at me, winking.

Tasha and I may have overpacked a bit, but we don't get away as two couples much. Even the trip to Texas over the summer, when the boys played in that league, was with Tasha and Whiskey's kids. It was a different dynamic than being on our own. And when we checked the weather for this visit, it showed a swing of thirty degrees during our stay, with a chance of both extreme heat and cold rain.

This place is weird. Fitting.

Despite Wyatt's warning that we might not be able to fit our luggage in the car, we all pile in with our bags just fine. It helps that Bryce rented an XL Escalade, which I hope the company or team is covering. I don't remember this kind of glitzy attention rolled out for my dad when he was a free agent. Of course, it was widely understood that things like fancy cars and celebrity parties weren't going to win over Reed Johnson. I hope the people pulling the strings now know that's not going to impress Wyatt Stone. I, however, could get used to riding around in an Escalade.

It takes about thirty minutes to get to the new stadium, built just off the waterfront. It's surrounded by glass buildings and brand-new storefronts with trendy restaurants and sidewalk seating in anticipation of big game-day crowds. It's nice here, and the temperature at this very moment is very appealing. But it's not home.

I should avoid comparisons. If we lived near the stadium in Arizona, we would be in the thick of things too. But the wide-open spaces in Arizona simply hit different.

Bryce parks in the circular drive-up right outside the business offices on the north end of the stadium. Nobody seems to be rushing to valet the car, and I can't help but feel we're breaking some rules by parking there. When three more outlandishly tall men dressed in dark green polos and dress slacks—the general uniform for retired NFL guys working in front offices, it seems—walk out to greet us, I relax.

"Welcome to Skyjack Stadium," the man in the center says, stretching a hand out to shake Wyatt's first. His hair is white, his beard peppered, and there's something about him that feels familiar.

"Jerry, great to see you again," Bryce says, shaking his hand before the man moves on to Whiskey. I mentally rummage through the context clues until my mind lands on Jerry Caswell, and my eyebrows shoot up.

"You played with my dad!" I blurt out.

The man's gaze scrunches as it lands on me, and a second later, his lip ticks up.

"Well, goddamn. Are you Johnson's kid? We must be getting old," he says, stretching his arms out for a hug. I glance at Wyatt in time to catch him rolling his eyes at Whiskey. The two of them constantly joke about how the world operates on six degrees of Reed Johnson. It might very well be five. My dad's reach is further than Kevin Bacon's. Jerry was his tight end for two years in Detroit.

"I forgot about that connection," Jerry says with a raspy chuckle as he takes a step back from me and elbows Wyatt's side. "You married into royalty, Wyatt."

"So they tell me," Wyatt laughs out. His teeth are pushed together, his forced smile making his jaw flex. I don't think anyone else notices how overwhelmed he is, but before it becomes obvious, I slide my hand in his and nestle into my husband's side.

"Wyatt broke all of Daddy's high school records," I brag. I know it embarrasses Wyatt when I mention that fact, but it will also go a long way to separating him from my father in this crowd. He's a standout on his own, and when I feel his bicep relax under my palm, I know he gets it.

"Well, how about we see if these guys can work out a deal so you can break the rest of them," Jerry says, flashing Wyatt his trademark toothy grin.

Jerry leads the group of us into the offices, and we weave through a few hallways before reaching an elevator. I can tell we're not all going to fit when everyone begins to pile in, so I hang back, partly wanting Wyatt to continue his chat with Jerry. I'm not sure what Jerry's role is with the Portland Cyclones, but if he has any pull at all, that six degrees of Reed Johnson thing might come in handy.

"I'll take the next one too," Bryce says, stepping out when he realizes I'm the only one hanging back.

I make eyes at Wyatt before he can offer to trade places, silently urging him to stay put. Those jealous tendencies are deeply woven into his fabric when it comes to my history with Bryce, and though he knows there's nothing there to worry about, his brain chemistry still reacts as if there is. I get it. I do the same when *anyone* eyes my man.

The doors close, and I exhale, the sound whooshing out of me a little heavier than I expect. I chuckle, a bit embarrassed to show how tense I was.

"That was a lot, huh?" Bryce says, his lip tugging up in empathy.

I shrug, then hold my shoulders up for an extra second before letting them drop. That felt good, too.

"It's all a lot," I confess.

He nods with a tight, soft grin. I hold his gaze for a few seconds, mentally debating whether I really want to know what's in his head. The tense grip this entire thing has on my chest is so strong that I decide I can't have too many details, and maybe knowing more about the dirty underbelly of sports contract negotiations will arm me with the tools to help Wyatt come out of this unscathed.

"Be honest," I say, lifting my chin a touch. My eyes dim on his. I doubt I need to say more.

"This is really happening, Peyt." His chest rises with a deep inhale, and it may have been years since he was my boyfriend, and he may have been an adolescent idiot back then, but I still know his tells. There's something he's not saying.

"I don't think we'd be here if there wasn't something to this. But I'm not a fragile ego you have to dance around, Bryce.

Neither is Wyatt. Tell me the truth—what are his chances? I know they drafted a quarterback. He's young, and he was in the Heisman conversation. Is this all for show?"

I was old enough to understand some of the political games that were played during my dad's final years when he met with certain coaches. Sometimes a visit is more about putting pressure on the other guy. And young players often need to be put in their place. I need to know if that's what this is. It won't matter, because I believe Wyatt will come out on top even if that's not how they envision him here. But I'd like to know how hard my husband is going to have to battle so I can fight along with him.

"Whiskey is an easier sell, Peyt. I won't lie. He's a league minimum, and he's better than a lot of the offensive line guys coming in. His injury profile is slim to none, and he's stayed in pretty good shape for a big man. He's not a huge risk for them. But—"

I quirk a brow.

"But," I echo.

Bryce glances over his shoulder, as if making sure we're alone. We are, but since the elevator doors open just then, he waits for us to step in before finishing his words.

"Wyatt's the one they wanted to see. Whiskey would not be here getting the look if I wasn't bringing Wyatt along with him. He's got some legitimate fans calling the shots."

I hold Bryce's gaze for a beat, the tightness easing a little in my chest. I also digest the things he didn't say just now. While Wyatt has some fans, he also has some haters. He's going to have to prove himself, but that's never been a problem for him. And six years away from a serious game or not, there's still nobody better than him behind the ball.

My focus drifts, and my eyes zero in on the elevator

numbers. The four lights up, and before the elevator doors open to the executive suites, I turn to Bryce one last time.

"If you make this happen, you're his guy for life. You know that, right?"

Bryce blinks, then offers a slight nod.

"I know, Peyt. I promise I'll work my ass off for him."

The ding of the elevator doesn't faze me, my gaze fixed on Bryce's face for every millisecond before the doors open and break this bubble of trust. And there is trust between us. I feel it. I see it in his eyes. He wants this for Wyatt, and I'm sure, selfishly, for himself. There's nothing wrong with that. If he continues to have integrity, we'll share this corner of our lives with him. He's earned my benefit of the doubt. Now he needs to earn Wyatt's.

Chapter Seven

Wyatt

I've always been better with coaches than the muckety-mucks. Thank God Jerry and Coach Elgin are coming to this dinner thing tonight. I'm not sure Michael "Mickey" Payne is a fan. To be fair, the Cyclones' owner is a bit hard to read. He's always been an enigma; at least, that's what little background I was able to dig up on him between our brief meeting in his office during the tour and this dinner lends to.

He owns a chemical company, and he's been sued a few times. Whiskey's position is that most chemical companies have, and I'm sure he's right. But it's the way those lawsuits were dashed away with speed and tidiness that strikes me as, I don't know, a yellow flag maybe? I'm not sure whether he loves football or the investment and name recognition this expansion team buys him. Maybe it doesn't matter.

I wish Whiskey and Tasha were joining us for dinner, and the irony that I'm wishing for Tasha's presence in a professional setting isn't lost on me. She's not known for being guarded with her language or her volume, but right about now, I'd take her welcome distraction. But Bryce made it clear that tonight is about my future with the team, not Whiskey's. I just feel bad that Whisk feels left out.

"Peyton, let me get your seat," Jerry says, swooping in to scoot back my wife's chair in the oddly empty dining room of this posh steakhouse. Everything in this joint is leather and wood, and the lighting is dim enough to make it appear that everyone is scowling, not just Michael Payne.

"Always the gentleman, Jerry," Peyton says, batting her lashes. If Jerry weren't her father's age, I'd be hot with jealousy. Of course, as Peyton likes to point out from time to time when she walks me through one of the books she's reading, age-gap is a very sexy thing. My wife is very good at turning double-standards around to bite me in the ass.

"So, how does a guy go from running seam routes in Detroit to the front office of a new expansion team?" I've been curious about Jerry's role here. I get that he's an investor, but his hands-on presence feels as if he's more than that.

"To be fair, Wyatt, I bounced around a lot of things between Detroit and this dinner we're having. It's been a decade." He chuckles as he pulls a pair of gold-rimmed glasses from his shirt pocket. He drops them down his nose as he peruses a wine list, but his gaze pops above the rims to meet my stare.

"I gave Mickey a few million. In exchange, I get to be involved in recruiting." He shrugs as if it's no big deal, but the message behind his words is pretty clear. He's the one who had his eyes on me. He's the reason I'm here. I just hope those few million buy some decent sway when it comes to making final decisions.

"Sounds like a pretty cool way to retire," I say, taking the wine list from him and immediately passing it to Peyt. I don't have a clue about fine foods and wine and shit, so at this place, I plan on ordering whatever she tells me.

"Who knows, maybe I'll be calling the shots on the field someday," Jerry says, winking across the table at Coach Elgin.

"Fucker, I'm not dead yet," Coach laughs out, his gravelly voice an indicator of just how many cigars the man smokes.

The rapport between Jerry and Coach is refreshing. There's a genuine respect between the two, which I'm sure comes from Jerry's first few seasons in Tennessee under Coach Elgin.

"So, who came to Portland first, Coach? You or Jerry? Who brought whom on board?" Peyton asks, and I'm glad because I've been dying to know. Everything sounds more casual when she asks. I feel like every question I put out there is immediately dissected and woven into my character for evaluation.

"Actually, Phillips was my first hire," Mickey interjects from the head of the table. His sharp tone seems to jar everyone, even Clark Phillips, the offensive coordinator sitting to his right. There's a brief bout of silence while we all wait for Mickey to expound, but he doesn't, instead leaning to his side and holding up a hand to usher one of the servers in our direction.

"Ah, yeah. He was, but he only beat me out here by a week. Ain't that right, Clarky?" Coach Elgin has the benefit of being a winning coach with thirty years of experience under his belt. Plus, the man is seventy, and as I've heard many times from Peyton's Grampa Buck, once you hit seventy, you don't give a shit what anyone thinks about anything, especially you.

Clark Phillips is in his forties, and I have a feeling he very much gives a shit what people think, especially his boss. I got that sense from our very first handshake in Mickey's office, something about the way he held my stare and squeezed my hand. He's the one I need to prove myself to. And he seems to have the owner's ear more than anyone else at this table. The fact he doesn't bother to respond to Coach Elgin's friendly jab speaks volumes.

"Okay, so you were first. Then Coach and Jerry. Nice . . .

nice." Peyton swallows down her own frail echo, blinking her gaze downward as a server sets menus in front of each of us. While everyone else seems oblivious to the heavy silence suddenly choking the spirit out of the room, their heads buried in menus, my wife seems fully aware. Our eyes meet in a sideways glance, and all I can do is lift my brows in panic. This doesn't feel as if it's going well, and I'm not sure how to fix it.

Mickey is the first to order, taking care of most of the table, deciding what everyone "needs to try" before insisting on a glass of some cognac he had them prepare for the night. I don't like brandy, but when he orders a glass for me, I resolve to choking the shit down and gushing about it afterwards. With a smile.

"I'm excited to see what you can do out on the field tomorrow," Coach says once our orders are in place and the server leaves.

"I can't wait to get out there," I say, rubbing my sweaty palms on my thighs. If I had to throw a ball right now, I'm not sure my jittery fingers could grip it.

"How long's it been? Six years? Seven?" Phillips says, leaning back in his chair and crossing his arms over his chest. His stern eyes study me, and I can read his skepticism.

"Only six, sir. Though I've played plenty of independent ball since college, and I've done the summer league with Whiskey Olsen a few times, which is where I guess y'all saw me."

"I didn't see you," Phillips adds quickly. He's dismissive, but I don't wince. The perk of living around Peyton's little sister is that I've been primed to handle even the sharpest barbs. Nobody cuts to the core as harshly as a freshly minted teenager.

"Got it," I utter. My lips part again, but I'm not sure what else to say. My short response just now seems to have only built another layer of bricks between me and Coach Phillips. My eyes dart to Peyton for help, but her shocked face indicates she's as stumped as I am. I wish like hell Bryce were here, but he said Mickey insisted he get me one-on-one, though it's much more of a four on two.

"I saw you," Jerry finally says, leaning forward, his forearms on the table. His towering presence looms large over the round mahogany surface, and I'd swear I felt the heavy table tilt just a hair with his weight. He's the largest man in the room, and I'm glad he's on my side—both literally and figuratively.

I'm picking up more clues every minute, and I'm pretty sure the biggest divide at this table exists between Jerry and Coach Phillips. I'd feel a whole lot better if they were both in my corner, but I guess I should be happy to have one of them.

"Yeah, that's right. You called me from the beach after spending the day watching a game, told me we needed this guy in our locker room." Coach Elgin pauses when his drink arrives, taking a sip before continuing as he gestures toward me with the amber-colored liquid swirling in his snifter. "Jerry here said he hadn't seen anyone throw like you since that Reed Johnson. Small world he's your father-in-law. Ha! Ain't that some shit?"

"Yeah, it sure is," I utter, glancing around the table as my connection to Reed is fully let out of the bag. It gets the reaction I expect from Phillips—a smug expression and slow nod, probably paired with the assumption that I'm getting special treatment.

"Never saw him play," Mickey bursts out. His eyes are focused on his drink as he holds it up to the light before taking a long, slow sip. His gaze settles on me, and it's as blank as it was a moment ago. How the hell this shark of a businessman found his way into owning a football team beats me, but I can see how he'd be tough to beat in a negotiating room. Too bad I'm the one in it now.

"Oh, you missed out. I would have given anything to have him on any of my teams over the years. Probably would have won a few more Super Bowls with that guy," Coach Elgin muses.

"You only won two," Phillips mutters over the rim of his glass before drowning his dig in a sip. It doesn't seem to faze Coach Elgin. Perhaps age has a similar effect to living with a teenager—well-practiced armor.

"Two more than you," Jerry coughs out, clearly offended on his former coach's behalf.

"Kids, kids. Cut the fighting," Mickey says. I think he's making a joke, but the even tone in his voice makes it hard to tell. His face is still devoid of any evidence of a smile.

The nerves I felt walking into this place are starting to fray, and the air is thick with all sorts of tension. Thankfully, Coach Elgin kicks off casual conversation about my college years, asking me questions about my preferred style of play, how well I can stick to the pocket, and if I still think I can scramble. I focus mostly on him, glad that Phillips and Mickey are content to listen rather than ask questions of their own. By the time our food arrives, I've regained some of my confidence, and I might be winning Phillips over a tad too.

"You had some injuries in college, am I right? Didn't that agent of yours say that's how you two met? He replaced you?" Mickey's sudden turn knocks me off balance again, and his handle on my history is obviously thin. I finish chewing my last bite of my filet and clear my throat.

"Not quite," I start, but before I have a chance to set the record straight, Phillips takes over.

"Yeah, but that's basically right. We don't need to know your soap opera story. We need to know what you can deliver on the field, *now*. You follow me? I get that you didn't miss a lot of time from your injury, but when Bryce Hampton transferred to

Arizona, you two split time your senior year. You know we don't run two quarterbacks at this level, right?" His soft chuckle evokes all the swagger of a high school bully, and all I can do is shake once with a hard, disingenuous laugh.

"Yeah, I'm aware," I say, a clear bite to my tone.

Peyton's palm flattens on my thigh, and I quickly cover it with my own, drawing in a deep breath through my nose. I'm sure Phillips can see how hot I'm getting. I don't fucking care.

"I think that's what sets Wyatt apart from a lot of other players, you know?" my wife says.

"How so?" Jerry encourages, both ignoring the tight smirk spreading on Phillips's face.

"A lot of players claim to be there for the team, you know, program first. No individuals. Brotherhood, and all that. But when it comes time to sacrifice a little bit of glory for the greater good, how many of them put themselves first? And how many times does it blow up in a team's face?" Peyton's words seem to resonate as nobody responds for a few long seconds, and Coach Elgin simply nods as he wipes his linen napkin over his mouth, then tosses it to the table.

"Maybe," Mickey finally speaks up.

He saws into the meat on his plate, spearing a bright pink piece of steak with his golden fork. He holds it up as if he were a hunter showing off a trophy, and his gaze squares with mine for the first time since we met. Until now, it's been short glances through his tinted glasses.

"You know the saying about horses, don't you?" His head cocks to the side, a tiny smile pulling up one side of his mouth, deepening the wrinkles that line his cheeks.

I shrug, my fingers now intertwined with Peyton's on my thigh. Both of our hands are hot.

Mickey pops the piece of meat into his mouth and chews a few times.

"They shoot horses, don't they?" He finishes chewing as a cunning laugh rumbles from deep inside his chest.

I don't entirely follow, though I'm sure he's not praising me. Peyton, however, seems to understand exactly what he's getting at. She unfurls her hand from mine, balling both of hers together on the tabletop as she leans in.

"You're talking about how horses can no longer race when they're injured," she says flatly.

"*Hmm*," Mickey grunts, popping another bite into his mouth before he pinches his lips into a tight, affirming grin and shrugs a shoulder.

"I'm not sure whether you know this, Mr. Payne, but my family owns a rescue ranch for horses back in Arizona, and some of them were once racehorses. Just because they were injured doesn't mean they don't have purpose." Peyton's not really talking about the horses now. She's not even talking about me. She's standing up for herself, but I'm the only one here who knows that.

"That's sweet," Phillips adds, drawing my gaze to him in a flash.

"It's pretty amazing, actually," I say, doing little to hide my ire. This guy can dislike me all he wants, but he has no right to be a dick to my wife.

"Oh, yeah, I don't doubt it. It's just . . ." He waggles his head.

"What?" I challenge.

He pushes his plate forward, folding his napkin on the table, then folding his hands together on top of it as he leans in and meets my glare.

"You wouldn't put one of those horses back in the race . . . ever. Which begs the question, would you put the broken guy in as quarterback?"

I hold my tongue between my teeth and guard my smile as I snicker. Leaning back in my seat, I blink my gaze over to Coach

Elgin, whose amused expression is a little reassuring. I don't think he believes a word coming out of this guy's mouth.

"I dare you to show me a football player in this league, no . . . . hell . . . on this planet, who isn't broken in some way. This sport, it's brutal. It's not for the weak. And anyone who steps onto your field with the false expectation that they won't get hammered into the turf from time to time is a fool."

I know my volume is up, and I sense the encroaching servers stepping closer to our table as if they might need to taze me or something. This evening is not bringing out my best side, and I regret that. But right now, I'm not even sure I want to play for an asshole like Michael "Mickey" Payne. And I'm not sure I want to let my best friend play for him, either.

"Oh, don't get your shorts in a wad," Mickey says before tossing the rest of his second brandy back.

He plunks the snifter down on the table and runs the napkin over his lips before tossing it on top of his plate. He leans back, hands threaded together, and stares at me long and hard. I cross my arms over my chest and give it right back to him.

"I guess we'll see what you've got tomorrow," he says, his eyes shifting toward Phillips. The two of them share a quick glance, and I straighten my spine, suddenly feeling as though I need to be ready to take a hit twenty-four-seven, and not only on the field.

"Can't wait," I respond.

And when Peyton's nails dig into my thigh, I know she wants me to teach these assholes a lesson tomorrow too. And then, I think, she might just want to murder them.

Chapter Eight

Peyton

I didn't sleep. I have my dad's temper and my mom's defensiveness when it comes to the people I love. Of course, I'm also a stubborn competitor despite my spinal injury, and when Mickey attacked my very core, whether he knew it or not, he lit my inner fire.

When I told Wyatt I had half a mind to show up alongside him and Whiskey this morning and lay out a few of the guys on Mickey's prized O-line myself, I was only half kidding. I may have been delusional, but I was pissed. And I'm not so sure I want our family tied to that man and his organization. What I am sure of is that the last thing I want to do right now is traipse around a winery with Tasha while Wyatt and Whiskey tap dance for that asshole. I'm not sure how I'm going to keep my mouth shut around my friend. If I repeat anything to Tasha about things said during last night's dinner, she's going to make a scene. It's her nature, and I love that she's so loyal to our family and friendship that she'd throw away her and Whiskey's future in solidarity. I can't let her do that.

Tasha's rap on the door to our suite comes a few minutes

earlier than I expect, so I toss one of Wyatt's T-shirts over my head and skip to the door to let her in.

"Girl, you aren't ready?" She gestures down my lower naked half.

"You're early," I protest, urging her to step inside so the rest of the hotel doesn't get a good look at me in my panties.

Tasha chuckles as she follows me into the living room and drops her giant leather bag on the loveseat, fishing out a hairbrush and a small makeup bag before jetting straight toward the bathroom.

"Uh, I need to use that," I say, trailing close behind her.

She waves me off.

"I've seen you pee."

My friend plunks her makeup bag by the sink and flips her head upside down, then brushes out her long black hair. Since it's obvious she isn't budging from this bathroom, I shake my head and squeeze around her to the toilet. I zero in on the tiny spot of red on my underwear the second I sit down, and my heart drops to the floor.

"It's warm out today, that's why I'm wearing this sundress. You might want to skip those jeans I saw folded on the back of the toilet and opt for shorts or something."

My friend's words are muted by the rush of blood suddenly whizzing by my eardrums. I don't realize I'm crying until I feel the first drops hit my bare thighs. I try to wipe them away before Tasha notices, but her head is already upright, her hair pulled tight into her fist as she holds a hairband between her teeth.

She blinks at me, and I can tell she reads my expression right when she drops her hair and tosses the band into the sink.

"Oh, honey," she says, leaning against the opposite wall.

I shrug and sniffle away my disappointment.

"It's fine. It takes time for some people. It's just . . . I feel like it's been a while. And part of me felt like maybe this was it."

I shake off my last bits of hope and do my best to clear my mind as I finish up in the bathroom and head to my suitcase that's parked on the stand at the foot of the bed. I toss a few shirts onto the messy pile of blankets in search of my girl products, then snag my only pair of unsexy underwear and my black cotton shorts.

"Fuck!" The anger sneaks up on me, and I hear my friend step out of the bathroom behind me. I hold up my hand without turning around.

"I don't want pity. Not today."

She doesn't respond, and I don't make eye contact with her on my way back into the bathroom. She gives me privacy this time, but I've numbed myself to dwelling on another month gone by without a pregnancy, so it doesn't take me long to change clothes and sweep my hair up into a bun.

"Ready?" I snag my favorite Kate Spade bag from the dresser and slide my oversized sunglasses up the bridge of my nose.

"How about we get day drunk?" Tasha's voice stops me as I exit the bedroom, and I turn to give her a flat look.

"That's the best idea you've ever had in your entire life."

She nods, also not smiling as we head out the door and into the waiting rideshare vehicle.

There are times for being silly with your girlfriends, and then there are times to go to work. These missions include late-night conversations about tasteful revenge plots for someone who wronged one of us, gossip sessions about someone we knew in high school getting married, divorced, or, *occasionally*, arrested, and self-medicating utter devastation at the winery while you both ignore the reason for it. Today, it's the latter. And neither of us cracks a smile until we're at least a bottle in.

Tasha was right about the temperature today, and by the time we make our way back to the hotel, my face is flushed from both too much pinot gris and the bright sun I sat under for most of the day. Drunk as I may be, though, everything from the morning and the night before is still lingering in my mind. It's turned into a mush of sad frustration, and it all comes to a boil the second I open our room door and see Wyatt stepping out of the bedroom with a towel around his waist and another in his hand that he rubs over his hair.

He drops the hand towel the second my lips begin to blubber. His arms wrap around me, holding my forehead against his chest. I feel his chin rest on the top of my head before he slowly moves his lips to my crown.

"What is it, Peyt? What can I do?"

I shudder in his embrace. I don't cry often, but when I finally let things out—man, am I a mess. I sniff up what I can and pull one hand up to wipe away tears that are replaced by more in half a second. I step back enough to meet Wyatt's gaze and bite the inside of my cheek as I lift a shoulder.

"I got my period."

I shake with a quick sob and slap my palm over my mouth to hold it in. My eyes flutter shut, and I feel a little stupid for being so upset. It's been a few months of actively trying, and I know these things take time. But it's those *what ifs* that attack me from all sides. I can't help but think about my injury and the changes it may have made to my body that we haven't discovered yet.

"Come with me," Wyatt says, weaving his hand with mine and leading me into the hotel bathroom.

It's nicer than the one we have at home. For all my father's fortune, the guest house at their ranch is modest. Even my parents' primary suite is basic, the one upgrade is a tub with jets that my dad put in when my mom asked for it.

Wyatt turns the water on for the double shower heads and pops open the glass door before turning his attention to me. He lifts my T-shirt up my body, and I lift my arms so he can remove it completely. I start to slide my shorts down my hips, but he moves my hands out of the way, taking over the job and dropping soft kisses on my belly as he pulls my shorts and unflattering granny panties down my legs. He drops his towel to the floor, then unties my sneakers and slips them off my feet, allowing me to step out of my clothes before he rolls my socks over my arches and tosses them to the side.

I slide my bra straps from my shoulders and reach behind my back to unhook the silk bralette, letting it fall to the floor between us. Wyatt's palms slide up the length of my legs, tracing the curves of my hips before slowly creeping up my sides until his thumbs brush over my nipples. My lips part with a soft breath and he tips my chin up to meet his mouth, sucking in my top lip and holding it hostage until his stretching grin breaks his hold.

"You know I love trying to make a baby with you, right?" His smoldering voice helps erase the lingering distress, and I tilt my head to the side, stretching my neck for him to taste. His tongue takes a swipe at my skin, and the low rumble of his sinister laugh fills my ears.

Wyatt walks me backward into the shower, the warm water pelting my back and soon cascading over my head. He fills his hand with a few pumps of lavender shampoo and works the lather into my scalp and hair. My eyes fall shut at the sensation. Sometimes this type of touch is what I crave—to be cared for and eased away from my spiraling thoughts for a little while.

"I love you so much," I whisper, my eyes still shut. I'm finding it hard to open them. I had a lot to drink today, and I fear I may pay for it in the morning. My vision is swirling, but

Wyatt's hand is on my back, bracing me. I'm not afraid. I'm simply . . . tired.

"I will always love you more."

And those are the last words I remember before his lips press to my head and he shuts off the water.

Cool air blows a few stray hairs across my forehead, waking me from the deepest sleep I've had in days, maybe weeks. I blink my eyes open, glad that the room is still dim. Wyatt steps out of the bathroom, fully showered and dressed to take the field. I'm not entirely sure what day it is or how long I was out.

"Good morning, sunshine," he says with a wry smirk.

He steps back into the bathroom briefly then comes out with a glass of water and what I presume is a handful of Advil. He hands me three pills, and I quirk a brow.

"I'm not the one taking hits on the field this week. I think two will do," I say, squinting as I pry my eyes open wider. He spills all three pills into my palm and closes my hand around them.

"I'm pretty sure you're in three-Advil territory. You sounded like Whiskey last night when I put you to bed." He chuckles and I wince, knowing full well what Whiskey sounds like when he sleeps. Like a bear. A fucking bear . . . gargling. A fucking gargling bear.

I toss the pills in my mouth and gulp down half of the water. That slight movement of my head sends a throb to my temples. I quickly hand Wyatt the glass and press my palms to the sides of my head before falling back into the pillow.

"Maybe four-Advil territory," I admit.

He laughs, setting the glass on the nightstand before crawling into the bed and nestling next to me. He smells fresh and clean, and like the hotel's lavender body wash. I'm thinking of plucking that bottle right off the wall, I like it so much.

"Why don't you go back to sleep. It's five, and I have a long day ahead. Then, maybe tonight we blow off Whiskey and Tasha for a date night all our own. How does that sound?" He nuzzles into the crook of my neck, his nose grazing my jawline before he nips lightly at my skin.

"*Mmm*, maybe we order in," I say, my body tingling with desire. If I didn't think I'd fall over from vertigo by doing it, I'd pounce on this man and pull those sweatpants he's wearing down far enough for me to sit on that hard-on pressing against my thigh. But moving any more than I already have might kill me. And nothing kills the mood more than a grown-ass woman rushing to the bathroom with a hangover.

"Only if you wear that dress I saw you pack. You know the one, with the low back, and that slit that goes up the side, and—"

"The red one?" I quirk a brow, my right eye opening a little wider than the left.

Wyatt lets out a guilty chuckle, then kisses my lips before getting up from the bed.

"That's the one. Six o'clock. Be ready. I'll take care of everything." He winks as he backs away, like the damn teenager he was the first time he did that. And I fall for him all over again, right before falling back asleep.

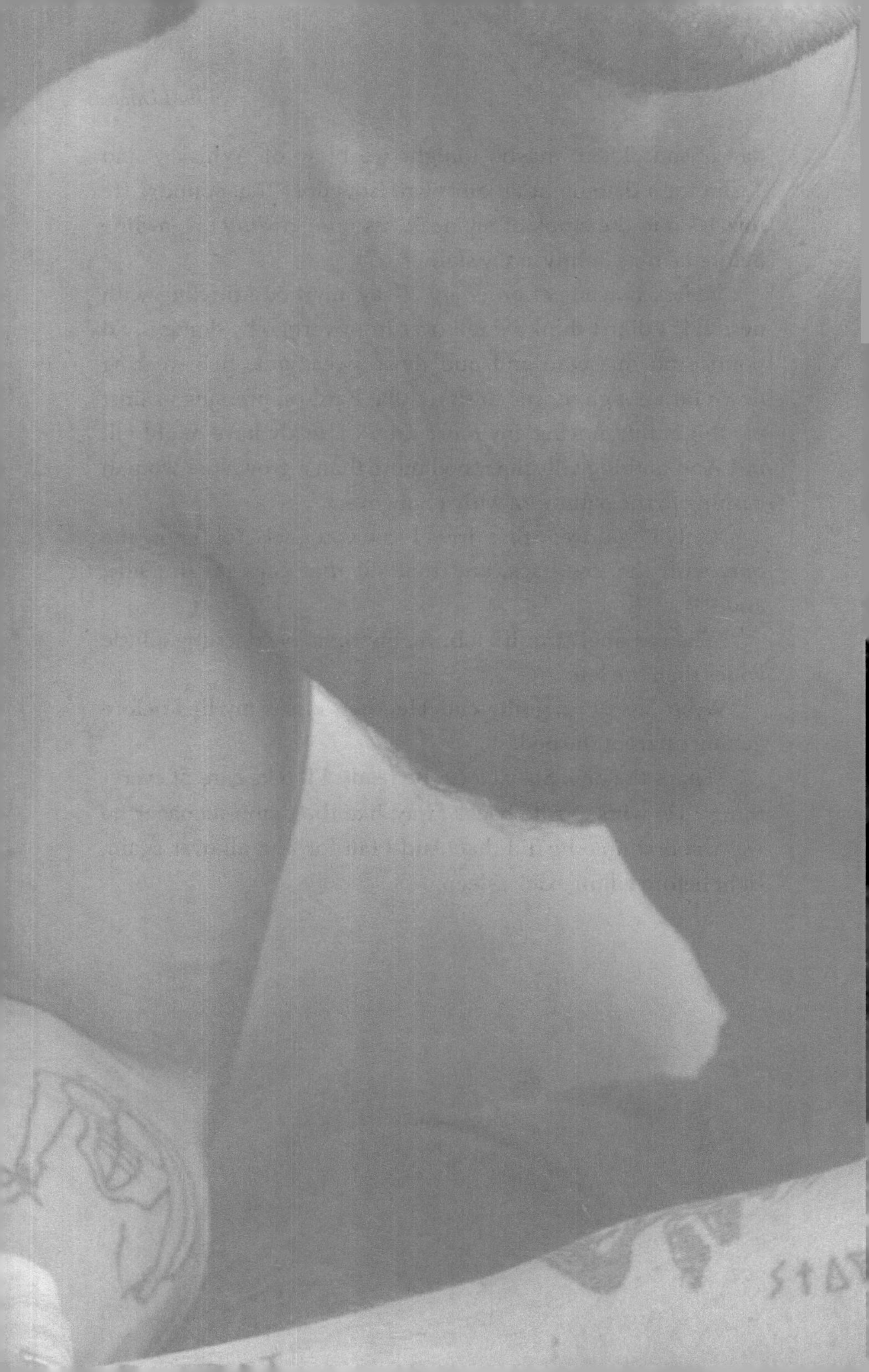

Chapter Nine

Wyatt

It wasn't Peyton's snoring that kept me up last night, though I didn't lie to her—she was sawing logs so loudly she may as well have been building a cabin. I've slept through her post-wine nights out, though, and what kept me up until two in the morning had nothing to do with my environment and every-thing to do with my head.

I know how much Peyton's heart hurts, and every time a month goes by without a hint that we may finally be pregnant, the hope and joy that lives behind her eyes grows a bit dimmer. Last night, seeing her fall apart with disappointment . . . I couldn't help but ask myself what the hell I'm doing here. The dinner with Coach, Mickey, and Phillips didn't help. I feel I'm being used, and in the process, it's taking a toll on Peyton. It would be one thing if it were just me here going through the ropes only to get let down in the end. I'm not sure I can take Peyton getting let down again.

Yesterday's workout was a joke. It's a good thing I had an hour to myself to cool off in the shower before Peyton got back to the hotel. I was pretty lit. I spent the afternoon running routes and throwing the ball at targets, and the entire thing felt like those pro-games Bryce and I would get invited to during college. Sure, my arm was fine. I think I looked fast, and I felt agile. But I could see it in everyone's face who was watching. *Indifference.* Fuck, even Bryce looked indifferent, and his job is to sell my ass.

"Pumped for today, man! Let's do this!" Whiskey flattens his palm into the center of my chest, knocking some of my wind away.

"Hell, yeah! See you out there, brother!" I put on a good face for my friend, but when he leaves the locker room, I drop my forearms to my thighs, balling my hands as I stare at the Cyclones emblem swirled in a mix of red, black, and blue in the carpet in the center of the room.

I can't walk away from this. It's not in my fabric. My dad would be disappointed, and I live my life by his creed. You finish what you start. And there are people who believe in me. I don't want to let them down. But I can't help this feeling that this game is rigged. I'm not sure I have a fair shot.

"Hey, there's my favorite client."

I chuckle silently at the sound of Bryce's salesman voice. Lifting my head, I snag my helmet from beside me and get to my feet.

"Dude, I'm your *only* client," I laugh out. I close the slick wooden cabinet where my change of clothes, phone, wallet— life—is stacked into a neat little pile. There's a security guard outside this room, and another two by the main entrance. And probably another dozen wandering around the stadium. I don't think we have any fans yet to keep out, but I guess it's the non-fans I should worry about.

Bryce slings an arm around me as we walk into the concourse together, and his grin is wide.

"What's got you in a good mood?" He's always been hard to

read in this way. This man can get excited about the dumbest shit. Hell, I remember he got a sponsorship deal that basically paid in free subs for the rest of the season when we played together that final year. You'd think he'd been given a new kidney.

"You do," he says, patting my chest in the same spot Whiskey attacked. I wish they'd quit hitting me there.

His arm drops from around me and he walks a stride or two ahead of me so he can spin and walk backward to look me in the eyes.

"No pressure in that. Wow, thanks," I say in a wry tone.

"Ha! I'm not worried in the least bit. I *know* you. And today? Today, we're gonna see the Wyatt Stone I know still beats inside that chest of yours."

His smirk makes me laugh, and not because his pep talk is working some magic, but because I think he might be full of shit.

"Looking past the idea that you supposedly *know* me, tell me, Bryce . . . what is it that's in store for me today that has you so sure I'm going to hit that turf suddenly a decade younger and a million miles faster?"

He makes a hard stop, and I halt a few inches before running into him. His palms land on my shoulders, and our gazes square up. A few seconds pass, and frankly, his smug grin is starting to piss me off. But then he tilts his head to the right, and I follow his direction, my eyes scanning the field behind him where Chance Hickory, the Cyclone's hyped QB draft pick, is tossing long balls into the end zone to Coach Phillips.

"Fuuuuuck," I groan.

"Right? Let's show this fucker," Bryce says, squeezing my shoulder pads and shaking me where I stand.

I think he misread my *fuuuuuck*.

My eyes flit back to his, and his smile drops a hint.

"What? You're not hyped for this? Since when does Wyatt Stone not thrive under competition? Man, this is where you're at your best! And this kid, he's a lot like me when I was in high school."

"A total dick?" I say, my lip twisted up on the side.

"Ha, ha, very funny," Bryce says. I move to walk forward, but he stops me, putting pressure on my shoulders again. My focus returns to his face, and I hold on to the stern look in his eyes.

"Okay, maybe a little. Yeah, he's a dick. And I was a dick. But he's also arrogant to a fault. And he thinks he knows everything. He thinks he's invincible. He thinks he's the second coming of the football quarterback gods. And Wy?"

I tilt my head a hair, mouth closed, brows raised.

"He's not. He's no god. He's a twenty-one-year-old with a whole lot to learn. And he is *not* the guy to lead this team when they host their opening kickoff in a few weeks."

I blink my attention back to the field, where Chance takes a ball from the basket and instantly drops back a few steps before flinging it fifty yards down the field. It looks easy for him. I bet it doesn't hurt his elbow the way it sometimes does mine. But I get what Bryce is saying. He's showing off. This little exercise is meaningless. And it's careless. If his arm is a commodity, I'm shocked Phillips is putting it at risk by letting him act like a fool. Which means maybe they're *both* like Bryce was in high school.

Arrogant assholes.

I nod slowly, then meet Bryce's gaze again.

"Yeah, okay. I see what you're saying." I slip my helmet on and come back to his waiting stare, letting him manhandle the sleeves of my practice jersey for a few more seconds. We nod at one another as if we're back in the tunnel at Arizona, ready to beat our rivals.

"Show them who you are," he says, sending me on my way with a swift slap to the ass.

I jog out to the sideline, meeting up with Coach Elgin and Jerry, who is dressed more like a coach today than a guy who bought his way into the front office.

"There's the man," Jerry says. I smile because all this ego-inflating is well-meaning, but fuck is it embarrassing.

"Morning, Coach." I pull my helmet off and set it on the sideline the way my dad always taught me. For every team of mine he coached, he would have us line our helmets up as we ran and stretched. We set up in perfect lines. We shouted in unison. We listened and respected, and I carried those lessons with me through high school and college, getting my team-mates to follow suit.

"Respect your equipment. Respect your teammates and coaches. And respect your family members who work hard and show up," my dad always said. It's the simple things that set the example, and treating this game with respect shows. I just hope Mickey is up there in that box watching.

"You ready to show this kid what's up?" Jerry's chuckle crackles, and he snaps the gum in his mouth as his grin pushes into his cheeks. He's wearing reflective sunglasses, so I can't make out his eyes, but I sense from the rest of his expression that he's amused. I think he's waiting for me to shame this kid a little, maybe knock him off his pedestal. I just hope I don't get knocked on my ass.

"Stone!"

My head swivels to the other end of the field where Coach Phillips is feeding balls to Chance.

I bend down, grab my helmet, and put it on as I jog over to him. I'm not sure what I'll do if he asks me to start throwing recklessly like his golden boy is. I guess I'll do it to make him happy, though I fundamentally disagree with it. This isn't how you warm up.

"Yes, Coach." I glance beyond his shoulder to Coach Elgin, who is standing on his own in the end zone. I think his eyes are on me, and I gulp. I don't want to disappoint him.

"We're gonna run a few routes today with the A and B squad. You're going to be working with B. You good with that?"

Phillips doesn't look my direction when he asks, instead tossing another ball to Chance, who I notice hasn't given me a single glance. I'm sure he knows who I am. That's the arrogance Bryce was talking about, I bet.

"You got it, Coach." I snag one of the balls from the cart and squeeze it between both palms as I nod toward Chance.

"Maybe we can toss a little? Get the arm warm?" I suggest.

Again, Chance's neck doesn't even break to look in my direction.

"He's warm. Grab one of the B receivers when they come out." Phillips physically turns his body away from me, leaving me holding a ball with nobody to throw to and a face as hot as a hatch chile.

"Got it," I say, knowing he's no longer listening.

Fine. If he thinks Chance is warm and this little showcase they've got going is all he needs to perform today, who the hell am I to correct him? I shake my head and laugh silently as I spin around and jog toward the center of the field. I set the ball down along with my helmet and begin my warm-up routine, finishing with a few sprints to get the blood pumping through my entire body. The rest of the team is trickling out when I jog to the sideline and fuel up on some electrolytes, and test the wrap around my wrists.

I recognize the third-string receiver from my late-night study sessions of the roster photos. His name is Jax, and he's greener than green. He was a late round pick-up from Iowa. I hope he can catch.

"Hey, eighty-six," I call out, getting his attention. He looks behind him at first, then turns his attention to me, tapping on his chest.

"Yeah, you're Jax, right?" I'm starting to doubt my memory.

"Yeah, that's me."

Thank God.

"Cool. I'm Wyatt. I'm throwing to you today. Mind helping me get a few reps in?"

Jax has dark brown skin, and he's maybe six inches taller than me. When Peyton told her dad Jerry was working with the team, Reed mentioned that the man has a knack for discovering talent. My gut tells me he saw something in Jax that others overlooked. And if Jax can catch on the run, I have a feeling he and I are going to show a few people up today. He seems nervous, though, so I'm going to need to give his confidence a kick in the ass.

He nods to me, and we both make our way to the sideline. The receivers have been running all morning, so I know he's good and warm. The two of us start off with some light tossing about ten yards apart, and I gradually grow it to twenty until I'm zipping the ball at him with enough force that it will stick whether he wants it to or not. My final toss lands square in his chest, but his hands collapse around the ball, caging it in place, and the grin that pulls up one side of his mouth settles my nerves about him.

"I'm good," I say, walking toward him. He tosses the ball back to me when I'm a few feet away.

"You know, I watched you play when I was in junior high," Jax says. His lips pucker as he fights to hold in his laugh.

"Yeah, yeah. Out here, I'm an old man. I get it," I say, and he finally lets the laugh spill out.

"It's cool, though. You were the shit for Arizona. When I found out they might pick you up—" He waggles his head and bites the tip of his tongue through his smile. "I got a little excited, I guess. Maybe a little star struck."

"Ha!" My turn to laugh. "I'll try not to disappoint you. How are you on the run? Like, if I lead you, make you stretch . . . will you get there?"

His deep inhale is concerning.

"Look, I'm not going to lie to you, Wyatt. I had a shit QB last season, and it damn near ruined my draft. I want to say no problem, but at this point? I have no idea what I can do with a real pass."

I nod, suddenly getting why his draft pick was so high. I like Jax. Humble guys tend to surprise people. I have a good feeling about today.

"Got it. We'll start easy, and then maybe see what we can do together."

"I like the sound of that," he says through excited laughter. We slap hands and bump fists, then join the rest of the team as everyone circles up to listen to Coach Phillips.

My gaze is glued to Coach Elgin, his hands comfortable in the pockets of his Cyclones windbreaker, his bushy eyebrows popping out above the rims of his blue-tinted sunglasses. He's old-school, with a whistle hanging around his neck and a hat that looks like it's been through a war covering his head. He rubs the scruff on his chin as he listens to his assistant run through today's plan. I have a sense he's feeling out Phillips as much as Phillips is feeling out me. I also sense he trusts him about the same amount I do.

Coach Phillips breaks, and we filter to our various positions, divided into two squads. I make it a point to introduce myself to every single guy on the B team, especially my O-line. That's something I learned from Reed, to make the O-line feel like the most important guys on the field. Because they are—at least as far as my skull is concerned.

Chance doesn't seem to be interested in getting to know anyone, instead gripping a ball in his palm and swinging it into his hip as he waits to get called to the line of scrimmage. I smirk in anticipation, and his first attempt at the Z-route goes about as well as I predict. It's hard to jump right in and throw to guys you don't know. But me? I know my guys. I've been saying their names in the order I learned them for the last five minutes while I stand back and watch Chance be exactly the guy Bryce told me he is.

Jax, Sumon, Taylor, Ben, Drey, Michael, Mo, Lenia, Felix, and finally, Cisco.

Cisco . . . he's the most important right now. B-squad center and the first guy to hold off the rush.

"B squad, let's go!"

The A squad clears out as we rush to the line. I flatten my hand on Cisco's back as he centers the ball.

"Deep breath, Cisco. We got this," I say, reassuring him.

I blink slowly, repeating those words in my head to myself, and I look to my right and left, putting faces to every guy on my line. I see Whiskey, even though he was on the A squad. Where Ben is lined up, I imagine Ratcliffe from Arizona. And Drey is also Jake from my Vista days. These are my guys.

"Oh, twenty-one! Oh, twenty-one! Hike!" The ball sticks to my hands, and I fall back a few steps, believing in my pocket. Jax hits his route as if he's been programmed by some AI, not missing a beat and crossing over just as the ball leaves my hands. My line holds off the sack, *thank God,* and Jax hits the forty right when the ball does, the catch near seamless—minus the slight twist he has to make with his shoulder to make sure it's snug before he takes off.

"Run it again!" Coach Phillips whistles, halting Jax before he can break for the end zone.

My squad scurries back to the line of scrimmage, and before I start the count, Coach Phillips growls, "Clean it up!"

"Looked pretty clean to me," Drew mutters to my right. I smile, and I catch the shake in Cisco's body as he keeps his laughter quiet.

"Yes, Coach!" I say, leaning down and turning my head to the right to catch Jax's eyes. I give him a nod, and he flashes a quick thumbs-up. We're gonna need to fast-track our plan. Mostly because I'm ready to show off a little.

"Oh, twenty-one! Oh, twenty-one! Hike!"

This time, the play goes off faster, the defense rushing with more energy, and the O-line breaks down right before I'm able to step out and sling the ball down the field. I take the hit, landing on my shoulder. It hurts more than I remember, but also less than I expect. Maybe they're taking it easy on me, friendly fire and all that.

I lift my head enough to watch Jax stretch his hands out and pull the ball into his chest about two yards deeper than the last time we ran the route. This time, Coach Phillips lets him run all the way.

"All right, A-squad. Get in there and show them how it's done," Phillips says. His whistle is secured between his front teeth, probably to keep him from cracking his molars.

We were supposed to run this five times, but it only took two passes for me to get under Phillips's skin. Jax jogs back to us, and we slap hands. I walk down the line and praise every guy on my squad, telling them to keep the energy up. It's been twenty minutes, but already we're bonding. Behind me, Chance and the A-squad are running one sloppy play after another. And when I glance at Coach Elgin and Jerry, the two of them are grinning with tight lips, matching toothpicks sticking out.

About a half dozen routes and two hours later, my body is drenched inside and out, and my squad looks a bit ragged, but we held our own. I'm pouring water down my throat—and the front of my body—when Keke, today's star pass-rusher, holds out a fist.

"Pretty good stuff, old man," he says. We bump knuckles, and I give him a nod and smile, catching Chance looking our way while Phillips fills his head with what I assume is unearned praise.

"Looked good out there today, Wyatt. You made a statement for sure." I turn at Jerry's compliment, my helmet still propped on my forehead. He's standing with Bryce, whose smug grin tells me he's pleased with my performance today. I wish that guy had a better poker face, but it feels good that he seems to think I did well.

"Thanks, but I'm not sure that message got through to everyone." I chuckle and spray another dose of water into my mouth before tossing the empty bottle onto the grass near the hydration table.

"Phillips doesn't matter here. Elgin makes the call. It's in his contract. Phillips is—"

"You don't need to finish that," I cut in, and the three of us laugh.

"Fair enough," Jerry says.

"I'll catch you inside, Wy," Bryce says, placing a hand on my shoulder and forcing my gaze to meet his. His eyes flicker with a flash of what I think is pride. Maybe a little greed too. He has a lot riding on this. He wants it to work as much as I do, if not more.

"Sounds good," I say, patting his bicep and nodding. It's weird being able to read each other so well, especially given our past. But I hear his silent words loud and clear—I stood out today, and Chance is exactly the kind of guy he said he is.

Jerry's hands drop into his pockets, and he gazes across the field to where a few guys from the defense are stretching out on the field. Lots of cramping today on the team. One of the perks of playing in Arizona for years is that I've learned everything there is to know about hydration. I don't cramp, probably because by this point I've morphed into part camel.

"Walk with me," he finally says when Bryce is far enough away. He nods toward the stands.

"Okay," I answer, my voice obviously full of caution.

Jerry laughs softly and gestures toward a group of field assistants gathering empty water bottles and cleaning up discarded athletic tape.

"Hey, Ryan, right?"

A skinny guy in glasses who looks fresh out of college lifts his head to meet Jerry's gaze, and swallows so hard his Adam's apple dips under his shirt collar and pops back into place.

"Yes, sir?" The kid's as nervous as I am. I'm not sure Jerry gets the power he wields out here.

"Take this in for Mr. Stone, if you don't mind." Jerry lifts my helmet from my head, leaving what feels like a deep crease along my forehead in its wake. He hands it to Ryan, who nods and dashes off to the locker room.

"That kid thinks you're timing him. Look at him go." The two of us look on as Ryan disappears through the tunnel a few seconds later.

"I am," Jerry says, pulling his watch hand from his pocket and glancing at it before quirking up the side of his mouth and shifting his gaze my way. "Kidding."

I shake with a light laugh, and my shoulders relax a hint as I walk alongside Jerry toward the first row of seats. He's funny. And of everyone out here with a hand in my fate, he feels the most kindred. But the bubbling in my belly that's shooting fire up my esophagus is still brewing, and I'm still not ready to let my guard down around anyone out here but Peyton.

I slide into the row and move down a few seats. Jerry takes the second one in, leaving two between us. I lean forward, resting my elbows on my knee pads as I nervously ball my fists. Jerry crosses one long leg over the other, his slacks lifting at the ankles enough to reveal a flashy pair of red and blue Cyclones socks. They match his coach-style polo.

"Mickey is going to want to go with Chance. You know that already, though," he says.

I nod, because in most ways I did. But hearing it anchors that thought in concrete and drops it into my gut.

"I figured."

My mouth feels dry, and I wish I still had a water bottle to drown my anxiety before it chokes me. I shut my mouth instead and swallow hard.

"He's not ready now . . . Chance?" Jerry continues. "He will be. One day. But he's too green. He needs a mentor."

I feel his eyes on me before I turn to confirm they are. As much as I knew this was the case, that the expectation was for me to ease the pathway for a younger talent to come in, it still tastes bad.

"You're ready now, Wyatt. Hell, you were probably ready years ago, but teams missed the boat. What I saw out there today? What you do naturally with the team . . . that's not something kids come out of college with. That kind of leadership is either in you or it's not. And if it's not, it's going to take a humbling experience to get you there."

I breathe out a short laugh and look down at the concrete.

"Is that my role here? To be a humbling experience for Chance Hickory?"

I give him a sideways look and wait for his response. He uncrosses his legs and matches my posture, meeting my eyes.

"Initially? Yeah, Wyatt. You're here to be the teacher. To be the motivating factor. To scare the shit out of a punk kid with raw talent and zero discipline."

I nod, my stomach dropping with my gaze.

"I won't lie to you, Wyatt. Ever. You have my word. You can ask your father-in-law what that's worth, and I hope he'd tell you to take it to the bank. So, know when I say this—"

I pop my head up and hold my breath as we lock gazes.

"I think that job is yours to lose. And that means I believe you'll take it from him. I already saw the wheels turning today. I see the tells. The way the team so easily leaned into your leadership. The reactions you got from the sidelines, from the defense, from the other coaches—from the guy up in the box."

"Now you're bullshitting me," I laugh out.

He shakes his head.

"I've been around this business a long time. And as stubborn of a son-of-a-bitch as Mickey may be, he's still a businessman. With you at the helm, the Cyclones make money. Not *eventually*. Now. As soon as you play a televised game in front of fans. As soon as you step into the media room and answer questions. The moment you connect with Jax or whomever in the end zone. Dollar signs, Wyatt. You will win. Chance won't. Not yet. And if you win, and win early, and keep winning? This gig is yours."

I exhale loudly, allowing my lips to actually flap with my breath, and Jerry laughs at my physical reaction.

"It's a lot," he says.

I thread my hands behind my neck and squint as I look up at the sky. The cloud cover is thin enough to be nothing more than a reflector for the sun.

"It's more than a lot. And it feels fucking impossible."

"Yeah," he says, standing and moving close enough to pat

my shoulder twice with his massive hand. "But that's kind of your thing, isn't it? Doing impossible shit."

He chuckles through his toothy smile as he lifts his sunglasses from his shirt collar and slides them back into place. It's hard not to notice the massive gold and diamond-studded ring on his hand—I've seen that ring on Reed's hand.

"Get some rest, Wyatt. I'll see you tomorrow."

I stay put until Jerry's out of sight. In fact, I wallow in my own doubts and fears long enough to watch the coaching assistants completely clear the field of equipment and debris. Eventually, Bryce steps through the tunnel and heads my way. I decide to meet him midfield.

"You ready?"

I know his question isn't about lunch or heading back to the hotel. I wear the weight of it, and it feels impossible. But that's what I do, isn't it? Carry the impossible into the end zone for the win.

"I'm ready."

And for now, I mean it.

Chapter Ten

Peyton

I felt bad the other night when Wyatt ordered room service and set up the balcony with dinner for two, expecting me in the red dress, only to end up with me in sweats and a deep desire to curl up with a heating pad.

I've been miserable the last few days, even after my period was done. And Wy's feeling his own stress. I'm still not sure whether he wants this starting job or simply wants to win and prove those doubting assholes Phillips and Mickey wrong. I'm not sure I care about his reasons as long as Mickey has to eat a little crow. A lot of crow. A *whole* lot of crows. A murder of crows.

As sad and lost as I've felt, though, something clicked for me today. And I want to celebrate.

While I was at lunch with Tasha, it dawned on me how much I need something of my own. I love working with my mom, and I'll never give that up. I've grown to share her passions. She inspires me, as do the clients we get to work with. The horses are great co-workers, too. But I've been craving more. And it took a Portland high school cheer competition and a hotel full of loud, glitter-covered teenage girls to realize what it is I want.

"I want to coach."

It's the second time I've said it to Wyatt in the last ten seconds. The first time, he was still staring at my hips in this dress. I guess I should be honored that he's more rapt with my body than the tantalizing filet sizzling on the table next to us. It's a little chilly in Portland in May, and this Arizona girl wasn't up for wearing a slinky dress in fifty-degree weather, so I had room service recreate his date night inside our suite.

"Oh, like . . . *coach* coach," he stammers, finally peeling his eyes away from my body to meet my gaze. I'm a bit overdressed, though I find his white T-shirt and gray sweatpants as sexy as he seems to find my dress. I pulled this date night off while he was in the shower after his second workout with the team today, and given his slack-jawed expression and wide eyes, I'd say I pulled the surprise off nicely.

"Is there another kind of coach?" I pop my hip out and twist my lips as I await his response. He shakes his head and runs his palm over his face and into his wet hair. He shoots me a sheepish grin and closes the distance between us, hooking his finger into the plunging neckline of my dress and tugging me closer.

"I'm a little distracted," he admits, dropping his mouth to the curve of my neck. His teeth graze my collarbone as he makes his way along my bare shoulder, and while I want to say *fuck it* to the gourmet dinner and conversation and let him have his way right now, I also very much want him to hear me out. Because this plan of mine affects him. It affects *us.*

My fingertips run along his stubbled jawline as I coax his mouth away from my skin and force his eyes to look at mine.

"*Mmm*, you're going to distract me if you don't stop—"

He growls and moves right back into the crook of my neck. I

giggle before backing away a full step and holding out my hands.

"Five minutes. That's all I need. And then you can do as you wish."

A sinister smirk takes up residence on his face. *I just gave him a hall pass for anything.*

"Yes, Wyatt. I want to *coach* coach. At Coolidge. They need someone, and I already talked to the athletic director about it. The job is mine to take, and I really want to do it. I think I *need* to, for my head and my heart."

I draw in a long breath and hold my mouth shut tight as realization paints his features. His lips pull into a tight line as his gaze drops down to the floor.

"Which means you'll be there, in Coolidge, while I'm here. Assuming they keep me."

"You know they're going to keep you. At least for the season. And knowing you as I do, probably for years after. Especially when they see the lightning in a bottle that is Wyatt Stone."

He chuckles, never good at taking a compliment, even from his biggest fan in the world. I knead my hands in front of me, wanting him to be more than okay with my proposal. I need him to encourage it, mostly because I'm a little nervous about how our relationship will shake out. My parents spent seasons apart, and while they are one of the closest couples in the world, I know firsthand that my mom had to fight hard to keep them that way.

"How would it work?" He quirks a brow and moves one of the chairs out to take a seat. I suddenly feel as if I'm auditioning for him, and it strikes me that I've never really had to interview for anything. Wyatt would push me to be and do whatever I want, even if it means selling his own soul, but I'm suddenly nervous now that he's put me on the spot.

"Well," I begin, pushing my tongue into my cheek. "I won't

need to be back in Arizona until August, for tryouts. And I've already checked the schedules for every Cyclones home game. I can take the first Saturday morning flight out and come back home on the following Monday mornings."

Wyatt's head tilts as his mouth quirks up on one side.

"You don't want to fly that much."

I shake my head quickly.

"No, I do. In fact, I can make four away games, too. And, well, the Arizona game is a no-brainer. And maybe, if I can get the squad to nationals, I can pair that trip with your Miami game, and then—"

"Peyt."

My mouth snaps shut when Wyatt stands and moves toward me with a playful smirk.

"Why are you trying to sell me on this? You've made up your mind. I mean, my gut instincts tell me you have a file full of details and itineraries stashed somewhere on that laptop."

He gestures to my work bag resting on the kitchenette counter. I blink at it a few times and lift a shoulder.

"I like to be prepared before a presentation," I say, a half second before Wyatt's palms cup my shoulders. I relax under his touch as my head swivels back to face him.

"You don't need to make a presentation. You want this. I understand, and I want it for you, too. We . . ." He moves one hand from my shoulder to tap a finger to his chest, then to mine. "We'll make it work."

I bite my lip and try not to cry. I've been a bit of an emotional mess the last few days, and when my husband says the perfect thing, it really hits that cluster of nerves around my heart.

"You're not worried about what it might do? To us?"

I need to hear him say it.

"I'm not worried about us at all. Ever. In fact, of the thousands of things that I will worry about over my lifetime, *us* will never be one of them. I know so."

He takes my hand in his and presses it to his chest. His heart thumps under my palm. His body is warm, and the cotton of his T-shirt is still a little damp from his recent shower and wet hair. He smells like the desert rain . . . like home.

I lift my chin and step into him, his eyes dropping down and zeroing in on my mouth.

"How do you know?"

His lip ticks up, showing off his dimple, and my eyes flutter shut from the instant intoxication.

"Because I'm yours, and you . . ." He pauses as his right hand slides through the slit on the side of my dress and wraps around my ass, tugging me into him.

"You are mine."

Wyatt drops to his knees, pushing my dress up my thighs and tugging my panties down my legs. I barely have time to gasp before his mouth covers my pussy, and my hands dive into his hair as I fight to hold myself steady and maintain my balance.

"What about dinner?" I pant.

"You are all I want to eat," he says as his fingers dig into my ass and his tongue flicks my sensitive skin.

"Ohhhh-kayyyy," I rasp, my voice quivering from his seductive assault.

Wyatt sucks me into his mouth and punishes my clit with his tongue until my legs nearly buckle, and before I fall to pieces, he slowly stands and brings my dress up and over my body along with him. Tossing the flimsy fabric to the floor, he lifts me and carries me to the back of the plush sofa that faces the stone fireplace and a wall of windows that looks out over the city. The sky outside is pink but quickly fading to purple, and the room is cast in a golden hue that makes Wyatt's eyes almost glow a cerulean blue.

My legs wrap around him as he discards my lace bralette, tossing it on top of my dress. His palms meet at my spine as he arches me back enough to give his mouth access to my breasts, and he sucks my nipple so hard that it throbs when he lets go.

"Wyatt," I hum his name, my need for him desperate as I unfurl my legs and part them wider.

I pull his shirt up over his head as he pulls his sweatpants down and fists his cock. The scratches along his sides from his workouts make him look rough, and I don't think his abs have ever been so toned. I let my hands roam over the hard ridges and down to his hips as he strokes himself while his eyes seer into me.

"Come here," he growls as he palms my ass and pulls me to the very edge of the sofa back, forcefully thrusting his cock inside of me.

"Mine," he says, moving his mouth to my neck as his hands grip my ass. His hips rock feverishly as he pummels me.

"Wy—" I can't even finish his name, every thrust hitting me so right, so hard, that it sends shocks throughout my entire body.

"Come for me, baby," he commands.

My body tingles, my insides tightening as I fight to hold off the inevitable. I don't want this to end, but I need to come. I can't take it much longer.

"That's it," he praises when the first whimper leaves my lips.

My open mouth lands on his shoulder, and my teeth dig into his skin as the first waves nearly knock me out. Wyatt doesn't let up, fucking me harder with every thrust until my climax is so sensitive that I lose my breath and have to dig my nails into his back to hold on. His cock swells inside of me, and

I warm with his cum as he thrusts a few more times, holding me to him through the very last pulse.

Our bodies sticky and tangled, Wyatt reaches for my thighs and pulls my legs tight around him, swiveling so he's now leaning against the back of the sofa while his cock still fills me. I rest my cheek against his shoulder. I'm a little out of breath, but the slow strokes of Wyatt's fingertips along my spine eventually slow my heart rate back to normal. I could sleep here, just like this, with him inside of me and our bodies melded as one.

"I just have one question," he finally says, sweeping my hair away from my ear so he can kiss the lobe.

I shift my upper body so I can meet his gaze, and he continues to run his hand through my hair, tucking what I can only imagine are wild strands behind my ear.

"What's that?" I ask.

"Do cheer coaches wear the uniforms?"

I laugh at his question but bite my tongue when I realize he's merely smirking. My brow pinches.

"Are you serious?"

His gaze moves to mine and his hands move back to my hips, pulling me into him as he grinds his cock into me, reminding me he's still hard and somehow ready.

"Deadly."

Chapter Eleven

Wyatt

A one-year deal.

Bryce isn't pushing. I respect him more because of it, too. Me signing is a huge win for him. Damn, though, but he hasn't brought that up once. If anything, he's been throwing out all the reasons I should walk out of here and give them a big middle finger over my shoulder.

"It's not even a respectable number," he says, spinning the paperwork back around on the wide mahogany table before leaning back in his chair to level me with his signature expression. "I say fuck 'em."

He means it, too. I can tell. If there's one constant about Bryce Hampton, it's that he's a shit liar. No poker face at all.

I breathe in deeply and flip through the boilerplate contract they give rookies one more time, as if something in these words is going to jump out at me and help make up my mind. Peyton left us in here fifteen minutes ago. She was so offended by the offer that she feared sticking around would only end with her storming into the front offices and wringing Mickey's neck. Of course, it wouldn't be Mickey; it would be his assistant. And then Jerry would have to help cover up the crime. It would be a mess.

"If you want, I'll call Jerry back in here. But you and I both know these aren't his numbers. This is all Mickey," Bryce says.

"And Phillips. I don't know what it is he hates about me so much, but there is no winning that guy over."

Bryce's brows raise, and he leans his head toward the currently closed glass door.

"Not yet. I'm still thinking about it."

Bryce's body slinks into the chair, and he lets out a heavy exhale. He spins in the chair while linking his hands behind his neck. He stops cold when he makes it a full rotation, and his eyes are on me again.

"I should have let Jason handle this, man. I'm sorry. I fucked it up."

I burst into instant laughter and shake my head.

"Dude, Jason couldn't have sold me any better. Plus, you got Whisk a solid deal. This isn't on you. It's just . . . what it is."

I lean forward and rest my chin on my fist to take one more hard look at the number on top of the contract—$840,000.

"I pulled in more with my last year of NIL deals," I laugh out.

"Fuck, Wy. *I* pulled in more," Bryce adds.

"Did you know I didn't want to play football at first? Back when I was a kid."

My confession makes Bryce sit back, and his brow draws in tight.

"Yeah," I chuckle. "My dad signed me up for this league, and I wasn't very good right away, and that frustrated me. But he made me promise to give it a year. *One year, son, and if you still don't like it, we'll find something else.*"

Bryce smirks at my imitation of my father's voice. My mom says I sound like him now that I'm grown. I like that I do.

"Looks like you changed your mind on the game," Bryce says.

I nod.

"By the fourth game, I was the starting quarterback. I mean, it was pee wee ball, so it's not like I was throwing long passes or anything like that. But I got to be in charge. I got to yell out plays that meant nothing. You know how it was when we were kids; we pretended we were the guys on TV."

"Ha, yeah," Bryce agrees, nodding as he smiles.

"That year changed everything," I recall. "I practiced every day in the front yard, throwing the ball with my dad. He'd get up early with me before school on the days he wasn't on shift just to let me get some reps in. By the time the season was up, I won most-improved player. My dad said it should have been MVP."

I chew at the inside of my mouth while I live in my memories for a moment. I can almost feel the blast of air from my dad's truck vents as he drove me home from the end-of-season pizza party. He glued that trophy to his dashboard, he was so proud.

"What a difference a year makes," I mumble, not fully aware my thoughts are out loud until Bryce responds.

"One year," he says.

Our eyes lock, and my upper lip twitches as my belly stirs with that long-lost fire. It's not about the money. It's about the disrespect.

I pull the contract toward me and grab the pen, clicking it against the table, then scratching my name across the signature line before tossing the pen and paper toward Bryce.

"I do one year, and then you get me the deal I'm worth."

Bryce stands immediately, rolling the contract up in one hand and reaching across the table to me with the other. I get to my feet, and we shake once.

"Hell fuckin' yeah," he says, before marching out of the room and down the hallway to Jerry's office. I sit in the quiet of the conference room for a few extra seconds, long enough to hear Jerry shout the same words Bryce did as he left, then I grab my phone from the table and call my wife on my way to the elevator.

"Well?" That's her greeting.

"One year," I say.

The line is silent at first, and my stomach tightens. I'm tougher when she's in my corner. I need her with me on this. I need her strength and stubborn will.

"One year," she finally echoes.

"One."

"*Hmm*," she sounds like she's pondering. "And then they pay you millions," she finally adds.

My mouth inches up as I step into the elevator and imagine the hardball look on her face. She doesn't have to say it for me to know that she might even push for half of my salary to be instantly donated to her mom's charity.

"See you in two minutes." I end our call and hold my breath for the short elevator ride, breaking into a jog when I pass by Janice, the sweet red-headed woman with twins at UofA.

"That looks like a good-news jog to me," Janice hollers after me. I spin around and give her a thumbs up. She's Jerry's secretary, and reminds me so much of my mom. Speaking of my mom, I have to call her next. She's going to worry that I'm settling, but she's also going to scream with joy. She's always wanted to see me set foot on a pro field. And what this all means for my dad is probably the biggest positive to come out of the deal. I know he's watching this play out, and I feel his hands on my shoulders as he tells me to give those doubters hell.

Our rental Escalade is idling as I step into the player lot, and I can tell by the way Peyton's hair is blowing in every which direction that she's got the air on full blast. I startle her when I yank open the driver's side door, but she quickly pounces on the center console, holding herself up with her palms as her body lurches toward me for a kiss. I cup her cheeks and cover her mouth with mine, and it feels as though time stops. I live in the bliss as long as I can before, eventually, we both need to breathe.

"I've already found an apartment," she says the second our mouths part.

I chuckle and shift into reverse, checking the lot behind me before pulling out.

"Of course you have," I say through a chuckle. "And let me guess . . . we need to move in this summer."

She doesn't respond, so when I reach the light to exit the stadium and enter the highway, I give her a curious sideways glance. Her guilty, tight-lipped grin says it all, but to punctuate things, she shrugs.

"Woman, you're not even going to be living here full time, and you've got me roped into moving trucks in June," I laugh out.

"It's a dry heat," she tosses in, and now we're both laughing. I'm not sure whether it's because we're happy or because we're scared. Maybe a little bit of both. But I do know there's no one I would rather be taking this gamble with.

Three weeks later

"There is nothing dry about this."

It's been raining for two straight days, the same amount of time we've been moving boxes, sofas, and bedroom furniture into the historic brick building in the heart of downtown. My shoes are sopping wet, the soles more like well-used Mr. Clean sponges at this point, and Whiskey gave up wearing shoes about four trips ago. The big man has embraced being barefoot.

"This is the last one, guys. I promise," Peyton swears over the expanse of the love seat she and I are carrying together. Her hair is matted to the sides of her face, and there's no mystery to what her bra looks like. Everyone can see it through the thin gray T-shirt that's now glued to her skin thanks to the downpour.

Whiskey pushes the button for the seventh floor on the freight elevator, then collapses into the armchair he carried by himself. I snarl at him because there isn't enough room for me to drop my end of the sofa, plus I wouldn't want to stick Peyton with the rest of the weight on her own. It *is* her fault that we didn't hire movers for this project of hers, though.

"Remind me again why I couldn't have just clicked around IKEA's website and had everything delivered?"

She levels me with a hard stare and a flat-lined mouth, and I immediately snap my mouth shut and nod.

"You're right." I gulp and drop my gaze to the bulky sofa arm hugged to my chest. "You will live here too, *though not a lot.*"

I mumble that last part, but Peyton still hears it, and she pushes the sofa into my gut. I grunt and cough out a laugh.

"Dude, this is why you don't complain. You simply do as they say. Tasha's gonna have us doing the same thing once she picks a rental. Only we've got two kids, and she wants a house, so this move will take days, and she'll be spreading it across rooms and streets and yards."

I exhale and lean my back into the metal wall of the eleva-tor. Tasha and Peyton like quirky furniture, and they both like to shop. I guess I should feel lucky that Peyton was able to find the pieces she wanted in two days. I have a feeling I'll be moving something around Whiskey's house every few days for the next year.

We get the last two pieces of furniture through the door, and while Peyton paces through the great room deciding exactly which way she wants things to face, I grab two beers from the fridge and hand one to Whisk.

"It's a nice sofa, man," he says, bumping my arm with his elbow. I nod and let my gaze drift to my wife, who insisted on the creamy chenille piece with a chaise lounge seat. I predict I'll be taking many naps on that thing, and when she's gone, I might end up sleeping there. I miss her too much when the bed is big and empty.

I'm about to tip my head back and take a swig of my beer when Peyton drops down suddenly and sits on the edge of the chaise section.

"You okay, babe?"

She shakes her head and leans forward, practically tucking her head between her knees. I leave my beer on the counter and hop over the love seat to sit next to her. My hand rubs circles on her back, her shirt damp and cold.

"You overdid it today," I say, feeling bad that I let her help in the first place. She hasn't had muscle spasms in a while, and she's so damn strong that I sometimes forget that physical exertion can take a toll on her.

"I'm just a little light-headed. I'll be fine," she says, lifting her head enough to give Whiskey a thumbs up from across the room.

"I can handle moving stuff around the room, dude. Why don't you take off and get back to Tasha and the kids. I need to force her to quit for the day and maybe take a hot shower," I say.

Whiskey guzzles the rest of his beer and leaves us with his belched words, "Sounds good."

I follow him to the door, then lock it behind him.

"He's a real romantic," Peyton jokes, holding her arms up so I can peel her wet shirt over her head.

"I could have gotten one of the guys to help, or hell, had your dad come up for this. I'm sorry."

Peyton shakes her head and grabs my arm as she lifts herself back to her feet.

"I know this place is temporary, and it's not really *ours* ours, but it's our first on our own. I wanted to decorate it my way, and do things on our own, and just . . ." She blinks a few times and sits back on the couch, pinching the bridge of her nose.

"Babe, we should get you out of the wet clothes. Let me carry you." I scoop her into my arms and carry her to the main bathroom where all her toiletries and our towels are still in the department store bags we bought them in this morning.

I flip the shower on to warm the water as Peyton slips out of her shorts and bra. She sits on the closed toilet to pull her wet socks from her feet when she suddenly freezes, her mouth falling open.

"You okay?" I drop to a knee and touch her chin. Her eyes flicker to mine but remain as wide as her mouth. I can't tell if she's in shock, about to be sick, or suddenly remembered something deeply important, like leaving a stove burner on.

"Peyt?"

She blinks a few times, then licks her lips before pulling them in tight. Her smile shows itself slowly at first, and I mirror her expression, mostly because I have no clue what is going on, and she's acting really weird.

"Wy, I think you need to run to the drugstore. Like, now. I need to pee on a stick."

I stand up before her words fully register but stop after taking a step toward the door. I flip around to face her again.

"Wait, you think . . ."

She nods, but her movement is subtle, like she doesn't want the universe to see her say yes.

"Shit. Uh, okay. Yeah. There's one down the block. I'll just . . ." I spin in place a few times before Peyton breaks me from my daze.

"Just go!" she tells me.

Panic rushes through my veins and I'm finding it hard to function. I can't locate my keys, my phone, or my wallet. I can barely find my way out of the bathroom. I center myself for a breath in the kitchen, where I spot my wallet and phone.

"Lock up behind me," I shout, flying out the door and down the hallway to the elevator. I press the button a few times, but when I don't hear any movement coming from the elevator shaft, I opt for the stairs.

The stairwell exits into the back of the mailroom, and I zip by a couple checking their mailbox as I rush to the lobby and out the main doors. The rain seems to have let up, but the sidewalks are wet and the roads puddled. I splash my way across the street, dunking my already soaked shoes at least six times before reaching the drugstore. I don't know what sort of test Peyton usually buys, and I'm not sure what the difference is between the fifteen-dollar kit and the thirty-dollar one, so I snag an assortment and rush to the checkout.

I ring myself out and forget to opt in to pay for a bag, so I gather up the five tests I chose and tuck them into my T-shirt the way I collected Easter Eggs when I was a kid. My shoes squish against the sidewalk, but I manage to make it back to our apartment without pouncing my feet into a deep puddle again. I'm about to knock on our door when Peyton flings it open, and I dash inside.

"Were you waiting there for me?"

Peyton nods, locking the door behind her as she guzzles down the last few sips in a twenty-four-ounce water bottle.

"I've been drinking water since the moment you left so I can go," she laughs out before waving me toward the bathroom.

I'm panting as I stride through our bedroom, the shower still going strong. The steam is making it warm in here, and coupled with the humidity outside and the dose of adrenaline that's soaking my organs, I feel a little bit like throwing up.

I drop the boxes on the counter before reaching into the shower and killing the spray while Peyton rips into the most expensive test kit I bought and reads the pamphlet.

"What can I do? Do you need me to get you more water? Do you need me to mix something or make you food?"

I have no idea how this shit works, and I feel pretty fucking useless.

My wife chuckles and hands me her empty water bottle.

"More water. I can't have too much water."

I nod, happy to get direction. I fill her bottle at the kitchen sink, making a mental note to set up the water filter tomorrow, then head back to the bathroom in time to catch Peyton about to go.

"Leave!" She waves me back out the door, and I flip around the corner and flatten my back against the wall.

"I've seen you pee before, babe. We've been together for a decade." I laugh at the absurdity of the moment.

"I know, but I don't want to get shy. I need to go while I can, and just . . . *shh!*"

I bite my lip and hold in my laugh before uttering a quiet, "Okay."

Several seconds pass, and I hold my breath until Peyton tells me to come back inside. She's setting the test stick on top of the plastic wrapper it came in when I enter the room. I hand her the water bottle, and she gulps some of it down, but her gaze remains fixed on the test strip.

I move in behind her, wrapping my arms around her body and kissing the top of her head.

"I love you," I say.

She squeezes my arm with her free hand and holds the bottle's rim to her lips with the other, no longer drinking. I can't tell if it's her pulse I feel or my own, but the thump is constant and racing. Our bathroom smells like wet shoes and shower steam, and my forehead is covered with a sheen of sweat.

"I love you," I say again, praying this test comes back positive. I want kids desperately, but more than that, I want this for Peyton.

Her body rocks side to side, so I go along with it and sway with her. My chin rests on top of her head, and I adjust my arms around her, holding her tighter as the test strip reveals a deep pink control line.

"We can take them all, too. Just to make sure. If this one doesn't say you're pregnant, maybe one of them will. I didn't know what I was buying. That's why I got so many, and I—"

"Wy? *Shh*," she whispers.

"Okay," I hum, lowering my mouth to the top of her head again and leaving it there.

We both stare at the small plastic cartridge on the marble countertop, such a rudimentary experiment to determine something so epic. Petyon's body tightens in my embrace as the first line emerges, and when the second one appears, her body quakes.

"Is that—?"

Peyton nods, and I peel one arm away so I can cover my mouth. I think I'm going to cry.

She picks up the test cautiously, cradling it in her palms as she turns slowly to face me. Tears are streaming down her cheeks, and when her gaze lifts to mine, I see nothing but joy in her eyes.

"We're going to be a mom and dad. You and me. Peyt, oh my God!" I cup her cheeks and kiss her forehead, everything still feeling fragile.

"I love you, Wyatt. I love you so much. I'm going to be a mom. I'm a mom."

The reality hits her hard and all at once. I take the test strip from her hands and move it back to the counter, then pull her back into my arms and rock us again. We dance to the music in our heads for nearly an hour and never make it to the shower. Hell, we never make it to the bed. We fall asleep on the carpet of our new apartment somewhere between the bathroom and the mattress with five positive pregnancy tests laid out between us.

One year just got a whole lot more interesting.

Chapter Twelve

Peyton

I used to think I was good at keeping secrets. Turns out I never had a really big secret to keep.

This secret? Being pregnant? It's hard to keep. I've almost let it slip a dozen times to Tasha. I kind of think she knows, though. She drops hints, like making comments here and there about me needing to buy more comfortable clothes for the fall football games now that I'll be coaching cheer. Comfort has never been a requirement for Tasha. An outfit is either cute or trash. And she's not shy about calling out the things in my closet that she thinks I should donate, or, as she likes to say, burn.

Between Wyatt's physical tests and media interviews and my work setting up the competition season for cheer, we haven't had much time to sit down and talk about the logistics of having a baby. In some ways, being busy for the first few weeks has taken the edge off my anxiety.

It's July Fourth at the Johnson house, and that's always a big deal. My dad's birthday is in August, and football camps are about to start at every level—at the high school and in Portland. My grandpa always insists that July Fourth stands as a non-negotiable family day, and he always goes all out. My dad took over the reins after Grampa's last stroke, but Buck Johnson still calls the shots, which means everyone is here.

Everyone.

Probably makes it a good time to let the family in on my secret.

"How are you feeling?"

Wyatt takes the two strings for my bikini top from my hands and ties them behind my neck before kissing my shoulder.

"I haven't thrown up again, so that's a win." I give him a tired, crooked smile over my shoulder.

"You think you're going to be down to eat today? You know your dad puts out a spread, and Rose made carnitas. I've been smelling it all morning."

"Ugh, me too," I admit, holding my arm across my mouth for a few seconds as a wave of nausea passes.

"Okay, if that smell is making you sick then you're really screwed," Wyatt says with a laugh.

I groan as the feeling passes. He's right. I am screwed, because my grandma's carnitas is pretty much the best thing on the planet, and the July Fourth spread is what I always say I would choose for my last meal. This is damn near close to my favorite holiday simply for the food alone. There is no way I'm going to be able to not raise suspicions if I don't fill my plate.

"I think I have to tell them all today."

"Thank God!" Wyatt sighs as he flops back on our bed in a giant letter X.

I shoot him a glare, then turn back toward the mirror on the back of our bedroom door to continue inspecting my belly. I feel like I can see a bump, but also, I've been checking for a bump every four hours for the last month.

"You know this means my dad is going to know we had sex," I say nonchalantly.

"Yeah, I'm over that," Wyatt says, waving a hand in the other direction. He sits up a few seconds later, though, with his brow pulled in tight.

"Over it, huh?" I say, moving toward the bed. I crawl over him, straddling him as he holds himself up on his elbows.

"Nah, your dad will always scare the shit out of me. But . . ." He flattens a palm gently over my belly. "Our baby? She's worth it."

I pucker my lips and tilt back.

"*She*, huh?"

Wyatt's hand moves around my waist, then up my back, his fingertips dancing along my spine.

"Yeah, I think it's a girl."

I hold his stare for a few quiet seconds, then nod. I have no feelings either way, and maybe that's simply because I'm so focused on staying healthy and navigating the next several months. This family does seem to have a thing for producing girls, though, so maybe he's right.

"Come on. Let's let the cat out of the bag," I say, patting Wyatt's bare chest with my hands before sliding off him.

I grab two beach towels on our way out the door and stop to lock up out of habit. I giggle when I realize I don't have keys with me.

"We aren't in Portland," Wyatt says, seeing my mistake.

"It's just so different," I say, and he nods.

Our home here is tucked behind gates and behind my family's main home. I wanted us to have our own place so badly, I didn't stop to recognize the benefits of living on a large property with people around to look out for one another twenty-four-seven. I definitely have a different sense of safety here than at the apartment. I'm not sure the Portland place is supposed to feel like home, though, anyhow. And if Wyatt lands a long-term contract next year and we put down more permanent roots there with a house, I'm still not sure that place will ever completely feel like home.

I tuck those thoughts away as we make our way along the path from the guest house to my parents' home. Their back patio is already filled with people, including a few guys from the high school team who have my family has sort of adopted for big occasions. That's what this family does. It grows with every person it touches.

"Hey, now it's a party!" My aunt Sarah is revving the blender at the poolside bar, making margaritas, and it takes her about fifteen seconds to pour one and march it over to me.

"Happy Fourth of July!" She's already had a few; I can smell it on her breath. I take the glass from her but set it down on a patio table and proceed to make my way through the rest of our houseguests, doling out hugs and learning the names of my dad's latest group of favorite players. My aunt's gaze keeps finding me as I weave through the group gathered inside, and I'm sure she's wondering why I'm not gulping down my favorite summer drink.

I spot Wyatt talking to my dad near the side door that leads to the grill and join them, weaving my hand with his and hoping he can sense my nerves through my sweaty palm.

"Good afternoon, Coach." My dad winks before hugging me and kissing my cheek. He was thrilled that I took the job at Coolidge, and he keeps talking about how we can drive to work together in the mornings. The idea warms my tummy, too, but right now all I can think about is how my aunt is going to blow my news before I get a chance to tell everyone myself.

"Tryouts soon. You got any players I can steal?"

My dad laughs at my joke but waggles a finger at me in warning. My junior year, two of his players defected from football to join the cheer squad. He was furious, though he tried to play the part of supportive adult. One of them, Aiken, was a star receiver. Turned out Aiken was also a phenomenal gymnast, and he ended up getting a full ride to UCLA for gymnastics thanks to his stunt team work.

I tug Wyatt's hand and tilt my head toward the back hallway. He follows my lead, and we dip out of view.

"Hey, I need you to drink my margarita. My aunt gave it to me, and she seems very aware that I haven't had a single sip."

Wyatt's mouth ticks up enough to dimple his cheek as his eyes scan over me toward the back yard.

"Why don't we just tell everyone now," he says, and he's right, except I need to work up my courage. I don't know why I'm so scared to say it out loud.

"Please? I need the perfect timing."

He chuckles softly, then leans in to kiss my lips, smiling against my mouth.

"Anything for my baby mama," he teases.

I swat his ass as he walks by, and he yelps playfully.

"Get a room!" Whiskey shouts from behind the kitchen counter where he is sampling one of everything my mom and Rosie laid out.

"Where's your wife?" I ask. I suddenly decide to tell Tasha the news first, sort of for practice.

"She's by the pool lathering up the girls with sunscreen." He nods toward the sliding glass door, and I spot Tasha on one of the lounge chairs, slipping a pair of goggles around one of her six-year-old's heads.

"Thanks."

I drag Wyatt along behind me, making a stop by the patio table for my abandoned margarita before weaving through the extra chairs my dad put out on our way to Tasha. I hand Wyatt my drink before sitting next to my friend, just as she sends her girls out to the pool with a final warning not to splash the adults. Their giggles as their feet patter toward the steps tell me they're breaking that rule right out of the gate.

"Were we that bad?" she asks.

I take in the innocent play happening on the steps, her girls already splashing the teenage boys in the pool.

"We were worse, but not by much," I joke.

"So . . . I wanted to tell you something," I say, my obvious lead-in clearly piquing my friend's curiosity as she pulls her sunglasses from her face and situates herself on her chair to meet my gaze.

"I—"

"Peyton Johnson, why the fuck aren't you drinking? Are you pregnant or something?"

My Aunt Sarah's voice carries across the patio, her finger pointing at my husband as he stands behind me with the rim of my glass against his lips. He's frozen, like the drink was before I let it melt. He didn't even get a full sip in before my aunt called us out. My body deflates, my shoulders sagging as I glance back at Wyatt one more time, then turn to Tasha. All that's left to do is give her a guilty shrug.

"I wanted to be the one to tell you," I croak.

I'm not sure what my worries were about. The instant the news sinks in, my best friend's hands cup her mouth and she lets out a piercing, joyous scream.

"Really?" Her eyes flash wide, and I nod as we both start to cry.

"Oh, my God, Peyt! I'm going to be an auntie," she says, folding herself into me and wrapping her arms around me tight.

"It's still pretty new. I'm not due until February." *Valentine's Day, according to my doctor.*

"Bitch, you're serious?" My Aunt Sarah pipes in, pushing my uncle and a few of my dad's assistant coaches out of her way as she climbs over seats to get to me.

I nod and get to my feet in time to receive Sarah's attack of hugs.

"Peyton, congratulations, honey! Your mom is going to be so pissed I found out first," she says at my ear. My pulse races at the realization, and I spin around with wide eyes, ready to hunt my mom down. I don't even get a step away, though, before I'm confronted with a massive bouquet of pink and blue balloons along with a basket filled with what looks like pregnancy treats. I blink a few times and realize my mom is the one holding the basket.

Her smirk gives her away.

"Wait . . . you knew?"

She shrugs a shoulder and sets my gift and balloons to the side before pulling me into her arms and rocking me side to side.

"Baby, a mom always knows. I could tell something was up when you were in Portland. Your voice had a tone."

"I had a tone?" I really can't fathom this super power my mom has. I don't think I acted any differently with her, but I've also been in my own head a lot.

"And don't be mad at him, but Wyatt confirmed the news. It's not his fault. I made your dad call him and ask, and well—"

"You told?" I swat at my husband, who backs away and downs the entire margarita out of panic and fear.

"Hon, I can't lie to your dad. And you know he can't say no to your mom. It was a well-oiled machine. I'm afraid today isn't just a Fourth of July celebration. It's a baby shower."

And as I glance around the patio, taking in my aunt's gloating grin as she claps, my Uncle Jason's belly laugh, Rosie's teary eyes, my sister's hand over her mouth, and my dad's raised beer as he stands in the back and tries not to cry himself, I realize I'm not in this alone. I rush to my dad and am swallowed up in the world's best hug. This massive Johnson family that only seems to keep getting bigger is all a baby needs in this world.

Chapter Thirteen

Wyatt

I'm starting to think I'm the oldest guy on the team. Our backup center, Cisco, looks like he's in his late thirties, but it turns out beards can be deceiving. That fucker's twenty-six. That new information has me second-guessing my assumptions about most of the O-line. I think the only guys I've got beat out here for sure are Phillips, Elgin, and Jerry. And I'm not so sure about Phillips.

It was hard to leave for camp. I'm glad Peyton is with family, though. And she's busy with tryouts for the upcoming cheer season. She seems genuinely excited about our future, and since I'm nervous as hell about it, it's good that one of us has a steady head on our shoulders.

Hell, I'm just hoping to keep my head attached to my body during camp. The hits are coming for real now. It's time to shine for every guy out here, not just me, and I've felt every single ounce of effort in that pass rush.

"Tackling is discouraged, *my ass*," I grumble to Whiskey as we undress after another grueling day.

"You know how it is, man. We all want a job." Whiskey chuckles as he pulls his pads off and plops down on the bench.

"You're getting a job, Whisk. You're killing it out there. I'm proud of you." I pat him on the back, and he groans as he tilts to one side to pull his layers of socks and tape from one leg.

"I don't know why you think you're not starting with me. Chance can't hit the cross pattern for shit. He's too green."

"Thanks," I say with a nod, holding in the fact I'm pretty green myself. It's not like I've stepped foot on a pro field before.

There's a clear line forming on the team, and I don't want to be the guy drawing it, but I think I am. The grinders out here, like Cisco and Drey, have bought into my style. We're always out on the field first, off it last, talking up everyone, celebrating the small wins. Most of the young guys, the two- or three-year players, along with the rookies, are into Chance's hype. My dad used to call it *me* ball. Funny that the last time I saw players hotdogging and getting away with it was when I was a kid. Maybe they've got it figured out, though. I've watched Chance out there, and he's full of so much raw talent it isn't even funny. He simply lacks discipline.

"Oh, fuck that guy at *Athletico!*" *Speaking of the immature punk.*

Chance busts out of the showers with his entourage behind him. *What kind of man can't shower on his own?* I swear, those guys follow him everywhere. Half of them won't even make the final squad.

"Did you know he was covering the MLB before they gave him the Cyclones beat? I bet he doesn't even like football," one of the guys laughs out, slapping hands with Chance as he flings open his cubby and lays out his after-camp clothes. I'm putting on jeans and my Arizona hoodie. He's rolling out of this place in a suit.

"Man, that Trujillo guy writes shit. I bet he thinks the old rickety man over there should start the first game. No offense," Chance says over his shoulder, as if I'm an afterthought. I'm not stupid. I know this entire conversation is about me. If I weren't in here, he wouldn't be having it.

I read the article he's talking about. It points out a lot of Chance's weaknesses, things that will likely result in embarrassing turnovers on the field if he's not careful. And Trujillo isn't wrong. He's usually not. Sure, he was covering baseball last season. That's after a decade covering the ins and outs of the NFL, though—for pretty much every outlet in the country. *But yeah. What does he know?*

Once I'm dressed, I fire off a quick text to Peyton letting her know that I'll give her a call when I get to the room. If she were here for camp, I might drive the hour back to our apartment. But since she's not, I may as well stay in the hotel with the rest of the guys. Maybe I'll spend some time in the bar and win a few of them over. I can be charming. *I think.*

"You coming out with us, old man? Or . . . you have a curfew with the old lady?" The few guys still lingering in the locker room with Chance snicker at his stupid joke.

Ten years ago, I would have knocked his teeth out by now. Sometimes, being professional isn't what it's cracked up to be.

I force out a friendly-sounding chuckle and shake my head.

"Yeah, you got me. She's got me wrapped around her finger, I guess. Hey, but good work out there today. Keep it up," I say with exaggerated enthusiasm, then pat his shoulder as I walk past him. He lets out a snort-laugh.

"Yeah, you too. Keep it up."

At least he and his buddies wait for me to almost clear the doorway before they burst into laughter. I don't like to wish for quarterbacks to eat turf; it feels like bad karma. But damn would I revel in seeing Chance get knocked on his ass a few times.

His time will come.

It's a five-minute walk to the hotel from the facilities we're using at the university. I'm not used to summer air feeling so chilly. I kind of like it rather than the oven-burn that comes along with living in Arizona. Late afternoons here drop below eighty, and there's this perpetual breeze that I could get used to.

I call Peyton the second I step off the elevator.

"Hi, Daddy."

She's been calling me that for the last week, and at first, I thought it was cute. But then Whiskey brought up Reed, and how funny it is that he's her daddy, and now I don't think it's cute at all. All I see in my head is Reed's wild eyes staring at me and telling me to watch myself.

"You're still sticking with that, huh?" I hold my keycard against the lock pad, and when it clicks, I push the door open and head straight for the bed.

"Wyatt, you're stuck with it. Because you *are* this baby's daddy."

The smile hits my lips automatically as I collapse on my back, my head sinking into the pile of pillows.

"Okay, maybe *baby* daddy, then. How's that?"

"I can call you that . . . *baby daddy*." Her voice is sultry, that touch of grit that's part of her signature sound when she's tired. I miss her.

"Tell me about tryouts?"

She groans in response, so I settle in on my side to hear what promises to be a long venting session.

"I picked fifteen. I should have stuck with ten, but I'm new, and I didn't want to cut half of the girls who came out, so I kept a few extra on the agreement that they'll be for practice and games, but not competition. Unless, of course, they earn it. But one of their moms is . . . *a lot*."

I smirk, my memory easily slipping back to Peyton's high

school cheer days. She never had to earn time on the mat. But she did run into some trouble with warring egos. And then there was the parade snub.

"I've seen you work wonders with your sister. I'm sure you'll be able to handle those teen personalities," I say.

"*Mmm*, it's not the teens I'm worried about."

I breathe out a laugh along with her.

"I get it. I miss working with teens. They're a lot easier than young college grads who think their shit doesn't stink."

I hear someone calling Peyton in the distance through the phone, so I sit up, figuring our conversation is going to get cut short tonight.

"I'll be right there," she says, her voice muffled, probably from tucking the phone against her chest.

"Don't overdo it."

She sighs at my parenting of her. It's one of her hot buttons, but I can't help myself. I'm worried about her pushing herself too hard with the cheer practices and still helping her mom. Her body needed breaks when she wasn't creating a second human inside. Now, she *really* needs to listen to her body's warnings.

"I'm being very careful, Wy. It's just Ellie. I created a monster when I helped with her hair. My mom gave her permission to dye it purple. I'm merely supervising this experiment."

I imagine Peyton with purple hair for a blip, and somehow, I swear she senses it. Before I say another word, she breaks into my thoughts.

"And no, I like my hair how it is."

"Damn, you really have that mom intuition thing going strong already, don't you?" I chuckle as she hums, "*Mmm hmm*."

"I love you," I say, cupping the phone and wishing she were here for me to kiss.

"I love you more. Now, go bond with your teammates. You can't have them thinking I've got you on a short leash."

I chuckle silently as she ends our call. She has no idea how spot-on her observation is.

It's not quite six yet, so a few of the guys are probably still lingering around the bar downstairs before going out. I'm not so sure I want to head to the club with Chance's crew, and I doubt they want to see me there. But I could hang out in the bar and grab dinner, maybe watch the Diamondbacks game, and lament that I didn't pick baseball instead of this brutal sport.

I freshen up, swapping out my hoodie for a more respectable quarter-zip, and shove a Cyclones hat on my head to avoid doing something with my hair. I hit the lobby in time to catch a few of Chance's buddies waiting for the valet to bring around their ride. They get quiet as I approach, so I make a point of stopping and putting my hand on one of their shoulders.

"Hey, we didn't get to formally meet yet. I'm Wyatt," I say, taking the guy's hand. His mouth is caught in this half-surprised, half-laughing position as his eyes bounce between me and the other two guys waiting with him.

"Yeah, uh. I know you. I'm Clay. This is Shawn, and that's Kenny."

We shake, and I nod and smile at the other two. I don't bother to memorize their names. They aren't on the team. They're just here to surround Chance in a bubble. It's a bad way for this kid to start. I get that these are his pals from college, and I know he's young and wants to keep the party going. I may be new to the pros, too, but I know enough to see bad habits forming. And the fact he put these guys up in the same hotel with him for the opening week of camp is a majorly bad idea.

"Hey, don't keep him out late, yeah?" I point at Clay as I

leave their group, and while my tone says I'm kidding, I'm actually not.

"Yeah, all right, Gramps," he responds.

I keep walking, and I nod before turning my attention to the bar. I hold my tongue until I spot a familiar round body nestled into the corner stool at the end of the bar. Coach Elgin looks to be finishing up a steak he probably shouldn't be eating, but he's still nursing a beer, so I take the seat next to him.

"Hey, Wy. You need a menu?" He runs a napkin over his mouth, then reaches across the bar and grabs a laminated page with maybe a dozen items printed on the front.

"I don't think I can eat that," I say, nodding toward his plate. "I'd be a slug tomorrow."

"Ha, well, good thing my job calls for slugs."

I peruse the menu and settle on the grilled chicken and veggies. I flag down the bartender and put my order in, adding a beer to join Coach as he finishes his.

"So, how we looking, Coach?" I've been dying to pick his brain about this entire situation, and since I have him alone, there's no better time. I'm not comfortable enough to come straight out and get his take on me showing Chance the ropes, and the knowing laugh that spills out as he pulls his beer from his lips is why. Nothing gets by this man.

"I'll tell you what I've told all my quarterbacks like you over the years, Wyatt. We're all here to do a job. Best advice I've got is for you to do it to the best of your ability." He lifts his beer and tips it back, draining the mug before setting it down next to his plate.

He wriggles his way from the stool, his legs not quite long enough to reach the floor. It's funny to see a man with his pedigree in a game of big men lumber around at five-foot-six. It's even funnier to watch him dismount from a barstool.

"Quarterbacks like me, huh?"

He pauses and quirks a brow.

"You picked up on that, did ya?"

I nod.

"Yeah, I did. And all due respect, sir, but I don't think you've ever coached a quarterback like me." My mouth works before my brain sometimes, and I instantly swallow, hoping that wasn't too bold.

The long, quiet seconds before Coach laughs are torturous. He finally does, his eyes crinkling at the sides like Santa Claus. His hand lands on my back as he leans in close, like he's about to tell me a secret.

"I'd love for you to surprise me."

He winks, then drops a hundred-dollar bill on the counter to cover his tab. It's the same wink my dad used to give me after dropping one of his classic lines. The same wink he taught me. I can't help but feel there's a sign in there somewhere.

Chapter Fourteen

Peyton

"Pick a hand."

My dad grins while standing in the open driver's side door with his arms tucked behind his back. It's the third gas station we've stopped at on our way to LA, so I could pee. I probably should have made him stop a few more times, but I'm stubborn and held it.

"Right hand," I say.

"Damn it!" He bows his head and hands over a pack of Reese's.

"Yes!" I fist pump with one hand and snag my snack with the other.

I could've flown to Wyatt's first pre-season game with both our moms and the rest of our family. I'm sure I wouldn't be stressing about getting there on time like I am right now if I did. But I would've missed out on this. My road trips with my dad have been fewer as an adult, and I'm sure they'll be even less when I add a baby car seat to the mix. I wanted this time with my dad. I need it.

"Okay, that granddaughter of mine starts messing with your

bladder again, just holler, yeah? I know every gas station from here to the stadium."

I rip into my candy while my dad revs up his truck.

"Deal, though I don't think the baby is kicking my bladder at this point. I read it's mostly hormones and my uterus getting bigger, and—"

"Yeah, I'm out when you start saying the word uterus," my dad jokes . . . *sort of.*

I'm about to hit the three-month mark, and half of my family has placed their bets that Wyatt and I are having a girl. I don't know, though. There's this thought nagging in the back of my mind that this baby might just break the girl streak my dad started. It's not like Buck and Millie, his late wife, had girls either; it was my dad and my Uncle Jason. And my mom's brother, my Uncle Mike, goes against that theory too. And Wyatt's family is split fifty-fifty girls to boys, and he carries the damn chromosome anyhow. But no way do I breathe a word of those thoughts out loud in this family. My dad and grandpa will be stocking up on shoulder pads and footballs for every size.

I've told Wyatt my thoughts, and he's still sure it's a girl. We have a wager on it for the first month of diaper duty.

We're about an hour out when my dad's phone rings through the truck's speakers with a call from Wyatt. Kick-off is at six, and it's three-thirty, which makes this a really strange time for him to be sneaking in a call.

"Shouldn't you be on the field or getting stretched or something?" I make eyes at my dad, both of us wearing nervous smiles.

"Yeah, I know. I'm about to get taped. I just wanted you guys to know before you get here . . . I'm getting the start."

My dad slaps the top of his steering wheel while my palms cover my mouth.

"Atta boy!" my dad says, and I'm glad he can speak because I think I'm in shock. Wyatt's the better quarterback, but Bryce warned me not to expect much right away. Chance is where the hype is.

"Baby . . ." I mutter, my eyes tearing up. My dad chuckles next to me and reaches across the console to hold my hand.

"Don't put too much weight on it, guys. Apparently, Chance has some elbow tightness, so it's more a precaution that they're going with me instead, but still—"

"But still . . . this is your time to show those assholes what a real quarterback looks like," I blurt out. I cup my mouth and make wide eyes at my dad as both he and Wyatt laugh at my fighting words.

"Wy, it doesn't matter how you get your shot. It's all about what you do with it. So get your head on right, spend a little time with Whisk before the game, sit with yourself, and talk to your dad. We'll be watching everything. We'll be there with you."

"Thank you, Reed." I can hear the hitch in his voice, the little break that lets me know this moment means something to him. It means *a lot*.

"I love you, baby. Give 'em hell."

"I love you, Peyt," he says before ending the call.

I break down into stupid pregnancy tears a half second later, and my dad keeps hold of my hand, vacillating between consoling my nerves and being amused at my emotional reaction. What he doesn't know is that Mom was like this when he played, at least for the big games. She cried through the fourth quarter of his last Super Bowl.

My dad and I roll up to the stadium with an hour to spare. Of all the perks that come with being a hall-of-famer, my dad's ability to park anywhere he wants at any football facility ranks near the top. He tosses his truck keys to the valet working the player's garage, stopping to shake the kid's hand.

If it wouldn't get the kid in trouble, my dad would offer to take a photo.

The second we enter the suite, I make a beeline for the restroom, proud of myself for holding it for the final miles through LA. Those miles can take hours, but my dad pulled off a few questionable traffic maneuvers that we both agree Mom doesn't need to know about.

I wash up and step out of the restroom into the buzz of our family and friends, who just learned that Wyatt's getting the ball tonight. Tasha hugs me first, then promptly switches into parent mode, filling her twins' plates with crackers, cheese, fruit, and way too many cookies. I think she's hoping for an early sugar crash. My mom's eyes are glassy when I finally locate her, and we laugh quietly, an unspoken understanding of how we both likely reacted to the news. She squeezes my hand and kisses my cheek before sending me off to hug my aunt and uncle, and then Wyatt's mom, Theresa, who is standing with his dad's old fire captain, Jeff.

Jeff was a last-minute addition to the suite, and Wyatt doesn't know he's here. His mom asked for him to come, and I know how much Jeff was like a father to Wyatt, having worked alongside his dad for years. Jeff's wife passed away three years ago, and he and Theresa have formed a tight friendship through shared grief.

He's been hanging around a lot more often, and given he lives in the city—about ninety miles away from Theresa's house —it definitely means *something*. However, Wyatt would prefer to keep whatever is happening between them a mystery. I brought it up when we were at his mom's New Year's party, which Jeff attended. He told me there was nothing there, but his attention stayed on them for the rest of the night.

"Good news, huh?"

I turn from my conversation with Theresa and Jeff at the

sound of Bryce's voice. I give him a hug, squeezing a little tighter thanks to the adrenaline pouring through me. I step back and meet his gaze.

"A start's a start, right?" I wear a toothy, nerve-wrecked smile.

"He's going to crush it, Peyt. Relax," he says, but I can't help but notice his shoulders are still ratcheted up to his ears.

"I will when you do," I challenge.

"Ha, okay. Maybe after a few of these," he says, cracking the tab from a microbrew he pulled from the large ice bucket.

"Totally not fair," I pout, twisting the cap off my water as Bryce chuckles.

"Hey, maybe I can represent the little guy one day," he says with a wink before heading toward my dad to talk business and football for the rest of the night.

Little guy. One more vote on my side.

I make myself a plate of bland food, trying not to wake the stomach gremlin that hasn't shown up as often as it did the first two months of my pregnancy. My insides are twisty enough on their own tonight; no need for me to fan the flames and tempt fate.

Wiggling into the seat next to Tasha, I squeeze her knee and the two of us kick our feet with our own private celebration.

"You can take the cheerleader off the field . . ." she begins.

"But you can't take the cheer out of the leader," I finish with her.

We clasp hands, our shared nerves making us both a little sweaty. I pick at my food, the rumbles in my tummy a cautious warning that keeps me away from the turkey slices. I slip out for one more bathroom trip and a refill on crackers and water before the team takes the field, and then *it's on!*

Wyatt's warm-up tosses take me back, not just to college but to that first year we met. He was special, even then. My dad saw it early, and was terrified of it. And then, when Wyatt broke his records, he respected it. Now, Wyatt's family.

"He looks good," my mom mutters from the seat behind me. I nod, too busy chewing on my nails to speak. She squeezes my shoulders a few times, then sits back in her seat, urging my dad to finally take his. He'll be pacing by the first set of downs. I'm certain.

The national anthem and coin toss are a blur, and before I know it, the Cyclones are on the field and Wyatt is lined up ready to count it off. I close my eyes and breathe out slowly, my lips puckering as if there's a straw in my mouth. I watched my mom do this when I was little and my dad played. She said she was able to block out everything but him. Now, it's my turn.

When my eyes open, everything sounds muted. Wyatt takes the snap and falls back a few steps before hitting his running back with a short pass that he carries for seven yards. I clap, then hold my clasped hands to my lips, keeping my peaceful bubble intact.

"Come on, baby. Let's go," I mouth, not even certain the words are aloud.

Wyatt hands the ball off two more times, gaining a first down before taking his first hit on a pass that barely misses his receiver's hands. My teeth gnash, and my mom's hands land on my shoulders.

"It's okay. I'm okay," I reassure her, hoping she understands what I'm doing, that I'm closing out the noise the same way she did.

Wyatt takes a teammate's hand as he gets to his feet, and my eyes scan every single muscle on his body looking for limps or hesitations. He seems whole. Unscathed. *This time.*

I'm so intent on bracing myself for another hit that I don't see the signs until Wyatt scrambles to his right, buying time for his receiver to sprint downfield before he launches the ball forty yards. He hits his guy mid-stride, and nobody's even close. He's in the end zone and we're up six with only two minutes off the clock.

I finally breathe.

My dad's pacing seems like a good idea by the time the second quarter starts, so I join him, popping in and out of the suite depending on whether we're on defense or offense. Wyatt threw a pick his last time out, which I will fight anyone to the death arguing it wasn't his fault. It literally bounced out of the tight end's hands. And other than the big hit during the first set of downs, he's been lucky. Or rather, the pocket's been good. Tasha says it's because Whiskey's protecting him, and I tend to think she's right.

Phillips has been warming up the third and fourth string quarterbacks for the last few minutes, so my gut tells me Wyatt's done before the half. My dad and I are about to head into the suite and hit the buffet to eat some *real* food when the monitors on the concourse show Wyatt's slow jog out to the huddle to close out the half. This time, there's something about the crowd that begs me to stay out here, to let the noise in—*all of it.*

"Dad, I'm gonna . . ." I gesture to the tunnel leading to the second level seats, and my dad nods.

We slip in without anyone noticing, which, when I'm with my father, is often a feat. It's cleared out up high, partly because this is preseason, but mostly because everyone up here is making a dash for the bathrooms and the beer lines. A guy a few rows behind us seems to be well versed on the team, and when he rattles off Wyatt's college stats, messing up his total passing yards, I grip my dad's forearm to keep him from turning around and correcting him.

"It's my damn record he broke," my dad grumbles, and I laugh softly while patting his arm.

"I know, but when Wyatt's their all-star in a few years, that guy will know better," I say, letting myself go there mentally for the first time since Wyatt started camp.

He really can do this.

The first few plays are running routes, one for a loss, the next two for the first down. There's a mad swap of players dashing on and off the field as the clock winds down, and I suddenly feel thankful that Wyatt got an entire half to prove himself rather than a few dwindling seconds. I'm also a little uneasy seeing Whiskey peel off for the final play.

Unfortunately, the new center isn't going to win over anyone as he snaps the ball over Wyatt's head. My husband scrambles to pick it up, and I brace myself for him to take a hit. But rather than crumpling under the two-hundred-plus pounds that try to wrap him up, Wyatt spins out and tucks the ball in tight, ready to run.

"Oh, fuck," I let out, getting to my feet. My dad joins me, echoing my words as we simmer on our toes.

Please keep his legs intact. And please let those tendons hold. And his head . . . God, please protect his head.

About a dozen more requests buzz through my mind while Wyatt breaks three tackles before clearing the field and sprinting forty-seven yards into the end zone for the score. My hands fly up along with my dad's, and we turn to face one another for a double high five while we shout nonsense so loud that both of our voices break.

Wyatt spins the ball on the grass, then skips toward a few of his teammates, bumping chests with two of them before rushing to the sidelines, where Whiskey waits to wrap him in a massive bear hug.

And then, somehow, he finds me. I blow him a kiss that he

grabs out of the air, and when the clock hits zero, I flop down in the miserable plastic seat and wonder how the hell I'm going to keep this up for an entire season. *Or more.*

Chapter Fifteen

Wyatt

I hurt more than I'll admit; I'm sure Peyt can tell. Nothing gets by that woman. She reads my eyes like one of her Kennedy Ryan books. Cover to cover.

Her dad probably knows too, but of all the people in this room I need to suck it up and be tough for, it's that guy. He took plenty of hits on the gridiron. He'd probably tell me today was child's play and I better toughen the grit. *He'd be right.*

"My boy!" My dad's old fire captain, Jeff, stretches out his arms the second I spot him.

"What is this? I had no idea you were coming. Did you do this?" I point to Jeff as I look Peyton in the eyes. She shakes her head and her brow ticks up in the direction of my mom, and well . . . *shit.*

"Oh. Awesome surprise, Ma! I'm so glad you got to be here for it." I remind myself that the heavy pats he leaves on my back during our hug are genuine and full of love even if lately, he seems to be spending an awful lot of time with my mom. Maybe that wouldn't be so bad.

"Your dad is smiling up there today, Wy. He's proud of you. We all are."

His words level my chest with an unexpected blow, and my eyes tear up before I can control my emotional reaction. I sniffle and wipe under my eyes with my thumb and index finger.

"Thanks, Jeff. That means a lot."

I move on to my mom and hold her tight while I steady my breath. I give her a chance to sniff away her tears against my chest, too. I don't know that we'll ever fully get over missing my dad. So many things he's not here to see. But I like what Jeff says, that he's watching from above. I hope that's the case. I'd like to believe in it, in something good . . . for him. If ever there was a human who deserved a heaven waiting for him, it was Todd Stone.

"I'm so proud of you," my mom says, tugging at the center of my button-down shirt. Like college, we dress for the media after a game. I did most of my interviews in my jersey without my pads, but the longer interviews were done in what I call my "big boy clothes."

Peyton, however, calls them something else. Rather, she sort of growls when I dress in slacks with a shirt and tie. It's fair to say we both have our versions of the red dress. Mine just comes in grays and black.

The room suddenly bursts with a new level of energy as Chase enters with his friends, along with a few extra media outlets who have been following him around like trained dogs. I get that he's an interesting story—a number-one draft pick that the country can't wait to see on the field. And the fact he didn't play tonight just feeds the frenzy. But the dude is going to burn out if he keeps up this pace of attention. Eventually, someone's going to catch him in a foul mood, or worse, doing something stupid. And that fall from grace hurts.

"Come on, let's get out of here," I say as I sling my arm

around Peyton. She grins up at me like when we were in high school, and I can't help but feel the flutters in my chest. My girl. Always my girl.

We all pile out of the lobby and wait one by one for our rides. Reed's truck comes along first, and my mom, Jeff, and Nolan pile in as Reed takes the keys from the valet and tips what looks like two hundred bucks. *Fuck, man . . . I hope I'm doing that well one day.*

"Tell Peyt I'll swing by the hotel in the morning and get her for the ride back," Reed says, and I nod.

Teams rarely get to spend the night after an away game, but we were the prime-time game tonight, and things ran long, especially for a preseason game. We knew there would be extra media, too, given that Portland's the new kid on the block. It's almost eleven, and half of us are still here.

The black SUV with tinted windows finally pulls into the player lot, and I wave to get the driver clearance from the gate guard. He drives around the loop, stopping in front of Peyton and me. The driver opens his door, but I quickly hold up a hand.

"Save your steps, buddy. I got it," I say, figuring the least I can do is be a good passenger since this cat isn't getting a two-hundred-buck tip out of me. He'll get a solid forty for now.

I open the back door and take Peyton's hand, helping her step from the curb into the vehicle. I slide into the seat beside her.

"You at the Lux with the rest of the team, sir?"

Sir. I don't think anyone's ever called me that.

"Uh, yeah. Thanks . . ." I lean forward to read his name on the badge clipped to his rearview mirror. "Daniel."

He smiles in the reflection.

"You're welcome, sir."

Sir.

"I see you locking that away, baby daddy," Peyton says in a hushed tone.

Damn it if I'm not blushing. Yeah, she caught me. I was imagining her calling me *Sir*. I think I like it. I waggle my head.

"You know, don't be afraid to mix it up if you'd like," I say.

She holds my gaze for a few long seconds, slowly licking her lips before catching the bottom one with her teeth.

"Nah. I'm sticking with baby daddy," she laughs out.

I cover my face, cringing, and I can't verify it, but I swear I hear Daniel chuckle from the front seat.

"Fine. You call me whatever you want."

The hotel isn't far from the stadium, but LA traffic makes everything feel far, even at this time of night. I can see the golden logo for the hotel through the windshield, and my gaze catches Daniel's as I lift to try to gauge how many lights we need to get through.

"You had a great game tonight, sir. If . . . if it's okay that I say that."

I sink back into my seat, my mouth agape with a hint of shock.

"Thanks, Daniel. I mean, yeah. You can say that anytime you want."

The three of us laugh.

"Good, then, you played great. I grew up in Portland, so I was kind of rooting for you guys. I hope we get more of you when the season officially starts. That young kid . . ." He bunches his lips, and I muse to myself over the fact Chance is probably the same age as this guy.

"Aww, Hickory's gonna be great. You know, it's kind of an honor to play the role of mentor. I guess that's what I am. The old man?" I glance at Peyton, and she rolls her eyes.

"Hey, Brady played into his forties. You're still a baby out here, sir. Trust me. People will be wearing your jersey one day."

Daniel's gaze lingers in the mirror for a beat, and I finally give him a nod and utter, "Thanks."

I decide to use the tap payment when he drops us off at the hotel, and I tip him a hundred bucks. Maybe that was his plan all along, and if so, good on him. It worked. But the whole idea of giving what I've got, maybe before I've really got it, feels nice. That's the best part about this ride, really. I get to be a big deal to someone, and tonight, I was a big deal to Daniel.

I rush Peyton into the hotel and through the lobby before anyone takes notice of us. A lot of the guests were lingering in the lobby before the game, probably wanting to get a glimpse of the team. I'm sure there are people here now, and who knows, maybe a few from *TMZ* or other tabloid socials. Mostly, though, I want to get my wife alone. I've missed her, and I'm ready to be selfish.

"You know that if they sell your jersey one day, you're going to have to get that guy one, right?"

"Oh, absolutely. And I'm signing it." I wave my hand in the air as if it's my signature.

Peyton laughs as she tugs the hair tie from her hair, letting her waves spill down around her face. Her oversized Cyclones T-shirt has a tiny mustard stain near the collar, probably from the snacks she ate in the suite. It's adorable, but I'm not going to tell her about it. She won't think it's cute.

"This doesn't feel very heavy," I say, testing the weight of her travel bag on my shoulder.

"There's not a lot in it," she says, with a smug, coy grin.

I bite the tip of my tongue, and my cock flexes inside these miserable dress pants. I glance toward the elevator buttons and press the seventeen a few extra times, as if that will magically get us to our floor faster. We make it quick enough, though, and when the doors open, I sweep Peyton up into my arms and carry her to the right and down the long hallway to my room at the very end.

I keycard our way through the door and drop our bags right inside before letting her body slide slowly from my grasp, her back against the door, my arms caging her.

"God, I've missed you," I say, my mouth suckling the curve of her neck as she works to undo my black silk tie. She pulls it from my neck and tosses it to the floor before moving her hands to my jaw, her cool fingers scratching against my stubble as she lifts on her toes and takes my bottom lip between her teeth.

"*Grrr*, woman," I growl, lifting her in my arms, then spinning her before walking us backward past the small sitting area and to the king-sized bed.

Her legs hit the edge of the mattress, but rather than sitting down, her palms slide to the center of my chest, and she breaks our kiss.

"Is that . . . a balcony?" Her head tilts back and to one side.

My eyes flit to the sheer window curtains, the city lights glowing behind. I nod.

"It is."

My dick is so hard right now, I think I might break this zipper.

"Why don't you wait for me outside, then. I'll just be a minute." Her mouth curves, her expression sly and dirty, and *my God, I have to get out of these pants.*

"Yes, ma'am," I say, taking slow, deliberate steps backward as I unbutton my shirt.

"I'm still not calling you Sir, baby daddy," she teases.

"Peyt, you can call me anything you want. Just let me fuck you before I come in my pants like a sixteen-year-old," I say through a genuinely nervous laugh.

Her lips merely tighten, her smirk growing.

"Off you go," she says, waving me toward the sliding glass door.

I do as she says while she grabs her travel bag and slips into the bathroom. I finish unbuttoning my shirt outside, the cool air helping me hold out while Peyton spends a good five minutes in the bathroom. I adjust my cock in my pants, leaving the zipper down since my boxer briefs are black and snug.

"Are you ready?"

Peyton's voice is soft, almost bashful sounding. I turn around to see her biting her fingernail as the breeze blows her hair across her face. She's wearing a cheer uniform, *actually hers.*

"Oh, that's . . . That's a very nice surprise," I say, sucking in my bottom lip and mentally begging myself to appreciate every second of this. I won't see her for another week. I need to build up some major memories.

"It's tighter, like . . . around here," she says, running her finger along the waistband and revealing the open zipper at her hip.

"It's because you have a baby bump," I say, my eyes softening as my palm moves to her midriff. I run my hand along her skin, her tummy definitely growing.

"I feel kind of weird about it," she says, squinting as she winces. I think she's embarrassed.

"Peyt, you're beautiful." I drop down on my knees and run both hands along her stomach, my thumbs tickling from her belly button around to her sides. I lean forward and kiss next to her navel.

"Yeah? You like my bump?" She sways her hips slightly, the skirt of her uniform swishing.

I chuckle and move my hands to the hemline, then gradually let them climb along the backs of her legs until I'm cupping her ass.

"Oh, someone is bare under here," I say, my cock pushing its way out of my boxers. I feel the cold air against the tip.

"I am," Peyton hums.

Her finger returns to her lips, and she holds her fingernail hostage between her teeth as her other hand moves into my hair. I look up as her fingers weave into the strands, and her eyes haze with what I think is the same need I have. She coaxes me closer, and I follow her lead, my hands sliding around to the front of her legs. I nudge them apart, then lift the front of her skirt to reveal her beautiful pussy, the thin strip of golden hair leading me to her swollen middle. I hold her gaze until the last second, until my eyes flutter shut and my mouth covers her clit, sucking it in as my tongue flicks it.

"Oh, fucking yes!" she moans.

She's not loud, but she's also not being bashful or quiet. I lean back for a breath, and to glance around our surroundings, every window near us dark, the next building far enough away that I don't think we're easily seen. It's good enough, and I dive right back in to feast on my fucking delicious wife.

My tongue slides along her sensitive skin, diving in and out of her folds as her hands move to my shoulders so she can steady herself. I suck her clit again, this time not letting go until I feel her legs wobble.

"Wyatt, yes. Please, right there."

I flick my tongue as her hand leaves my shoulder and covers mine, dragging it up higher along the inside of her thigh. When my thumb finds her wet, swollen pussy, she lets go, leaving me to push my thumb inside of her while my tongue continues its assault.

She whimpers, and in seconds, her body is quivering. I hold her steady with one hand wrapped around her leg while I work her with my other. Her hips slowly rock as she rides my tongue, her pussy pulsing against me with every wave of pleasure.

Once her body falls limp, I lift her up over my shoulder and carry her inside, and she giggles as I playfully smack her ass. I drop her gently on the bed, and her legs part willingly.

"I'm going to come so fast, Peyton," I admit, wasting no time tugging my pants down my legs and crawling above her to guide my cock inside.

"You can't get me pregnant again, at least not right now," she giggles out. I laugh with her, but as I sink deep into her warm pussy, I lose myself.

"Fucking hell, I've missed this," I say, dropping my mouth to her neck as I force myself to control my speed. I want to pound into her, but I also want to be gentle and loving. And I want this to last more than ten seconds.

"This has missed you," she says in a sexy, hushed tone. Her hips lift to meet my mine as I push in deeper, and I have a feeling she's talking about her sweet cunt.

She pushes her cheer top up her body, stopping when her bare breasts are uncovered. Her nipples are so hard that I can't help but bite one as I brace myself on one arm and pump into her faster. I'm drunk on this moment, the feel of her sweat dampened skin, the way she smells of coconut shampoo and sex, every memory rolled up between us. Every single time I've been inside of her, every minute I've filled her with my cum.

"Oh fuck, I'm coming," I groan, pushing in a few more times as I empty myself inside of her. She grinds into me as if she's savoring every drop. Her body is covered in a sheen of sweat, mine somehow halfway out of my dress shirt. I collapse on the bed next to her, my cock sticky from our sex.

She rolls to her side and slides her hand along my stomach before wrapping her palm around my dick and coaxing out a few more tiny drops of cum. She coats my tip with it, running her thumb over me then sucking her thumb in her mouth as she peers up at me with pouty lips and a hunger in her eyes.

"Ha, they say the LA defensive line is tough. Woman, you're going to kill me."

I shift to my side and drag my fingertips along her bare chest, circling her left nipple, then pinching it lightly.

"They say women are insatiable when they're pregnant," she utters, biting her lip.

"Oh, *they* do, do *they?*"

She nods.

"And who are *they?*"

Her fingertips drift to my shaft, keeping me hard.

"I am. I'm everything, and all you need to answer to . . . *Sir.*"

Well, fuck.

Chapter Sixteen

Peyton

I have an ongoing mental list of texts I don't like waking up to. There was the time he texted me that he was going to miss our anniversary because of the football rally fundraiser. I was only mildly mad because . . . *football*. Then there was the text that only said, "Sorry." It took me a while to realize what he was apologizing for, and when I saw the cracked windshield on the Jeep, I was relieved it was something so trivial.

I think this is a new level, though. There's really no way to *not* freak out when reading this. And then for him to not answer my texts on top of it—that's the kicker.

"You hear from Wyatt yet?" Tasha asks as she snaps gum and flips through social media in the chair next to me. She's clothed and not covered in ultrasound gel while awaiting someone to roll a device around her stomach.

"Aren't you supposed to be on *my* phone . . . you know . . . filming *this*?"

Tasha drops her phone into her purse on the floor and fumbles in her seat.

"Oh shit, right," she stammers, flailing my phone around her lap before getting it situated the right way so she can record. "Okay, you're live, baby."

I grimace.

"I don't want to be *live*."

She levels me with a look that reads, "Duh."

"I know, I was being creative. It's a saying. I mean, I'm recording. Now, smile and tell us what we're doing here."

I roll my eyes until my focus lands on my doctor's waiting gaze.

"Sorry," I say, ignoring the frustrated expression barely concealed behind Dr. Mazel's glasses.

"Hi, Wyatt. Here we are. It's the big three-month check-up. Are you ready?" I hold up two thumbs.

"Good work, Mamma," Tasha says, encouraging me. I'm in a bit of a funk today, and not only because of the mystery text Wyatt sent warning me of impending doom.

I miss him. And I don't want to lean into those feelings because he'll feel bad. I know he misses me too. He wanted to be here for this, and I wish he were. But football is his dream. And he's good at it. *Gah! He's so good.*

"That's the head," Dr. Mazel explains. Tasha captures the blur on the monitor. It doesn't look like much yet, but the heartbeat is strong. I see our baby, and I know we can't tell yet, but I swear it's a boy.

"Want to hear it?" the doctor asks.

I nod, and she turns up the volume on the monitor, the regular swish of our tiny human's heart flooding my ears. The tears come fast, for me and for Tasha.

"Wyatt, I hope you can hear this. That's our girl right there," Tasha says, throwing in her opinion. She's the most vocal with her guess. Or should I say, her statement. She insists she's never wrong about this. I don't remind her that she thought she was having *one* baby, and she thought it would be a boy. She's oh for two.

"I'll make you a digital recording. You should be able to send it to him."

I nod and sniffle at the doctor's offer. While she clicks around and measures a few things, typing various numbers that don't seem to raise any alarms, Tasha captures a few more seconds of my appointment before ending the recording and giving me back my phone. I text Wyatt the video, hoping maybe that will get his attention and he can fill me in on the freak out I'm not supposed to have.

My phone buzzes in my palm about thirty seconds later, and I answer without even thinking.

"Hey, babe. Did you get it?"

I get a glare from the doctor and cup the phone with my hand.

"Shoot, sorry."

She shakes her head and chuckles, seeming to finally lighten up.

"We're done here. Go ahead and get dressed, and I'll meet you outside," she says.

Tasha rests her head on mine, and when I pull my phone back up, she butts in to brag to Wyatt.

"Your baby is beautiful, Wy. So beautiful! Mwah!" My friend mouths to me that she'll meet me outside, and when the door shuts behind her and the doctor, I exhale and put the phone on speaker so I can get dressed.

"I wish I was there," Wyatt says.

"I know. Me, too. But we got good video. And really, you've seen me in a paper dress before. I'm just wiping jelly off my stomach and pulling on my leggings." I discard the napkins and toss my paper gown into the bin before shaking out my leggings and moving to sit on the edge of the exam table.

"I do enjoy watching you hop around when you put on leggings," he teases.

"Ha ha. I'm not hopping, thank you very much." Only because I'm afraid I'll fall on my face. I'm trying to be cautious about everything right now—no horses, no tumbling, and zero wardrobe hopping.

"So, I'm guessing you haven't seen it yet," Wyatt says.

I freeze with one leg dressed, the other bare.

"Is this the freak-out thing, Wyatt? Why am I going to freak out?" My heart is pounding so hard I may need to press the medical button to get my doctor back in here.

"Well, you know how we were on the balcony?"

Shit. Oh no.

"I guess *someone* saw us and took a pic, and then they posted it, and it's kind of trending."

"Wyatt!" I shove my other leg into my pants and scoot up to fully sit on the table so I can flip through my phone. I quickly find what he's talking about.

Because by trending he means it's the number one search on everything!

"Oh, God," I breathe out, covering most of my face, though I can't seem to avert my eyes.

"The team PR person said not to worry. She said it happens all the time. It will get replaced by something else later today."

"Oh, *she said.* Great. Anonymous PR woman said not to worry, so it's fine. I'm fine. It's *fine!*"

"Peyt? You don't sound fine."

"Because I'm not fine!"

Tasha cracks the door open, probably because the entire back office and waiting room can hear me. My body is so hot. I know my flesh is beet red. I hand my friend my phone, and she immediately covers her mouth to hold in her laughter.

"It's not funny, Tash."

"Okay, Peyt. It's kind of funny."

"See? It's not that bad," Wyatt says.

"Oh, hey, Wyatt."

The two of them banter for a moment while I snag my phone and stare at the photo again. Coming down a tick from the height, I do see how it could be worse. Nobody can see any . . . *parts*. Wyatt's on his knees, and I'm in front of him. In my cheer outfit. I know what he's doing, but it also just looks like he's adoring me. My belly. It's explainable. And that *did* happen. It's just not what's happening in this photo.

I take Wyatt off speaker.

"Okay, I'm calmer."

"Oh, good," he sighs.

"I didn't say I was calm. I'm simply calmer. Wyatt, this is going to be a thing."

"I know," he admits.

I don't have to say it. We both can read the tea leaves. There are a few people in the Coolidge Schools system who are rather . . . conservative. One of them happens to be the parent of one of my athletes, and she's not my biggest fan. But frankly, her daughter is not very good. I kept her because, well, her mom scares the shit out of me. I've heard the woman take on the town council and the school board. I wanted to be under her radar, not square the fuck in it.

"I love you, Peyt. I'm really sorry."

It breaks me to hear him sound sad. Especially about us.

"Wyatt, you weren't alone in this. And you know what? We didn't do anything wrong. We're married! I've seen a lot of football players in Coolidge skate by with a lot worse on the Internet. Being appreciated by my husband should be pretty easy to explain away."

I wish I believed everything I'm saying as much as it sounds like I do. I am rather angry about it. Well, pre-angry. But it's only a matter of time before I will have to deal with Adrian Sommers, cheer mom with a vengeance.

"Okay, I'll call you tonight. I've got film with Phillips all day. More teaching opportunities," Wyatt says in a wry tone.

"Soak it up, baby."

I blow a kiss into the phone and end the call.

"I know you're worried about the school district, but Peyt . . . this is showing up on the teen socials. Which means . . ."

"Fuuuuuuuck," I groan.

This is going to impact Ellie. At the start of a school year. A rather *important* year. Eighth grade.

I give Tasha the keys to the Jeep, and she drives us home while I scour every app on my phone, taking stock of the chatter. It's mostly harmless. Of course, there are a lot of "atta boys" slung in Wyatt's direction. I'm sure this will be great for his reputation, which again, is bullshit. By the time we reach the driveway, I've culled dozens of copies of the image, and none of them appear altered to show something that isn't there, and they all show Wyatt's mouth on my stomach. You'd have to have joined us on the balcony to know where his hands were, and truthfully, it's possible he was only kissing me at that time. I rather recognize the particular tilt of my head, though. But again, that's personal. *My* details.

I breathe in deeply and right my head. My mom is out in the pen with a client, so I can make my way to her before approaching my sister. My mom's good with a PR crisis. She's been through most of the obvious ones that come along with being a pro-athlete's wife. The number of times people printed photos of the two of them on vacation and claimed my mom was another woman could fill five years of calendar photos.

"You good?" Tasha says, handing me the keys as she pushes open the Jeep door.

I shrug and take them in my hand.

"Good . . . *ish?*"

She laughs, and I fake one. I hug her outside the Jeep, then head to the arena while my friend heads to her parents' house to pick up her girls.

My mom spots me as I approach and says something to the father and son walking in slow circles with Torrid, one of our mini horses. They nod and wave to me, which fills me with relief. Not everyone spends their entire day looking at social media. I'm sure they haven't seen the photo.

"Appointment go well?" my mom asks, moving right in for a hug.

I let out my breath during our embrace and adjust my hands along her back to hold on for a while.

"Something wrong?" Her worried tone spikes my pulse.

I shake my head along her shoulder.

"No, the appointment was great. Everything is perfect. Right on time. She thinks we can find out the gender soon." My words are happy, but my expression is being pulled to the earth. My mom can't see it, but I think she senses it, because she begins to rub circles on my back.

"I need some advice," I begin, backing away enough to pull my phone from my purse. I show her the picture, and she spends a few long seconds swiping through the several screenshots I saved. Her face is devoid of judgment, and that's probably the only reason I'm not crying.

"I mean, it only looks bad when someone writes a headline saying it's something bad," she says, handing my phone back to me.

My shoulders relax a little, but I can still feel my pulse in my belly.

"Okay, but what about the uniform? That's not good, is it?"

The way her face bunches up is answer enough.

"Ugh," I groan, pushing my hand into my hair.

"You're the worst sister in the entire world! You ruined my life! I hate you!" The barrage of vitriol hits me without warning. I didn't hear the bus or her bike. And I'm so stunned and hurt by her words that I can't even make sense of the scene until she's halfway across the driveway on her way to the house.

"Ellie! Talk to me!" I move to follow her, but my mom grabs my wrist to stop me.

"Give her an hour. Let her process on her own. She'll be ready to listen then. Well, *more* ready."

I feel sick.

My sister's bike is at the start of the driveway, lying on its side. She probably tossed it and sprinted with rage when she saw me. I barely got to take in her face. Was she crying? She was definitely spitting. I saw teeth. Lots of teeth. This is awful.

And just when I thought my universe had bottomed out for the day, my phone buzzes in my hand. Not a call, but a text. From the president of the school board.

DISTRICT OFFICE: *Peyton, your presence is requested at 6 p.m. Tuesday. The board has some questions for you, as a decency complaint has been filed. Thank you for your understanding in this matter. Your athletes have been notified that practices are on pause until the board makes its determination.*

And just like that, my day got infinitely more . . . awful.

Chapter Seventeen

Wyatt

Twenty-two-year-olds can be real assholes.

Chance Hickory is twenty-two.

I'm sure he took that photo, or one of his buddies did, but I'm trying *really* hard to give him the benefit of the doubt. I've seen their likes on social media, the snarky comments some of them have made about the woman in the photo, questioning whether I'm stepping out on my wife. My gut tells me the reason Chance did it, or at least didn't stop any of it. He wants to see my character take a hit.

He's young. And he's been given all this attention and power so early in his career. He's not ready for it.

I bet someone said that about me my senior year at Arizona. I do my best to live up to my father's standards, to mind my emotions, do the gut checks before speaking and acting out. But I'm sure I've messed up a time or two over the years. Especially when I first entered the draft. I get that saying about hindsight, now that I've got a few years to look back on.

When I took a year off to help Peyton, I went into the draft the next season with expectations—not of myself, but of the people who I felt would be stupid to pass me by. And when I didn't get picked, that fucked with my head.

How could they not see what I had to offer?

What I should have considered, though, was what I didn't bring to the table. Looking back, I left a whole host of things out of my first, second, and third impressions with a lot of the teams. I didn't lead; I followed. I didn't take risks on the field; I played it safe. I didn't put in the extra hour of work; instead, I called it a day early. I didn't stand out.

Chance stands out. Maybe a little too much. And I can't let this photo thing go completely, not without words.

I stare him directly in the eyes as I enter the locker room. He took it easy at our workout today. And he was late to film this morning. I went extra hard—partly to let out some aggression, but mostly because I've decided I want this, and if Chance is the heir apparent, he's going to have to sweat a little to take his crown.

"What's that look for?" He spits out a laugh with two of the young receivers after I pass by where they're sitting.

"Just taking a mental picture of you, man. You know, for my collection." I don't bother to turn around. I strip off my jersey and pads before glancing over my shoulder in time to catch them whispering.

"You know, if you want a photo of me, you can just ask. Here, I'll even pose for you." He gets up from his chair and walks to the center of the room, shirtless and in his boxers. He flexes a bicep and acts like he's about to kiss it before laughing and waving me off.

I scoff. "I'd rather wait outside like a creeper and catch you in your apartment, or maybe the next team hotel. I hear those photos go for a lot. You know, the kind that invade someone's privacy."

Chance chews at the inside of his mouth as he takes his seat again and stares at me. I hold his gaze, internally willing my pulse to slow. I pick up the towel hanging in my cubby and twist it rather than forming a fist.

A slow smirk stretches across Chance's face as he tips his chair back, balancing on the two back legs.

"Nah, you won't get the good pics that way. I'm careful when I'm out with the ladies. You know . . . I like to keep shit private. Balconies, though? Oof, yeah. They'll get ya."

I run a palm over my mouth and let my focus drop to the floor while I nod slowly. I'm gonna lose my cool. I feel it, and my grip on my self-control is slipping. I pop my gaze up, making eye contact with one of the young receivers who thought Chance was funny a minute ago. He's not laughing now, though. Neither is the other guy. These guys haven't seen any time on the field. They know they're probably getting cut after camp. But if they want to find their way onto a roster again for the next camp, they'll step out of this situation fast.

"You take that photo, Chance? Or was one of your buddies trailing me in LA?" I slam my cubby door shut and saunter toward him. His friends quickly disappear toward the showers. Smart.

"Look, Wyatt Earp, I don't know what you're talking about—"

I hook my foot under the front rung of his chair and lift, sending him tumbling backward. He braces his fall, straddling the fallen chair before kicking it to the side and stepping into me. Our chests nearly touch. I've got him by an inch, but sore elbow or not, his arms look as though they could choke me out. It would be worth it. I bump into his chest with my own, and he stumbles back a step, then comes right back at me. I take the hit like a champ.

"Come on, Wyatt Earp. Man up a little. Take a joke," he says, his laugh sounding less sure this time.

"You keep calling me that, and I assume it's about my age. But you know Wyatt Earp was the sheriff. And you need to have someone lay down the law with you."

"*Pfft*, okay! Yeah, you go ahead. Lay down the law," Chance mocks.

I catch him off guard with a quick slap to his jaw, and his eyes flash wide with shock when his head snaps back to face me.

"Don't start shit with me. Not unless you're willing to take it to the next level."

I slap him again, then shove him back until his back is flat against his cubby. He pushes into the center of my chest with his fists, shoving me off him, but I come right back at him, pinning him to the door and staring into his wild eyes.

"I'm gonna tell you this, and I'm only going to tell you once. The woman in that photo is my wife. I think you know that, but you thought it was funny to disrespect her anyhow. And the thing is, Chance? I don't let people make assumptions, spread stories, disparage, or threaten my wife. And what you did? What you *let* happen? That was a direct attack on the woman I love. The mother of my child. My *unborn* child.

"Your young punk ass is too underdeveloped to grasp the gravity of being a man on the verge of becoming a dad. You can't fathom the strength that comes from having a family of your own, of having something so precious in your life that you're willing to throw away an NFL career defending them when they're attacked. So you go ahead and snicker with your friends in the corner like some high school cafeteria bullshit all you want, but I swear . . . you ever take a photo, share a photo, fucking comment on a photo of *my* wife again, I will make sure that sore elbow of yours hurts for the rest of your fucking life."

I pound my fist against the wood paneling next to Chance's head before I finally step back. His teeth are gritted and his breath ragged as his fists ball at his sides. I walk backward slowly, almost taunting him to keep this up, to make a move and come at me. Peyton would be so mad if she were here. She'd tell me to put my caveman in check. Sometimes, though, the caveman gets shit done.

"We have a problem here?" Coach Phillips says as he steps into the room filled with obvious tension.

"We're all good. I was just giving Chance some photography tips. You know, for his hobby." I glare at Chance, noting the way his eyes flicker. I'm sure he's thinking of what he can say to make sure he's still Coach's golden boy. Phillips will take his side no matter what, though. That's the difference between us. I don't give a shit what Phillips thinks. I'm still the better QB. And I'm a fucking way better man.

"Yeah, Wyatt was just giving me some tips." Chance blinks a few times, his mouth stuck in a hard line.

"Anytime," I say, turning my body to face my cubby.

"I don't like drama, boys. Drop your shit at the door. If it shows up on my field—"

"No drama here, Coach," I say, not bothering to face him again as I finish stripping down for the shower. I wrap my towel around my waist and fling my cubby door shut, giving both Coach and Chance a wink as I pass.

Todd Stone would be proud.

Chance doesn't seem to want to stick around to shower at the practice fields. I'm glad because my bravado fades under the hot water, and I am not ready to go another round with him. I think he got my point. If he decides to keep stirring shit up, he's just a dick. And feeling threatened.

I'm stuffing my headphones and my dirty T-shirt into my

duffle when my phone buzzes with a call. I palm it, then shut my cubby door before checking the name on the screen. My heart kicks like a teenager in love when I see my wife's picture and name.

"Hey, babe. How'd you know I needed to hear your voice?"

She laughs softly.

"I don't know. Maybe because I needed to hear yours, too." She lets out an audible sigh.

"I'm sorry we didn't get to talk more this morning," I say, hating that I had to let her go after dropping such a huge bomb in her lap.

"It's fine. It's not like talking would have done much. If it helps, I'm a lot calmer now. In fact, I'm basically emotional putty. I'm not sure I can feel anything."

My heart squeezes at her words. My truck's the last one in the lot, other than some of the support staff and Coach Elgin's SUV. I click the fob and climb in, putting Peyton on speaker before buckling up.

I want to tell her about my conversation with Chance, leaving out some of the details, of course, like the part about slapping him. And shoving him. But I don't think she needs to take in anything new tonight.

"You talk to your dad yet?" I figure Reed's seen the news. I'm a little worried about his reaction, for obvious protective-father-for-life reasons. But he'll be as pissed as I am when I tell him about my chat with Chance. I have a feeling, given the opportunity, he'll have a talk of his own.

"Not yet. I did get an earful from my sister, though. Apparently, I've ruined her life."

Shit.

"I didn't think about how this might show up . . . you know . . . in the teen world."

We both sigh.

"I mean, they basically live on their phones. Even more than people our age do. I'm giving her the evening to cool down, but I told my mom I'm going to take her to breakfast in the morning before school. I figure letting her skip the first couple hours and signing her in late may buy me her willingness to listen . . . *a little*."

"Yeah, that's a good idea. Maybe I can buy your dad breakfast too. You know . . . so he doesn't kill me," I say with a short laugh.

"He's probably going to be busy burning down the school district offices, so you may need to have that breakfast in jail."

My face puzzles as I say, "Huh?"

"Seems my cheer coaching gig was short-lived. I'm suspended pending a decency hearing."

I punch my brakes in the middle of the parking lot, coming to a hard stop at her revelation.

"I'm sorry, decency?"

I've had a solid twenty-four hours to study that photo, and I've decided there is nothing indecent in it. Peyton's clothed. I look fully clothed. Nobody would know that my shirt was unbuttoned. Can people make suggestive insights? Yeah, probably. That's because we're all basically perverts who love that gotcha shit.

"Yep. I'm sure my dad's heard about it. The district gossipers are quick to do damage, and people around here love to start fires. I stand in front of the firing squad tomorrow at six."

"I'm coming," I say, without giving any thought to the logistics. I don't care what they are. There's zero chance I'm not showing up for her. For this.

"Wy, stop it. You can't possibly—"

"I'm coming," I cut in.

The line is silent for a few seconds. Peyton must realize she would be just as insistent if the tables were turned.

"Fine, but let me defend myself. You can stand in solidarity, but this fight is mine. Got it?"

I'm already scrolling on my phone for flight options.

"Got it. You run the show. I'll just be background."

I find a flight that leaves at two tomorrow, giving me just enough time to make morning practice before jetting to the airport and heading to Tucson. I'll just need a lift from the airport.

"I can't talk you out of this, can I?" Peyton says as my purchase goes through.

"Nope. Flight forty-seven-sixty. American. I'll get my mom to pick me up. Calling her now. Love you."

I hang up before Peyton has time to talk reason into me. I shoot her a quick text before calling my mom, one simple word —*please.*

PEYTON: *Okay. Sir.*

I chuckle as I dial my mom. Of all Peyton's gifts, her ability to find humor when the world is on fire is one of the best. It's kept me from spiraling during stressful times.

My phone rings in my truck a few times before the speakers finally crackle with the sounds of someone picking up.

"Hey, Wy. What's up, son?" Jeff answers.

I snap my mouth shut and stare blankly at my mom's photo on my phone screen, wishing I had one of Peyton's funny quips to get me out of this very awkward long pause.

Jeff answered. He's called me 'son' many times, but it hit differently this time.

"Uh . . . hi, yeah. Sorry. I was just—"

I was just falling down the rabbit hole of acceptance that you and my mom are likely a thing.

"Let me get your mom," Jeff says.

"Yeah. Yeah, uh. Mom. Thanks." I swallow down the dry razorblades.

Stick to the plan, Wyatt. You need a ride from Tucson to the district office tomorrow. It's a quick turnaround. You'll be in and out. You'll fill her in on everything during the drive. Everyone's fine. I'm fine. Peyton's fine. The baby is fine. I simply need a ride. Nothing else on my mind.

"Wyatt, what a surprise," my mom says, her voice wavering with the guilt of a kid literally stuck inside the cookie jar.

"Are you and Jeff fucking?"

I think that went well.

Chapter Eighteen

Peyton

I've been pacing outside the district offices for at least thirty minutes. I sent my parents inside, along with my dad's coaching staff, who all showed up for support. I know they mean well, and the show of strength probably plays in my favor, especially when it comes from the football side, but my mind keeps wandering to the size of my audience rather than the content on my notecards. I have some major points to make, and I don't want to get rattled.

It's particularly hot out; August in Arizona doing its thing. I'm so sweaty, I consider swapping out my suit pants and blouse for the dress I brought as backup. The bead of sweat slowly crawling down my spine almost pushes me over the edge, but thankfully, Wyatt's mom pulls into the lot with my husband in tow. Something about knowing he's here helps shore up my resolve. I'm glad he came.

I hold my cards at my side, my lips moving with the words as silently I run through my opening while Wyatt and his mom walk up to me.

"How are you feeling, hon?" Wyatt's mom gives me a quick hug.

I draw in a deep breath and let my shoulders fall with my exhale.

"I'm definitely prepared."

She runs her palms over my shoulders, brushing away loose hairs from my deep purple jacket.

"Well, you look like a prosecutor. Go give 'em hell."

She gently tugs my lapels, straightening my jacket before giving me a reassuring smile and glancing at her son.

"I'll be right in," Wyatt says, kissing his mom on the cheek before she heads into the public meeting room that is starting to reach capacity. I'm thankful I have yet to see anyone from the media. I'm sure the reporter from our local paper will tune in to watch the stream of the meeting online. That's better than a bunch of cameras parked out front.

"How was the drive?" I ask him once we're alone. He told me about his bold reaction when Jeff answered his mom's phone. I figured the hour drive from Tucson would give them some much-needed time to talk.

"Well, we talked about you. The photo. Your hearing tonight. The baby. The last ultrasound. Oh, and what I think my odds are for starting the next preseason game. So, yeah. It was eventful." *His sarcasm is showing.*

"You know, you could have brought it up, too. It's not just on your mom to come forward and share her personal life."

I give him a wry smirk as he stares at me blankly for a full breath. He looks to the right as he exhales and hunches, probably from all the valid points I just piled on his shoulders.

"It's not like she's been hiding things. They've both been out in the open about spending time together, showing up places together, *being* together. Maybe—and now, just hear me out, but maybe—your mom simply assumed you knew and were okay with it."

My husband blinks his focus back to me, his lips pursed.

"She's been a widow for a long time. And honestly, if she had to catch feelings for someone, wouldn't you want it to be a man like Jeff?"

His shoulders sag as his lips flap with a frustrated breath before relenting.

"Yes. I know you're right. Damn it, you're *always* right. It's just . . . weird." He pulls me in for a hug, and kisses the top of my head.

"Life is weird, Wyatt. It's a series of one weird thing after another. Now, put on your big-boy pants and go sit with your mom while I practice a speech about why it's okay to be affectionate with my husband."

His chest rumbles with his chuckle.

"Fair enough. And hey, pencil in some time to be *affectionate* later tonight. I fly out in the morning."

"*Mmm*, we'll see. Kinda depends how this thing goes." I step up on my toes to give him a quick kiss before he heads inside.

I run through my note cards two more times before tucking them in my jacket pocket and everyone heads inside. I make a stop in the ladies' room to shake out my nerves and touch up my lip gloss. When I push through the door, it flings open as someone pulls the handle from the other side, and I stumble out.

"Sorry, Coach . . . *oh* . . ."

I pull myself together quickly at the sound of Alissa Sommers' voice. It's not her fault that her mom is pushy. Honestly, I like Alissa. She's a terrible tumbler, and she can't project worth a damn, but she works hard and is a huge help at practice. I've dubbed her team manager for a reason. Her mom thinks her daughter is someone else, though. She thinks Alissa is the same loud, athletic cheerleader she was when she was in high school. And the fact Alissa isn't going to perform with the squad in competition baffles her. What Alissa needs is to be valued for exactly who she is.

Not your place, Peyton. Keep your mouth shut. Especially now.

"It's okay, Alissa. I'm a bit of a mess. I'm sure I would have tripped all on my own." I force a pleasant smile on my lips, but it breaks down when Alissa's mouth quivers and her eyes tear up.

"I'm so sorry," she says, her hands flying to her mouth, cupping it.

I shake my head and glance around the foyer of the meeting room. It's clear, so I shake my head and pull down my emotional mask for a moment.

"It's not your fault, Alissa. And no matter what, you will continue to have a place on the squad. You're a natural leader. And not all leaders have to be loud."

She nods as her hands slowly drop to her sides.

"Thank you," she says, her voice a whisper.

"No. Thank *you* for everything you've done to help the team." I stop myself from apologizing for her mom acting the way she is, because as ugly as her attack on me is, I know the root of it is because she believes she's defending her daughter.

Alissa attempts a smile, however tepid, then heads into the restroom. I make my way into the full meeting room, taking a seat in the very back, next to the other speakers who have been called on for tonight. Granted, the guy right next to me is presenting on the quotes the district received for replacement concrete for one of the elementary schools, and the woman next to him is asking for a budget for an eighth-grade winter dance. I wish I could trade places with her.

To spare the other guests from a late night, the board president, a retired teacher named Chuck Darwin of all things, shuffles the agenda and lets the two other presenters go first. The wait has me sweating, but it's too late to dip into the bathroom and swap the suit for a dress, though the thought of dashing out after a superhero-esque change is tempting.

"Now to the matter of the indecent photo—"

I get to my feet the second Chuck utters that word. *Indecent.*

"Excuse me. I would like to speak and correct what I suspect may be some dangerous misrepresentations of, well, me."

"*Hmm,*" he grumbles into his mic.

The applause from the audience buoys me as I step up to the podium in front of the dais. There is one section of the room that's quiet, the one where Alissa's mom is sitting with her cohorts. Strange how those are the parents of the girls I either cut from tryouts or offered non-performing roles.

Football doesn't have to put up with this shit.

I clear my throat and adjust the mic, the snickers from my haters catching my ears. They must catch my mom's too, because she levels an audible *shh* that carries across the room. I breathe in slowly through my nose rather than cringe. Mom is defending me. And that's what Alissa's mom thinks she's doing. Maintain composure. Stick to the message.

"I didn't come here tonight to defend a photo. I came to defend my name. My family's name. A name that means something because of the things we've all done for this community. My grandfather put this place on the map. Leading the high school to its first state football championship. Opening the first auto dealership in town. Serving as the president of this very board when my dad was a baby."

I glance to my right to find my father leaning against the wall alongside his coaching staff and several of his players.

"My dad carried that torch, and he didn't need to come back. I won't lie, there were times when I was sixteen and . . .

well . . . acting my age, and I thought 'Man, it would be nice to live in Malibu instead of a desert that tops out at a hundred and twenty-three degrees in July.'"

The crowd chuckles. Heat jokes always play well in this place.

"But nah. Not Reed Johnson. He wanted to come back to his roots. He wanted to help guide the inevitable growth. To pour money into the sport here, to the place that gave him a career in the first place. The man spends more time on that high school field than any of you ever have. My mom, too. And the ranch she's built, the way she's helping people, families, to find joy and to feel a connection through animal therapy. Yeah, the Johnsons are good for Coolidge."

I'm feeling my rhythm, which is probably why Chuck feels the need to clear his throat in his mic right now. My eyes flit up from my note cards to meet his. I haven't had to look at them much, but so far, I've stayed on message. But the way he's looking at me, boredom drooping his face, means my words aren't really sinking in.

I set my cards down on the podium and take a step back for a moment, dropping my head and shaking it. I'm going to have to go off script. I approach the mic again, this time gripping the edges of the podium and taking my time to meet the gazes of all five board members.

"You know, we wouldn't be having this meeting if I were the football coach. If this was a football parent filing a complaint. If this, what did you call it . . . *indecent?* Yeah, if this indecent photo was of my dad, one of his staff, one of our beloved players or alumni who wore the jersey, we wouldn't be having a meeting at all. Hell, I bet at least one of you on that board would turn it into a meme or a Christmas card."

Travis, who played for Coolidge with my Uncle Jason years

ago snaps his gaze to me. I smirk, and he cracks a little under the guilt, smiling back on one side of his mouth.

"It's interesting that I'm not the only person in this photo, yet I don't see my husband being dragged before you all to be embarrassed."

"Mrs. Stone, your husband is not a member of the faculty—"

I hold up my hand and utter, "Ah ah ah."

I glance at Wyatt, and he leans forward, sitting up tall.

"Hey, sweetheart? What was that thing you got in the mail the other day, you know, right before you left for training camp?"

My husband smirks, then stands, causing a wave of chatter and whispers to filter throughout the room.

"It was a letter stating I would be considered 'on sabbatical' until further notice. The football boosters were hoping I could maybe contribute to the spring program, help with workouts, and motivate the kids."

"So, basically, remain on staff," I lead, quirking a brow. I may have missed my calling as a lawyer.

"Basically. Yeah," Wyatt says, giving me a wink before taking his seat.

This time when I turn back to face the board, Chuck, along with Tammy Neddles, another retired teacher who always votes his way, are both sitting back with their arms crossed. They look pissed.

"We probably should have booked more time for this meeting, then, right? I mean, clearly, you're also going to evaluate how this sordid situation impacts my husband's role at Coolidge High. We're in the same photo. You know, both clothed, and married, and showing we love each other. To be clear, I did not take this photo. My husband also did not take this photo. We thought we were in the privacy of our hotel quarters, reconnecting after a few weeks apart. And he's kissing my belly because, not that this is anyone's business, but we're having a baby."

Maybe this is what I should have said in the first place, because the second my news breaks, the crowd becomes excited. There are a few whistles, some sweet *awws,* and there's applause. Plus, it's probably not a good look to come after the pregnant lady.

The gavel coming down on the dais startles me, along with many in the crowd, and decorum comes around. I have one last shot to make my case. The board members are all glancing at one another, leaning in and whispering. *Conspiring.* Yeah, I was wearing a Coolidge High cheer uniform. I paid for the thing when I was eighteen. I should get to wear it anytime I want. And again, I was *wearing* it. Not stripping out of it. And as far as anyone can tell, we were simply embracing—showing love.

"You know, a lot of things have been swept under proverbial rugs around this place when it comes to football. A certain fire my senior year comes to mind. And the underage drinking and skinny dipping in the river are a very public secret rites of passage. Oh, and I think there was a drag race or two between Coolidge players and Vista players. And—"

"Your point is made, Mrs. Stone," Chuck says, not wanting me to list more of the town's dirty laundry.

"It's Stone-Johnson," I correct, making sure to note that Johnson name in the record. I may as well cash in on it if it helps.

"Noted," Chuck says in a dry, emotionless tone.

"Thank you." I curtsy, mostly because I'm nervous, then head back to my lonely chair in the back of the room while Chuck makes a public appeal for any more speakers on the topic. I've become a topic.

I stare at the back of Adrian Sommers's head, my molars

smashing together while I hold my breath. When the tight, blonde bun wiggles as she shakes her head, passing on the chance to judge me publicly, I spit out my breath and let my back rest against the hard metal of the chair.

The board ultimately votes to dismiss the complaint against me when I skate by three against two. Chuck, of course, votes to suspend me, as does Tammy. I'm not surprised by their decision, but I am a little shocked by the outcome. This town likes to act small when it's convenient, and when it's about something gossipy at the expense of a woman, it gets small real fast.

Chapter Nineteen

Wyatt

"So much for this story going away. "

I hand my phone to Peyton while I finish getting dressed. The Cyclones' PR department has been working overtime. It seems a few people posted about Peyton's speech last night at the board meeting, some of them sharing video snippets that have now gone viral. For the most part, the response has been positive. Yeah, there are the occasional assholes who hide behind their fake profile pics and keyboards to tear her down, but the positive comments have been overwhelming. They've also piqued the curiosity of a lot of media ready to talk about double standards in social media and sports.

"I should probably put out a statement or something. I can't keep answering these with the same information over and over." She folds her legs up in our bed and cradles my phone as her thumbs fly along the keyboard.

"That's not a bad idea. For what it's worth, though, I'm proud of you." I lean over and kiss the top of her head.

"Thank you," she rasps in a sleepy voice.

This time together was too short. I hate being apart. By

the time we got home last night, we were both exhausted. I could barely keep my eyes open long enough to take a mental snapshot of her in my arms. I don't even think I dreamed.

"There. Sent. I'll call Jason this morning." She looks up into my eyes as she returns my phone. She seems sad.

"I'll just quit," I say, running my hand through her hair once, then holding my palm to her cheek. She leans into it and hums through a soft smile, turning just enough to kiss my wrist.

"We both know neither of us are quitters."

She's right. I laugh faintly.

"Yeah, I know. But right now, I wish I were."

She sucks in her bottom lip and scoots to the edge of the bed, wrapping her arms and legs around me the way a toddler does when they don't want their parent to drop them off at daycare.

"This isn't helping." I chuckle.

"Gah!" She lets go of me, and I help her to her feet. "Fine. I'll let you go."

My phone buzzes in my pocket, and I pull it out to see a message from my mom.

MOM: *In the driveway. No Jeff. How about we talk?*

I squeeze my eyes shut and show Peyton the message. She laughs and pats my back.

"You can do this, Wy. Have a talk with your mom. A *real* talk. You'll feel better. Then, call me tonight after practice."

I kiss her and take my phone back, shutting my eyes once more as I breathe her in.

"See you again in one hundred and four hours and sixteen minutes," I say, a ballpark guess, but I'm close.

Peyton gives me a sideways look on her way into the bathroom.

"I'll see you first since you'll be on the field," she teases, shouting from the bathroom as I head down the hall.

I don't reply, but the truth is I always see her first. I find her instantly, every time. She's the first thing I see when I step on the field, and the only person I want when the lights go off.

My mom lifts her brow as I approach her SUV, and Peyton's pep talk—and truth session—from last night plays in my mind. My mom's making the effort. I need to be ready to listen. And to be open.

"Thanks for being my rideshare. It's a tight turnaround," I say, dropping my travel bag in the back seat, then sliding into the front passenger side and buckling up.

"You know I like that you call me for things like this. It means a lot."

Our gazes meet, and we share a short knowing smile. It was Mom and me for a lot of road trips when I was young and my dad was on shift. She handled a lot of the back and forth to practice or to sports camps, too.

"Well? Shall we?" She shifts into reverse, and I nod, aware that she's not only talking about hitting the road.

"I'm sorry about how I reacted, Mom. That was . . . *oof!* Not my best moment." I wince, recalling what I said to her on the phone the other day.

"It was definitely not how I saw this conversation starting," she says as we hit the main road.

"You know, Peyton's kind of known for a while," I say.

My mom snort laughs.

"Son, I think the entire town has known. Along with half of the Valley fire departments. You might be oblivious."

"Really?" I lean forward, and she glances my way before belly laughing.

"Yeah, really. We didn't really hide it. His house is for sale, for Pete's sake. We're moving in together."

I flinch at that reveal. I definitely missed the clues for that level of relationship.

"Okay, okay. In. my defense, you maybe *could* have said something to me. Even if it wasn't right away. Like, say, 'Hey, Wyatt. Jeff and I have been seeing each other, and things are getting serious.'"

Her smile slips a tad, and she sighs.

"I know."

Her heavy sigh is a relief. I feel less crazy now. She didn't exactly share things with me.

"You could have told me, even if it was obvious."

She glances my way again with a brief, tight smile.

"I was . . . scared."

Her confession hits my chest hard. She's had a lot to be scared about in her life. The thought that she was afraid to talk to me hurts my heart.

"I wouldn't have been mad. I mean, I may have been surprised, but not . . . mad. I love Jeff. Like an uncle. Or apparently, a *stepfather*."

"Whoa, oh oh oh, slow down. Nobody is getting married anytime soon."

We both settle into nervous laughter, and slowly our conversation morphs into stories about Dad and Jeff on the job. I have a lot of nice memories with the man, and my mother does too. She doesn't say it outright, but I think perhaps that's part of the attraction. He's comfortable. He's also kind. And probably the man most like my dad out there—besides me.

As we close in on the airport, I promise to reach out to Jeff when I get some downtime this week. I'm sure he's feeling awkward in all of this, but it's important to me that he knows how I feel about him and that I approve of this, despite my initial surprise.

"You know, it's funny," I begin as my mom enters the departures lane for the airport.

"What is, honey?"

I gather my thoughts and sit with my embarrassment for a minute.

"I really was daft, wasn't I? I mean, now that we've talked about things, and you've pointed out the dozens of times you two showed up at something as a couple, and I was literally *right there!*"

My mom pats my knee.

"Well, it's a good thing you're handsome," she jokes.

"Aww, that's cold, Mom!"

We're back to us, and it feels good. In fact, it feels better than before. My mom seems genuinely happy. Less lonely. And if I'm really going to do this thing for more than a single season, I like the idea of her having someone in her life to give her comfort. I like Jeff.

She pulls to the curb, and I hop out to grab my bag before gazing back across the passenger seat to say our goodbyes. Before I speak, though, she pulls out a package from the nook in her door and hands it to me.

"What's this?" I arch a brow.

"Something I found the other day that I thought you might like to have. You can open it when you get inside." Her coyness makes me suspicious. It would be like my mom to buy me one of those embarrassing shirts, and I can tell by the floppiness and size of the wrapped item that it's fabric or clothing.

"Okay, then. Drive safe, and I'll call you." I blow her a kiss.

"You better," she says.

I push the passenger door shut and check the time on my phone. I still have forty minutes before my flight. I adjust my bag's strap on my shoulder, then pull at the twine my mom fashioned into a bow. Whatever this is, she wrapped it in re-used tissue paper from Christmas, the pale blue paper covered in snowflakes, wrinkled and torn in a few places. I unravel it as I walk inside, and at first glance, the garment doesn't look familiar. But then I unfurl it and stop in my tracks.

It's my name printed in red across the back of a white jersey. It's also my dad's name.

STONE

My fingertip runs along the stitching, the sharp corner of the T scratching my skin. It's my father's old public safety football jersey. Fire played games against police every year for charity. I loved this thing, and I wore it for Halloween at least three times when I was a kid. The first year, my mom had to pin the hemline up nearly in half so it didn't drag on the ground as I walked the neighborhood on a mission for candy. I wanted nothing more than to be him every chance I got. Halloween was the ideal time to act it out. In total, I think I was either a firefighter or a fire football team captain eight times over the years. As far as I was concerned, Todd Stone walked on water.

I fold the jersey, careful not to crease the letters on the back, and tuck it inside my travel bag. I pull my phone from my pocket and dial my mom as I head toward the security checkpoint. She answers right away.

"I love it."

"I knew you would. It seemed like something that should live with you." There's a softness to her voice, a tell of her emotions. She's not sad, though. She's reliving moments. I recognize the tone because I speak in it myself at times.

"You think it fits?"

I didn't really stretch it out enough to tell, but I remember it being large.

"Well, he never quite had *your* biceps, but I imagine you can pull it off."

"Good. I'm going to wear it under my jersey if I can, at least for practice. Thanks, Mom. I love you."

She echoes my affection, and I end our call as I step into the security line. A boy who looks to be about eleven or twelve is standing in front of me in line with a man I assume is his father. He gives me a double take before tugging on his dad's jacket sleeve.

"Hey, that's Wyatt Stone," he whispers, and not very quietly either.

I feel my cheeks warm up. I'm not dressed up as I should be, but I have on a button down and slacks, so at least I'm professional-looking.

"How you doin'?" I say, nodding to him.

"Good," he mutters, biting his bottom lip while he twists in place with nervous energy.

"Hey, great game, man. We were rooting for you. Pretty cool having an Arizona guy out there representing," his dad says. He reaches out his hand and we shake.

"Thank you. I'm trying. It's hard to keep up with those young guys, you know?" I kick myself internally when I realize he's probably about a decade older than me.

"Oh, I don't know about that. You looked comfortable to me. I think they had a hard time keeping up with you. Hey, good luck, man."

"Thank you," I say, tucking his words into the corner of my mind to dwell on later. *Was I really that good?*

His son keeps looking over his shoulder as we move up in the line. I feel inside my bag for anything that might work for an autograph, and I come across my pen and the coffee receipt from my trip to LA. I pull it out and scribble my signature along with a short message that I sort of borrow from my favorite quarterback growing up. Kurt Warner signed a ball for me once, and he wrote, "Always play with heart." It stuck with me, so maybe it will with him.

"Here," I say, handing him the makeshift keepsake. "You'll always know I take my coffee with double cream and sugar."

His dad laughs, and the kid holds the paper up in front of him while wearing a grin and wide eyes.

"Thanks, Mr. Stone," he says.

"Yeah, thanks, man." His father glances at my message, then back to me, nodding. He gets it.

As we shuffle through the checkpoint and approach the scanners, I set my bag on the conveyor belt and leave my palm on top for an extra beat.

Play with heart. I think I will.

Chapter Twenty

Peyton

My phone buzzes in my palm and I open the photo Wyatt sent of himself wearing his father's old jersey. He's right; it is a little tight. But it's also perfect.

"What an incredible gift," I say before taking my phone off speaker and heading out the door to the Jeep.

"Yeah. So many memories of my dad wearing this thing. You think it's stupid to wear it for practice?"

"Not at all."

I set my duffle bag in the passenger seat before moving to the driver's side. I sync my phone with the Jeep and head down our driveway, pausing at the empty road. Not a car in sight. I'm a little stressed about practice today. A few of the parents sent me messages of encouragement last night after the meeting, but I can't get over the look on a few of the faces in the crowd. They were demonizing me.

"You okay?" Wyatt breaks the silence.

"Yeah," I sigh out. "Sometimes, I just like having you on the line, even if I don't have anything to say."

"I know what you mean."

I give my pause a few more seconds, then turn onto the road, heading toward the high school.

"My mom told me the best way to shut everyone up is to win state," I say.

"*Hmm.* She's not wrong. Not in Coolidge anyway."

Everyone loves you when you win.

"I don't know if this is the squad that can do that, if I'm being real. They're scrappy, and I have a few tumblers, but the program doesn't have the support like it did when I was the captain."

Or the talent.

"So, find yourself a *you* and make her captain."

I ruminate on Wyatt's advice for a few seconds. I'm not sure there's a girl like me on the squad.

"Thanks, babe. That's good advice. I'm gonna look for someone."

I may need to find that person outside of the team and beg them to join, which wouldn't be a first for any sport at Coolidge. Hell, the underhanded recruitment that happens with high school football around here crosses state lines. I merely want to poach a volleyball player, or maybe a hidden gem who never tries out for anything.

"I gotta hit the field. I'll call you as soon as I get to the apartment tonight. Love you."

I blow a kiss into the phone before he ends the call, then finish my drive to the high school, pulling into the lot a few minutes before students file out to head home or to practices.

I park in the faculty section and grab my bag, heading inside before I have an audience. I feel as though this entire thing has put a new spotlight on me, like when I was a student here and my dad was still playing. It's strange how a high school campus can make anyone feel like an awkward adolescent again. The whispering. The name calling. This place sometimes assigns people in roles whether they want them or not. Bullies, nerds, loners. I've worn each of those titles at some point.

The gym is quiet when I step inside, the last PE class for the day done. I sneak up the steps to the mats upstairs, then pause at the large white board. Maybe this whole thing should be democratic. It takes me a few minutes to write every team member's name on the board, and by the time I click the cap back on the pen, half of the squad is upstairs with me and stretching.

I step in front of the short senior who is going to be our flyer this season.

"Kyra, how long have you been cheering?"

She stretches an arm across her body as she scrunches her face in thought. "Seven years? Yeah . . . seven."

I nod and mutter, "Thanks."

When Lily, the other senior on the team, arrives, I ask her the same question. She came up through the same cheer club I did, so I'm not surprised when she says she started at eight.

It would be easy to make the two of them co-captains. They don't fall into the bully category, and they're talented. But neither is the kind of leader who inspires. Or maybe I simply don't see it. And that makes a team vote feel like an even better idea.

"Hey, Coach? You can take Alissa's name off the board. She quit," says Amosa, a sophomore like Alissa.

My gut drops, and I can't help the audible sigh I let out.

"Why did she quit?"

I know why. Because her mom made her. And because she's the center of attention in a fight she didn't pick.

Amosa shrugs, but our gazes connect for a beat, long enough for a shared frowning expression.

Amosa and Alissa are friends. I've seen them together

outside of practice. I remember them both at games as freshmen, sitting in the stands, cheering with glitter on their faces. They were into school spirit without the hype of a cheer uniform. I get the feeling that both tried out simply to have something fun to do together and to be part of a team that liked to support the Bears as much as they did.

I turn to the board and pick up the eraser, hovering it over Alissa's name for a few seconds while I imagine this squad without her. I can't even imagine today's practice without her, honestly. She has this way of showing effort that's infectious. I honestly think some of the stronger girls try harder just because Alissa does.

I put the eraser back and flip around to face the squad, folding my arms over my chest.

"What's with the names, Coach?" Lily asks.

I pull my lips in tight, giving myself a second for a gut check before floating a wild idea out there.

"I was considering holding a vote today for team captain. I think you ladies are talented enough to really compete, but you're missing that extra drive. When I was cheering here, and at Arizona, we had strong leadership that pushed us all to be our best, together."

Amosa clears her throat, and I lift a brow as I glance at her.

"Sorry, Coach. But . . . weren't you the captain here?"

I smirk, realizing I did sort of indirectly brag about myself. I waggle my head and roll my eyes, feeling the burn of embarrassment.

"Yeah, but it wasn't just me. I wasn't always the captain. I learned from some awesome upperclassmen, and there was a system in place where the seniors chose their successor before graduation. I'm not sure why that practice stopped, but maybe . . . we should bring it back."

The girls look around the room at one another, a few of

them lifting their brows. They seem excited by the idea. My gaze settles on Kyra and Lily, and the two of them turn to look at one another with what I think is a sense of unease crinkling their eyes. I didn't think they wanted the captain roles, which is another reason I didn't simply pick them for it. I can see their hesitation now.

"I'm not coronating you, guys. Relax," I say, and Lily lets out a nervous laugh and shakes her head as she stares at the ground.

"No offense, Coach," Kyra adds. "It's not that I'm not ambitious. It's just that I don't think I'd enjoy being captain. And I have a lot on my plate with academics. And—"

I hold up my hand, stopping her from giving herself anxiety.

"I understand. And I wouldn't ask that of you, unless it's something you want."

They both nod and exhale through their noses, their smiles returning.

"But"—their smiles drop again; hopefully this proposal will be all right with them—"as the seniors, maybe it is fitting that you two get to decide who leads this team. It's your last year, and you've both been at this for a long time. You know what works and what doesn't. You have insights none of us have, not even me, because these are your peers. This is your last year in this uniform, and you deserve to help decide the direction. How does this program go from here?"

I can tell they're taking this role in thoughtfully, both blinking as their gazes drift to the empty space. I give the rest of the squad a gut check, glancing at the other girls to see if I sense any jealousy or bitterness. Mostly, it's smiles. A few girls look relieved. And all of this tells me that the person who should lead this squad isn't in this room. But I can't be the one to make that call.

"We'll do it. Or, well, I'll do it. Lily?" Kyra looks at her friend, and she nods.

"Great. I'd like you to think about it today, through practice. We're working on basic skills all afternoon, and that will give you a chance to observe the others, or pull anyone aside and talk to them, or—"

"We don't need to do that, actually," Lily says, biting her lip and lifting a brow at Kyra.

"No?"

My body floods with tingles, and I'm not sure whether I'm excited or terrified. I think both.

"Uh uh," Kyra confirms. "We all know it's Alissa. She's the heart and soul of this squad."

My belly buzzes, and my eyes well up a little. I blink the emotion away, but I'm pretty sure half of this room saw it. I smile and nod, looking Kyra in the eyes first, then Lily.

"Do you think you two can run skills practice today? I'll have the weight-lifting teacher sit in, but he doesn't know what we do. I need to go talk to Alissa's mom." My stomach roils with a wave of nausea. Why is doing the right thing so fucking hard sometimes?

Both girls nod. I direct the team to line up in groups, then pass the reins off to the two seniors to get the squad started. I pick the eraser back up next and wipe away the names from the board, all of them but one. I doubt this is what Wyatt had in mind when he gave me that advice earlier. He's going lose his crap when I tell him I walked up the Sommers's driveway today and rang the doorbell. I hope I don't also have to tell him I got punched in the face.

It takes me twenty minutes to get to Alissa's house. Her mom works out of the home office most days; she's a realtor. Her face is plastered all over this town, even on the one bus that runs from the library to the dairy farms down south. Her white

Cadillac is in the driveway when I pull up, which likely means she's at home today.

"Peyton, what the ever-loving fuck are you doing?" I whisper to myself as I touch up my lip gloss in the visor mirror. I'm not sure if I'm saying that in my own voice or my mother's.

With the same gusto it always took me to hype myself up for a tricky tumbling pass, I focus my thoughts and suck in a deep breath before getting out of the Jeep and marching up to the Sommers's front door. I press the button for the bell and take a step back when I hear the deep growl from the other side of the door. Of course they have dogs. That woman probably has attack canines trained on my scent.

"Sugar, down!" I recognize Adrian's voice through the door and smile on one side of my mouth hearing her dog's name. I would never guess that sound came from something named Sugar.

It's quiet and still for a few seconds, and I lift my chin and smile, figuring she's probably checking to see who's here through the peephole. I'm not sure whether she considers me a solicitor or not, so I adjust my feet and hold my ground while she works the locks. Our eyes connect the second she opens the door.

"What could you possibly want?" I figured she would come out hot. Frankly, I'm relieved she doesn't pop the screen open and poke me in the chest.

"I was hoping we could talk for a minute," I say, ignoring the acid crawling up my esophagus.

"Mom, who is it?" Alissa's voice sounds from the distance.

Adrian drops her gaze to the floor as her shoulders lift, then suddenly drop.

"Come in," she finally says, pushing open the security door for me and holding the front door wide while an overweight basset hound lies at her feet.

"Huh," I say, glancing down as I pass.

"Yeah, I know. She sounds worse than she is. That bark is all deterrence," she explains, her tone almost light, maybe even pleasant.

"It's effective," I say as she guides me into the living room.

"Not *that* effective. You still stuck around," she mutters.

I snicker at her burn, but she doesn't laugh with me, so I swallow down my amusement. Clearly, we aren't going to leap right to the less hostile, shit-talking level of our previous relationship. She's probably still hovering around the lawsuit territory.

"Oh—" Alissa stops between the kitchen and living room, a plate of crackers and cheese in her hands. She looks petrified.

"Hi, Alissa." I drop my hands into the side pockets of my leggings and do my best to relax my stance.

"Hi, Coach. I'm sorry I didn't tell you myself, but . . . I quit the team. That's why I'm not at practice." Her eyes dart around the room, periodically meeting mine.

"I figured it out," I say. "I was hoping the three of us could talk about that. What do you think?"

"*Umm*," Alissa says, her focus going to the stack of cheddar in her hands, then flitting to her mom.

Adrian shrugs, then drops herself into the corner cushion of her sofa, pulling a pillow into her lap.

"I told you that quitting things doesn't mean you can just stop cold turkey. You have to be professional about stuff. People depend on you, even when you don't think they do," Adrian says.

I blink a few times, shocked to hear her words. *It wasn't her decision to pull Alissa from the team? Alissa quit on her own?*

"I know. I'm sorry, Coach. I didn't mean to cause any inconvenience. I can bring my uniform in tomorrow and leave it with the equipment manager, if that's all right."

I shake my head and move to the chair across from her mom, still mentally working out what she's telling me. I pop my head up to meet her worried-looking expression, her eyes squinted as her taut mouth pulls in even tighter.

"Alissa, do you mind me asking why you want to quit?"

She glances toward her mom.

"Don't look at me," Adrian says, throwing her hands up.

I grimace because, well, she could show more grace.

Alissa brings her hands up over her face and groans before moving to the other end of the couch to sit. She uncovers her face but keeps her gaze on the floor, her knees pulled in close and the toes of her shoes pointing inward. She's making herself small.

"Is it the attention?" I ask.

Her eyelashes flicker as her gaze flits up.

I nod slowly, understanding her more than she'll realize. While being the center of attention doesn't scare me—*unless, of course, it's when being attacked for a paparazzi photo*—the idea of everyone looking at her never held much appeal for my mom. She and my father are an opposites-attract story in that way. Not that my dad loved the limelight. He simply didn't give a shit. He was loud and who he was, regardless of other people's opinions. It took my mom years to feel comfortable in her own skin. Everyone's journey is different.

"I have some news from the team. I'm wondering if I can share that with you, and if you'd be willing to think about it and see how it aligns with your comfort level?"

I can feel Adrian's heavy brow looming nearby as she stares at me suspiciously, but I keep my focus on Alissa. This needs to be her choice—quitting, or coming back and leading. She gives me a timid nod.

"I gave Lily and Kyra a responsibility, as the seniors on the team. I asked them to choose who should serve as our cheer captain this year."

"Okay?" Alissa says, her voice wavering. Her mom sits up tall, moving to the edge of the cushion as she discards the pillow she was clutching and instead folds her hands together at her knees. I don't like the idea of Adrian feeling vindicated, but I don't want Alissa to sell herself short because of this.

"They selected you, Alissa."

"Oooooh," Adrian coos in a drawn-out sound. I flash her a warning look but quickly soften my expression. I don't need to poke the bear and stir her up again.

"Oh, that's really . . . nice, I guess?"

"Alissa, that's a big deal!" her mom pipes in.

I pinch the bridge of my nose and close my eyes, shaking my head. I have to steer this thing.

"Your mom is right. It's an honor. But—" I give Adrian a pointed look, risking ticking her off. "This absolutely needs to be your decision, Alissa. You should only take on the role if you truly want it. Also, a few things you should know. One, the entire squad supports this. In fact, one of your teammates referred to you as the heart and soul."

Alissa tilts her head, and her mouth inches up on one side.

"They did?"

Miraculously, Adrian doesn't speak.

I nod.

"They did. And . . . you should also know that you are not expected to be on the mat for competitions. I firmly believe that you do not need to be the best athlete to be the best leader." My gaze drifts to Adrian again, and when I do not sense her opposition, my muscles relax some.

"Okay, so I could, technically, come to competitions but not have to, you know, perform?"

She's really considering this.

"Yes. Absolutely."

Her gaze dips down again as she fidgets with the edges of the small plate. I stand, and her mom quickly stands to match me.

"I don't want you to feel you have to decide now. You can think about it. Let me know tomorrow, maybe?"

I move toward the center of the room while her mom balls her hands together as if she's about to plot how to take over the world. Alissa's gaze lifts, and I hold out a hand to shake on our deal. She chews at the inside of her mouth for a few seconds, then shifts her plate to the center cushion and stands. We shake on it, and her firm grip gives me hope. I lean in before we part.

"And if you have questions or need to talk, without . . ." My eyes glance to my left, toward her mom. "You have my number."

She giggles silently and nods.

"Thank you, Coach."

"No. Thank *you*, Alissa. I appreciate you weighing your options."

I head to the door, but Adrian rushes ahead, opening it for me. Sugar is snoring in the same place she was when I arrived.

"Thank you for stopping by," Adrian says. Her tone would make anyone eavesdropping think we're old pals, but I know that's not the case. Just as I know she doesn't feel bad about putting me through a little hell or judging me.

"Have a good night," I say, leaving her with a polished smile that I keep in place until I climb back into my Jeep and pull away.

I roll the window down at the end of the block, the late August humidity and harsh afternoon sun cooking me. I reach across the seat and point the air vents in my direction so I'm being blasted by all four at once, and when I glance at my reflection in the mirror, my hair is blowing like a pop star in a music video. I yank my water bottle out from the tight-fitting console and flip back the lid, holding the spout to my lips.

And that's when the cramping begins.

I've dealt with this a lot since my accident. Spasticity is triggered so easily for me, and dehydration and stress are both culprits. I'm sure that's part of the problem now. But the way my arms and legs are tightening feels somehow different, and I can't help but worry it's because my body is different. Because I'm pregnant. And the litany of worries that follow that thought sends a rush of adrenaline down my spine.

I press my mom's contact button on my phone screen and flip the Jeep around to head toward the medical center. I know she'll panic, but I also know she's home and has her phone on her. And of everyone that will panic, she will remain the most level.

"Hey, sweetheart, what's—"

"I don't feel right, Mom. Meet me at the hospital," I say, leaving her on speaker as I drive.

"I'm on my way. Do you need me to drive you? Should you pull over?" I can hear her hands flailing around the kitchen counter for keys and probably her handbag. Her SUV rumbles to life within seconds, which means she's probably sprinting.

"I'm okay to drive. My muscles are just acting up. Can I just keep you on the phone and not talk?" *Unless, of course, I need to yell and scream.*

"Of course." Her steady voice moves in. It relaxes me enough to stop the thundering pulse sounding in my ears.

This is a panic attack, and I will win against it. I'm certain of it. I'm also certain of something else. This baby is a boy, because no female would stress out another woman like this.

Chapter Twenty-One

Wyatt

I can't miss today. Every pass is on the money. Even Phillips gave it up for me a few times. I caught the whistle he let out when I dropped a fifty-yarder on a dime, hitting Jax in the end zone.

I'm still not Phillips's guy, but today, for the first time, I don't feel as though he's actively rooting against me.

"Maybe you should wear weird-ass vintage jerseys out here more often, Stone," he jokes.

"Ha, maybe," I say, keeping the origin of my jersey to myself.

The only person out here who knows the meaning behind it is Whiskey, and he hasn't seen it yet, other than the photo I sent to him and Peyton earlier. The line will show up soon so we can run through a few plays before we break for dinner. We have a lot to clean up from the first pre-season game, and it's a short week for us with our next game Friday afternoon. At least we're home this time. No travel break.

Chance has been throwing short passes near the sideline while I've been practicing targets. He's itching to get out here, but the head trainer doesn't seem keen on letting him go full throttle just yet. I could tell him why his elbow hurts if he'd just listen to me, but I'm not sure he's ready to ease up on the showboating just yet. I knew the moment I saw him throwing those rocket passes for warm-ups the day we met that he would end up this way. I didn't expect it to happen so soon.

I make my way to the water station, careful to keep my distance from the nearby press area. Peyton's statement after her hearing yesterday seems to have made the rounds, and everyone wants me to comment. I haven't read it yet, so I'm not even sure what I'd say. Besides, I'm not the guy to be talking to the media out here. I get the sense Mickey wouldn't care for me looking like I'm the spokesperson. He seems to like Phillips for that.

I toss back some water, then prop a foot on one of the benches to adjust the wrap around my right lower calf. Chance must be done with his reps as he heads my direction, setting the ball down by my foot as he passes. We don't make eye contact, which is probably for the best, but regardless, I get a good feel for his hostility.

"We wearing rec team jerseys out here now?" He laughs at his own joke as he guzzles down water behind me. I grit my teeth and do my best to ignore him.

"Hey, don't knock it until you try it, Hickory," Phillips says. It's a rather backhanded way to defend me.

"Oh, yeah? You saying I should spend a few years playing rec ball like Stone here?"

The back of my jersey tugs up as someone picks at one of the letters in the last name. I shrug the touch off and turn around to catch Chance walking backward with a laugh.

"Don't do that," I warn.

"Oooooh," he needles, holding his hands out to the sides and wiggling them.

Nobody else is laughing, so I continue to bite my tongue.

"You make fun of it, but Stone was making throws on a rope today. That rust is coming off." Phillips holds a fist out for me. I bump it and nod back as I utter, "Thanks."

"*Pshh*, he's just loose. When I get this elbow feeling right, I'll show you how quarterbacks do it today. It's probably a good thing you don't get too comfortable in our uniform. You'll be riding the bench soon, collecting your little one-year deal for pension. Hey, maybe you can take it to Goodwill and buy yourself some more piece of shit jerseys when the season is done."

I straighten my spine and crack my neck at his words, and I'm about to get in his face when Whiskey cuts into the space between us, doing it for me.

"Let's stop talking about shit you don't know anything about, yeah?" Whiskey's let his beard grow out, and he looks like a wild man who wandered in from the Oregon woods to play some football. He's also about twice the size of Chance.

"This is a beef between me and him," Chance explains. Whiskey pokes him in the chest in response.

"Understand this. A beef with him is a beef with me. You have a lot of growing up to do, toddler." My friend barks when he's done, literally saying the word *woof* as he snaps his teeth and lunges toward the young QB. It takes every ounce of willpower in my body not to break into laughter over the way Chance looks as though he's about to shit his pants.

Before any of us can stir up more trouble, one of the training assistants taps my shoulder as she holds out a cell phone that isn't mine. My face puzzles as I take it into my hand, but then she says, "Peyton," and my heart flies wildly around the inside of my body.

"Hey! What's wrong?"

I walk toward the tunnel, fighting the temptation to run.

"I'm fine. Everything is okay. Please do not overreact."

It's weird how her words do the opposite to my physical chemistry.

"Peyt, tell me," I huff out, picking up my pace as I pass through the tunnel and turn right to head toward the locker room. I pause near the security office and duck into a small nook for privacy.

"I was having some muscle tightening, so I went to the hospital . . ."

I drop down on my haunches and drop my forehead into my palm. *Hospital.* I feel sick.

"Wyatt, you're not listening. Everything is okay. I'm okay. I came here as a precaution because it was much worse than it usually is, and I didn't want it to affect the baby. The heart rate is fine. I'm fine. They're doing some massaging and PT with me."

She's fine. The baby is fine.

I slide into a sitting position, letting my back fall against the concrete wall as my stomach finds its way back to where it belongs.

"I'm sorry I'm not there."

"No, Wyatt. Don't." She's quick to answer me, but it doesn't take away the fact I really wish I was with her.

"Are they keeping you overnight?" I'm sure her mom would stay with her if they were. She's got family there. She's taken care of.

"God, I hope not. But I'll be fine."

There's a machine beeping in the background, and I can't help but think it's counting heartbeats—hers, our baby's. My whole life.

"Do they know what triggered it?" I ask. Her spasticity has been under control for the last two months, and her doctor thought she might be one of the few lucky spinal injury patients who doesn't have flare-ups with pregnancy.

"Well, my doctor did mention stress," she says in a wry tone.

I chuckle softly and close my eyes.

"Yeah, I guess life has been a bit extra recently."

"*Hmm*, you think?" Her laugh soothes me.

"What's crazy is I was turning things around today when it happened. I did something big, and I think you'll be proud of me once you get over your initial shock."

I swear my wife is an expert at doling out information in such a way as to fuck with my nervous system. I pinch my brow.

"What did you do?"

"Well . . ."

Her over-the-top guilty tone forces a hard laugh from me. Jerry passes by and stops when he hears me, scrunching his face and holding his thumb up, then tipping it down as if to ask if I'm okay. I nod and point to the phone, mouthing, "Peyton." He nods, but his brow stays furrowed. It's a strange time for me to be on this call.

If I were any other guy out here, or hell, any guy trying to *get* out here, I'd wrap things up now that I know she's okay. But that's not how I operate, and it's not the way I ever want to. This game will always be second to her. And Mickey can tell me to pack my bags if he has an issue with that.

Peyton proceeds to tell me about her day, and she was right, I flip out a little when she shares that she went to the Sommers' house. But once I calm down and hear her out, I get her reasons.

"Do you think Alissa will show up tomorrow?"

Peyton's quiet for a few seconds.

"That's a hard question to answer, because yes, I think she'll show up. I'm just not sure whether she'll be handing me her uniform or accepting this new role. But I'm okay no matter which way it goes, ya know? It's about letting it be her choice."

My smile creeps into my cheeks.

"You're good at this. Coaching?"

"Yeah?" I can tell she's proud of herself. I'm proud of her, too.

"Yeah. And Peyt? You're going to be a great mom."

Her breath hitches on the other end of the call, and after a long second, she whispers, "Thanks."

The clatter of cleats on concrete stirs me out of my complacency. I get to my feet and peek down the corridor, where a dozen or so linemen file toward the field. I grab the back of my neck, wanting nothing more than to stay right here in this little concrete shelter away from responsibility, and talk to Peyton a little longer.

"Hey, I gotta get back. But maybe we can do that thing tonight where we fall asleep on the phone, like teenagers?"

"It's a date," she says. "Oh, and Wyatt, one more thing. I can't travel. Like, at all. So—"

"So . . . no visit this weekend."

"Or the next."

The line is silent with our shared, heavy thoughts. This sucks. But it's important. She has to stay healthy and safe, and traveling for a few football games isn't worth the risk. Football became number three when we found out she was pregnant.

"There's always the Arizona game," she finally says.

I do the mental math, but it's too far away to count to the first week of November. Instead, I'll count the hours until I can call her tonight.

"I'll be in the apartment by seven sharp."

"It's a date."

Chapter Twenty Two

Peyton

My sister hasn't spoken to me since she ran into the house proclaiming I ruined her life. I tried a few times to crack her armor, but she's thirteen; her world is not as big as it's going to be, so her feelings are valid, given the scale.

I distinctly recall at least five times before I was sixteen when I thought my life was ruined. Turns out, my life only got better from each of those points. And one of the greatest changes in my life was the birth of my sister.

Our mom told me she was worried when she found out I was in the hospital. Honestly, half the reason I wanted to get released early enough to come home was to get a chance to tell her I was okay before she went to bed. But she was asleep, or at least *playing* as if she was, when I rolled in at ten.

Ellie's running late for school this morning. I've been watching for movement in the garage for the last twenty minutes while Mom and I work with Macon in the arena. Unless she found a way to get her bike out and clear our property unseen, she's hiding out upstairs and plotting a way to stay home "sick."

I'm about to ask my mom if she minds if I leave her with Macon so I can check on Ellie when the garage door slides up.

"She's probably going to need a ride at this point." My mom says with a tilt of her head toward my Jeep.

My lip tugs up, and my gaze shifts to Macon.

"I feel like I'm always ditching you."

"Eh, I like the horse better than you anyway," Macon teases with a smirk. He waves a hand at me from his spot atop Otis. He's sitting so much taller than when he first started working with us. He's relying less on his walker, too, at least on his trip from the car to the arena.

"Thanks," I say with a nod before jogging toward the garage to intercept my sister.

When I step inside, I find she's not pulling her bike out at all, but shoving an abnormal number of T-shirts into her backpack.

"Those are going to wrinkle," I say, unintentionally startling her. She stands up quickly, dropping her open backpack to the concrete. A few of the shirts spill onto the garage floor.

"I just need them to make it to school. It's fine."

She crouches down and snags the loose shirts quickly, shoving them into the side pocket of her bag while simultaneously zipping the top closed. She snags one in the zipper, so I reach in to pull it free, but halt when I notice words printed on the front. She freezes, and I recognize that move—it's the same one I made when I got caught doing something I preferred to keep to myself, good or . . . *not so good*.

"El, what's on the shirts?" I could probably yank one out and read for myself, but I'm hoping she'll tell me.

Her eyes zip up to meet mine as her mouth hangs open. My head leans to one side, and I mentally sift through every context clue I can. She's not teary-eyed, and she's not exactly trembling. But she's clearly nervous.

"Can I see one?" I ask.

Her gaze drops to the one caught in the zipper. She slowly nods.

I work the fabric out of the zipper teeth and unfurl the light blue shirt to see the phrase DO BETTER printed on the front in large letters, with my name small underneath. It's my quote, from the statement I had Jason help me send out to the media.

I wanted to point out the hypocrisy, the way I did during the school board hearing, the way women are treated versus men, the way this town gladly makes excuses for football players but excoriates cheerleaders for the same behavior. They're at the same parties, drinking the same beer, jumping in the same rivers, and being reckless in the same cars. Yet the football players get a slap on the wrist after wrecking a car in a drag race, but the cheerleader who sat in the passenger seat or stood on the side of the road is suspended for merely being present. One is vitally important to play a stupid game, while the other won't be missed yelling from the sidelines.

"Your response has kind of gone viral," my sister explains.

I lift my gaze, my brow drawn in tight.

"I found a box of shirts from the pep rallies in the garage, and I made the graphic with Mom's Circuit. I was up all night."

"You stayed up all night making these?" My tone sounds angry, and I don't mean it to. I'm just surprised, and a little confused. Maybe a little moved that people paid attention to something I said, too.

"A lot of the girls want to wear them at school today, sort of to make a point. Maybe it's stupid." She starts to pull the shirts from her backpack, but I stop her, wrapping my hands around hers.

"Ellie, that's not stupid at all. That's . . . wow. I didn't think anyone would really read my comments if they made it into a story, but your peers did, and it resonated . . ."

Her shoulders lift to her ears as her eyes dart to me, then back to her school bag.

"I mean, you're making it sound kind of old, but yeah, basically. We liked what you said. *I* liked what you said. Especially the part when you called out football players."

I chuckle over the fact she called me old in a roundabout way, but I'm so flattered that she put in all this time because her friends like something I said. I'm not stupid, though. Part of this is my sister's way of jumping on a popular trend and maybe scoring social points at school, but also, she seems to really get the sentiment. I meant what I said in that statement—football culture needs to do better.

"How about I grab a box and we fold these? I can drive you to school too," I offer.

My sister's gaze lifts to meet mine, and this time she maintains eye contact long enough to see my proud smile. Her lips curve up faintly, then without warning, she lunges at me, wrapping her arms around me and burying her face in the curve of my neck.

"Oh, Ellie . . . thanks for that," I say, rubbing her back as we hug.

"I'm sorry I got mad at you," she mumbles against my shoulder.

I laugh softly and let my smile grow with this instant relief she's given me.

"I'm sorry I embarrassed you. I wasn't trying to," I say. I remember how hard her age was to navigate. Kids are cruel, and they don't always see the big picture. Name-calling and memes are so much easier.

"You didn't do anything wrong," Ellie says, finally pulling away. Our eyes meet briefly, and in that small moment, I see just how much my sister has grown up, and I am so fucking proud.

I stick around Ellie's school long enough to help her pass out the shirts she made to the dozens of junior high girls who clamor around her at the front gate. The box is nearly cleaned out when the bell rings, so I take it with me, leaving my sister with a couple of extra shirts in her bag. I snag one for myself, too, and when I get to the Jeep, I slip it on over my plain white tee.

I fill my mom in when I return, and she decides to order a few new reams of vinyl in case my sister wants to print more, along with some sweatshirts so she can expand her offering. We joke about how she missed an opportunity to monetize the trend, but really, spreading the message is worth so much more. Besides, it's not like Ellie pays for the supplies.

I spend the few hours before cheer practice catching up on what I clearly missed on social media. Ellie was right, *DO BETTER* does seem to be trending, and I'm getting credit. I'm not sure how much more attention I want from this incident, however, and when I go down the rabbit hole of various comments from keyboard warriors, I decide I probably should focus on the positivity of my sister's T-shirt campaign and leave it at that.

I hope the chatter questioning whether my statement was not-so-secretly directed at Mickey Payne and his Cyclones organization doesn't cause any problems for Wyatt. But the truth is, yeah . . . my words were for him, the team, and every other part of the football machine that needs to hear them.

On doctor's orders, I take it slow most of the day, my greatest exertion coming from the morning walk out to the arena with my mom, and some shirt folding with my sister. While Dr. Mazel advised against me returning to cheer practice right away, I decide to compromise—without telling her, of course—and instead promise myself not to assist in or demonstrate a single skill on the mat. I'll hold my notepad, and I'll wear the whistle. I am grounded from the rest.

I put on my DO BETTER shirt for practice, and instead of arriving early, I show up right as the students are filling the parking lot. I maneuver my way to my reserved spot and slip out of the Jeep without waiting for the sidewalks to clear. There are a few glares at me, some people zeroing in on my shirt, then smirking as we pass, and a few of the female students I pass on my way to the gym hold out their hands to high-five me.

I'm feeling so high from the difference in today's attention compared to the immediate aftermath of the photo scandal that I'm not totally aware of my surroundings when I clear the steps and walk across the mats in the cheer room. When one of the girls clears her throat, though, I turn around and am instantly faced with a twenty-foot-long paper banner reading *We love you, Coach!*

And then, the greatest gift of all. Alissa steps around the line of girls holding the banner to hand me flowers and a get-well card.

"We were worried about you, Coach. We're sorry you had to go to the hospital," she says. "I hope it's all right, but as Team Captain, I used some of our funds to buy you these flowers."

My grin is immediate, and I pull her in for a hug so fast that some of the water from the grocery store vase splatters our shirts.

"I'm so glad you decided to take the job," I say, my tone low enough that my words are just for her.

"Thank you for offering it to me."

I nod over her shoulder as we break apart.

"Thank them. They basically demanded it."

Alissa turns to face her teammates, and they whistle and clap for her return. Meanwhile, I decide to take advantage of my good fortune and listen to my doctor. I pull a folding chair out of the storage closet and hand over my practice plan, as well as my whistle, to my new captain.

Chapter Twenty-Three

Wyatt

Play with heart.

I've been thinking about that phrase ever since I signed a coffee receipt for that kid in Arizona. I think that's why wearing my dad's old jersey has so much power. It reminds me to keep my perspective right, to have fun playing a game that—*oof,* beats me why, but—someone is willing to pay me to do. Even if only for a year.

I hit the call button on my truck screen when I'm about two miles out from the stadium, and Peyton picks up on the first ring.

"So, did you decide to wear it?" Her first words instead of, *hello.*

"I did, even though running it through the wash seemed to make it tighter," I say, chuckling as I tug the collar of my dad's jersey away from my neck. I can still move my arms with full range, but I hope the fabric relaxes after I wear it for a bit. It only needs to make it through warmups before I change into full pads and the game-day jersey.

I debated bothering to wear it again, but then Peyton

pointed out that I was letting a grown-ass man bully me if I didn't. Besides, this might be the last game I get to start. Chance is set to play the last preseason game, and if his elbow holds up, I'm sure he'll be the season starter.

"I was thinking," Peyton says. I can hear the chatter of her family in the background, her uncle and aunt laughing while her mom shouts at them to quit being immature. I can picture them all piled in the living room, waiting for my game to start, playing poker or Monopoly for money, which they sometimes do.

"Not sure how anyone can think in that room," I joke.

"Right? Quiet is not a Johnson trait, it seems. Hold on." Her voice sounds muffled. She must be moving to another room.

I pull up to stop at the light before the main road to the stadium. It's four hours before game time, but newly-minted Cyclones fans are already tailgating in the expansive parking lot. The community part of this game is pretty cool. All someone needed to do to bring it to Portland was plant a billion-dollar seed.

"There. I can hear you now," Peyton says.

"There are so many people here already," I tell her, when suddenly a man walks by wearing a Cyclones jersey with my name on the back.

"Oh, shit!"

I cover my mouth and punch out a laugh.

"Please say you didn't hit someone," Peyton says, I think only half kidding.

"Babe, someone just walked by in a Stone jersey. I shit you not. Dude spent a hundred bucks to show up to a preseason game with my jersey. What the actual—"

"That's how good you are, Wy. Take it in. Own it," she says.

I rub my palm over my face as the light turns green and someone honks at me from behind. I shake myself out of my daze and pull through the intersection, but I crane my neck as I pass my first non-familial fan.

"This is wild," I whisper.

Peyton's soft giggle snaps me back to the present.

"Sorry, you were saying something about thinking?"

I wonder how many of those things they made. Or where that guy got it. The surprised thoughts keep coming.

"I love this for you, Wy. I wish I could see it," she says.

I miss her. But I don't want her feeling guilty for not being here.

"You've seen my name on a jersey before. You aren't missing much," I joke.

"That's what I was thinking about, actually. Or rather, your dad's jersey," she says.

"Yeah?"

I run my palm down the fire logo on the front, my thumb finding the small tear my mom repaired for my dad with her sewing machine. The white thread she used doesn't quite match the jersey.

"I think you should tell Chance why it's so important. Tell the team, maybe. If they knew the meaning behind it, maybe they wouldn't be so intimidated by it."

I chuckle at her choice of words.

"Peyt, I don't think they're intimidated. They're just dick-heads who like to bust balls and make fun of things."

"Maybe," she hums. "But at least one of them is intimidated."

She means Chance.

I nod, then utter, "Yeah, maybe."

He's threatened, for sure; I can understand that. Hell, I'm threatened by him. I simply have the comfort of knowing I'm not the QB who is part of the team's future. He is. Though, I am going to try like hell to change their minds. I suppose that's intimidating.

"Who made you so smart?" I say, slowing as I approach the security gate by the team parking lot. I roll my window down, and Earl, our head of security, bumps my fist, then waves me through.

"Well, one of my parents got straight A's. The other played football."

Ouch!

"Ha, I'm not sure if that was a dig at me or your dad or all of us."

She doesn't answer, so I assume the latter is probably right.

"I love you," I tell her as I pull into my spot.

"Love you. I'll be cheering for you. Close your eyes and try to hear me."

I promise to try, then end our call.

Whiskey pulls up next to me as I'm dragging my duffle bag across the back seat of my truck's cab. He and Tasha have made this entire thing feel a little more normal, letting me join their family for dinner a few nights a week. Whiskey likes to joke about how I help even the score in his house, but he's crazy to think I would ever vote against his wife in any situation. Tasha will always scare the shit out of me.

"You getting bigger, Wy? Or is that thing getting smaller?" He tugs at the center of my jersey, the slack a lot less than it was before I washed it.

"A little of both, I think." I grab his hand and pull him in for a bro hug.

We make our way inside, the scent in the training room already strong with pre-wrap spray.

"Bro, I've missed this. It's damn good to be back," Whiskey says.

"No doubt," I agree, dropping my stuff on the bench in front of my cubby. My chest tightens at the thought of not being here with him next season. It's such a strange tug-of-war, being pulled between home with Peyt and the field with my best friend.

"Fuck, with this again?"

Chance's remarks come out in a mumble, but it's clear enough for me. It was meant for me in the first place. Unfortunately, his words reach Whiskey, too, and my friend slams down his pads to march toward the young hotshot. A few of the other guys get up, and I mentally play out the brawl that's about to start.

Before I'm fully aware of what my body is doing, I find myself standing between Whiskey and Chance, my back to the quarterback and my hands on my friend's chest.

I dip my chin to give him a hard stare that I hope calms him. The big guy's nostrils are flaring.

"I got this."

His eyes flinch.

"I'm sure," I say.

He nods and takes a step back. I turn my attention to Chance, whose gaze is still fixed on Whiskey. I snap in his face, forcing his attention to me, because I'm a little irritable. When his friends flinch, though, I back off.

"Take a seat for a second." I keep my expression composed, my eyes soft.

Chance resists at first because he doesn't like to be told what to do. That's going to be problematic for him down the road, but that's a talk for another time.

"Please," I add.

He finally takes a step back and sits down. I gesture for his friends to do the same, as well as Whiskey, and within a few seconds, the dozen or so guys in the locker room are all seated and ready to listen to me.

If they knew the meaning behind it, maybe they wouldn't be so intimidated by it.

"I know you guys don't know me, my story, how I got here. I get that. I'm not Hickory over here, coming from Heisman talk, college playoffs, one of the best showings at the Combine since—"

"Ever," Chance adds. Yeah, he's going to need to work on arrogance.

"Right, good for you." My response gets a small chuckle from those who understand I'm mocking him. Of course, he doesn't. In a way, I envy his ability to be naïve to other people's opinions of him.

"My story is a little different. I broke a lot of records in high school and set a few more at Arizona in my first two years. I didn't have the same numbers after that, partly because my girlfriend at the time, who is now my wife, broke her spine. She had to completely relearn how to do just about everything. And I wanted to be there for that. I *chose* to."

The quiet in the room is palpable. This might be my only shot to win these guys over.

"This jersey I'm wearing . . . it was my dad's. He died before my senior year of high school. Cancer. He was a firefighter, and there are risks. They don't really tell you about the cancer risks when you sign up for the job. People like my dad dream of being firefighters. It starts in childhood, with the red firetrucks and the cool hats. Kind of hard to make cancer a part of that conversation."

My gaze drifts around the room, the solemn faces staring back at me. Whiskey nods as he stands with his back against the wall, arms crossed over his chest.

"My dad was the quarterback for the Arizona Fire team. Sure, it's not the pros. But don't tell any member of Arizona's public safety that. Those games are always serious. And my dad's teams won it all a few times."

I look down at the logo and smile to myself.

"Wearing this jersey reminds me to be the man he taught me to be. I don't have the hype. I'm the old guy. But I'm also Todd Stone's son. And this jersey, however corny you all seem to think it is, reminds me to be the best version of myself."

I hold my open palms out and shrug, looking Chance's friends in the eyes before slowly turning to face him again.

"We cool?"

I hold out my fist for him to bump. He chews at the inside of his mouth for a second, then tilts his head to one side, cracking his neck before bumping my fist.

"Yeah, we cool."

And for now, I think we are.

Chapter Twenty Four

Peyton

My dad is right. Finding out the gender of your baby is an incredible thing. It's also super hard to hold in your hand without peeking. And it's not the kind of news you want to share over a video call or the phone.

Which is why my dad rented an RV and drove my ass—along with my mom, sister, aunt, uncle, and grandparents—twenty-two hours to Portland for Wyatt's second pre-season game.

"Your doctor said not to fly. He said nothing about relaxing in a tour bus," my dad said when he explained his spur-of-the-moment gesture to my mom.

He also insists we call it a tour bus because RVing makes him feel old.

It's an RV.

"You think he bought it?" my dad asks? He was hovering as I spoke with Wyatt, biting his knuckles to keep from blurting out that we're here.

Those tailgaters Wyatt was talking about? We're one of them. And that jersey he saw? There are lots of them around.

My dad bought one from a vendor on the corner when he went out to rustle up some food. The guy tried to give it to him for free, something that happens a lot with my dad. I've always found that strange because it's not like my dad can't afford to pay for things. People get starstruck, I guess, and gestures like free coffees or knock-off jerseys with your son-in-law's name are how they show appreciation.

We chill in the RV, as well as on the makeshift porch my dad set up for our picnicking until an hour before game time. My dad called in a favor with Jerry to have the video screen guys put up the gender at the first timeout. It's crazy to think that the only people who know if my baby is a boy or a girl are my doctor, Jerry, and the video tech running master control.

Since we brought my Grampa Buck along for the game, we take the ADA entrance so he doesn't have to leave his wheel-chair. The elevator dumps us out on the suite level right by our box, so we're not lingering out in the corridor for long. My mom and Rose get my grandpa set up so he has a clear view while I text Tasha our location. She's in a different suite on the other end of the stadium, but when she gets my message, she and her girls make their way over to join us.

"Okay, folks. Here's how this is going to work," my Uncle Jason says, drawing our attention to the counter in the back of the suite. He sets two buckets on the counter and holds up two rolls of raffle tickets—one blue and one pink.

Are we really about to gamble on my baby's gender?

"It's a twenty-dollar buy-in, and you can pick a blue ticket or a pink one. Whatever the gender is, I'll draw the winning ticket from that color bucket. You can enter as many times as you want, and the winner gets the whole enchilada."

My stomach growls in response to my uncle's choice of idioms, but I'm soon distracted by the sudden flash of cash every member of my family seems to have brought along for this game.

"Hey, do I get to play?" I fish out a twenty from my wallet and wave it in the air until my uncle acknowledges me.

"I don't know. You might have some special intuition that gives you an edge, being the mom and all. Reed? What do you think?"

My eyes zip to focus on my dad, and he twists his lips in thought before lifting his chin a touch.

"What color would you pick?" my dad asks, his eyes dimmed with suspicion.

My brow crinkles.

"If I really have some special power and I say my opinion out loud, isn't that like securities fraud or something?" I reason.

"*Hmm.*" My dad rubs his chin and continues to stare at me.

"Ugh, fine! I think it's a boy. I think I'm having a boy. I want to buy a blue ticket. Happy?" I hold my twenty out for my uncle to take, but he consults my dad through a mutual glance for a few seconds. Suddenly, the two of them laugh, and my uncle takes my cash, then scribbles my name on a blue ticket and drops it in the bucket.

"What's so funny?"

"You." My uncle chuckles.

"Right? She thinks this family can produce a boy," my dad adds. "No way she has special insight."

I know they're joking, but also, *ouch!* Maybe I do have insight. Maybe that *is* a thing, mother's intuition and all that. Maybe—

"I'll take ten blue tickets, please," my grandpa says, craning his neck as he holds two hundred-dollar bills over his shoulder.

The laughing stops when he throws in his two cents, or two hunny, rather.

"That's interesting," my uncle says, rubbing his chin.

"Are you serious? *His* intuition counts more than mine?" I'm baffled by the logic, but I give up and decide my grandfather is simply adding to the pot. And when I move to sit in the seat near him, he reaches to his right and pats my knee.

"When we win this bet, the cash is yours, sweetheart," he says.

I hold his gaze for a second, my lip inching up on one side as his does the same.

"Thanks, Grampa," I say.

He winks and mumbles what sounds like "a bunch of idiots," and the two of us laugh until the Cyclones take the field for pre-game.

"What about me?" My sister waves a hand from the first row of seats.

"Do you have twenty bucks?" my uncle asks.

She shakes her head.

"Then maybe you can save up for the next family baby pool," he laughs out.

Ellie's brow furrows, but when our eyes meet, I mouth that I'll share my winnings. She seems happy with that, popping her ear buds back in and turning her attention to the field.

"I love that he does that," my dad says over my shoulder. He reaches over and points out to the field, where Wyatt is taking his time to talk to every player and shake their hands.

"I wonder where he got that from?" It's something my dad was always good at when he played. He does it still, at practice with the high school kids, and when he's playing a charity exhibition.

"I didn't teach him that, though. He just knows to do it."

Sometimes, I really wish there was a way for my father and Wyatt's to meet. I wish I had known my late father-in-law. I would have thanked him for making such a great son.

We stand for the national anthem as a local Portland

guitarist plays, and my gaze zeroes in on Wyatt's profile—his helmet clutched behind his back, his broad shoulders, and the slight curl of his hairline along his neck. He hasn't had a cut in a while. Superstitious things. He told me he'd cut it when the season ended.

As the anthem finishes, Wyatt turns, first reaching to his left to pound the fist of one of his receivers, then walking down the line of players to hug Whiskey before resting his helmet on his head and popping in his mouthguard. I should sit down so I'm out of sight, but something is pulling me to stay on my feet. I want him to know I'm here—now, before the reveal. I want him to go out there knowing he has me behind him, in person. I stay on my feet as his gaze scans the crowd. The closer he gets to our suite, the warmer my body becomes, until eventually our eyes lock.

"Did he literally spot you?" Tasha tugs my arm down to urge me to sit.

I giggle and hold up a hand.

"Yeah, he felt my presence, I guess."

Tasha scoffs out a laugh, but she simply doesn't get it. Wyatt and I are bound together with something so strong it can weave through thousands of people to connect us.

Wyatt shades his eyes from the lights as he holds up his hand in return, then flattens his palm on his chest. I do the same, then blow him a kiss that he catches.

We get the ball first, our return team setting Wyatt up with good field position at the thirty-seven-yard line. My man seems to have an extra hop in his step as he bounds out to the huddle, tossing his arms around his teammates next to him before clapping to break. That extra energy results in a twenty-yard pass to the sideline for a first down. The quick plays keep coming at a fierce pace, the Denver defense barely set by the time Wyatt has the next play running. It's a great mix of running and passing, and Wyatt drives the team down the field for a touchdown in seven plays.

"Listen to this," my dad says over my shoulder. I tilt my head for better hearing as my father cranks up the television in the suite so we can hear the commentary.

"Blake, I don't know about you, but I don't think I've seen a quarterback come out this hot for a preseason game, well, ever," the announcer says.

"I agree, Tom. Wyatt Stone may have been an unknown a few months ago, but he's someone people are watching now. And they're paying attention. Credit goes out to minority owner, Jerry Caswell. I've known him for a long time, and he has a knack for finding diamonds in rough places. He may just have one with Wyatt Stone."

"That's our boy!" My dad turns the television down and moves toward me to hug me from behind. I grab his forearm around my neck as my body fills with butterflies.

Then the in-game hostess takes over the video screen with some familiar words.

"What a great Cyclones drive! What fans may not know is that quarterback Wyatt Stone is going to be a dad!"

The stadium erupts with cheers, and my cheeks burn hot. The camera is going to point to me, and I'm afraid I'm going to look like a weeping cherry. I cover my cheeks with my palms and bite my lower lip as my grandfather reaches to his right and pats my knee. I should have dressed better for this instead of the oversized Cyclones long-sleeve tee and leggings, but things are starting to fit weird. Maybe this moment should have been different, celebrated at home. I could have waited. Wyatt would have understood.

"Well, Wyatt. We have some news for you today."

Oh, God. Here comes the camera.

My face is on the screen a second later, so there's no going back now. I keep my palms over my mouth, partly to stave off the sudden desire to vomit. My gaze lands on Wyatt as he stands with his hands folded over his head, his helmet on the bench behind him, his body rocking side-to-side with obvious nerves.

The graphic video begins, and tears prick my eyes as a cartoonish baby football player starts running down field, carrying the ball to the end zone and spiking it before slowly pulling off its helmet. There's either going to be a whole lot of hair, pink cheeks, and extra-long lashes to look like a girl, or a mini version of Wyatt staring at me.

"It's a boy," I whisper, knowing it in my gut. My words come out a half second before the reveal, and then I'm looking at the cartoon version of my son—*our* son—on the video board as thousands of strangers cheer.

Wyatt's hands fall to his chest as he slowly turns to face me, the camera back on my tear-stained face, my dad shaking my shoulders behind me, my mom clapping at his side. Tasha hugs me sideways before I lean to my left and kiss my grandfather's cheek. Taking a deep breath, I wave to the camera and form a heart with my hands. The camera shifts to show Wyatt doing the same, and when I see the tears falling down his face, I know Denver is in for a rough day. Today, my baby daddy is going to be impossible to stop.

Chapter Twenty-Five

Wyatt

That may have been the game of my life, but it's the last thing I want to talk about. I can't get through press fast enough, and every question that comes to me about finding out I'm having a boy only makes me want to bust out of here faster to get to Peyton.

Thankfully, after twenty-five minutes of interrogation, our PR rep cuts me loose, and I tear out of the locker room to find my wife and her family waiting for me. I scoop her into my arms and kiss her within seconds of seeing her face.

"You're going to make me dizzy." She giggles as I spin her in circles.

I put her down on her feet but keep her face cupped in my hands so I can admire her smile, her eyes, the tears pooled at the corners, the dimple from her mouth pushing into her cheek, the faint line that creases her forehead when she grins.

"A boy."

I shake my head, still in shock.

Peyton shrugs.

"I told you."

Her family laughs along with me.

"She told all of us," Reed adds.

"Yet I'm the only man smart enough to listen to her," Buck pipes up. "Speaking of—"

He holds an open palm out toward Jason, and Peyton moves to stand by her grandfather with her hand on her hip.

"Pay up, buddy," she says.

Jason shakes his head, then pulls a wad of cash out of his pocket.

"Dude, you guys aren't stupid enough to bet on the game, are you?" My chest flutters with panic.

"Ha, no! We bet on your baby," Jason says.

"Not *all* of us," Ellie gripes, crossing her arms over her chest.

"Grampa and I won," Peyton says, taking the cash and dividing it in half. Her grandfather pushes his half away when she offers it to him.

"I told you to keep all of it," he says.

Peyton's head falls to one side for a moment, then she bends down to hug Buck.

"Looks like I have a crib to buy," she says, her eyes flitting to me.

She's been dying to get to work on the baby's room. We decided to invest most of the money from my deal and eventually put it toward our dream home. The guest house has a small second bedroom that will work for now.

"You pick it all. You have much better taste than I do anyhow," I admit.

Peyton grins and then pockets her fun money. I drop my chin and lean in to kiss her softly, holding her gaze as I pull away.

"So, what happened to no traveling?"

I hope she didn't risk anything.

"Technically, it's no flying. So, guess who got an RV?" She quirks a brow, and I glance over her shoulder to her dad.

"Uh, tour bus, thank you very much," Reed answers, holding up a set of keys.

My mouth hangs open with a quiet laugh over the extremes this family is willing to go to, then my eyes focus on the jersey Reed is wearing. I flinch.

"Is that—?" I whirl my finger to ask Reed to spin around. He obliges, looking over his shoulder at my name, then at me.

"Got it for a real bargain, too. Forty bucks. It's a knock-off."

"Ha! I'm legit enough to have knock-off jerseys! Fucking wild!"

I walk to Reed and pinch his sleeve to test the fabric. I'm impressed with the quality for a fake jersey. I'm about to ask if there's enough time to hit the stand for one of my own when her mom tosses a plastic bag to me that I catch against my chest.

"No way!"

Nolan nods, wearing a crooked smirk.

I pull out my own fake jersey and instantly pull it over my head, pushing my arms through the sleeves. It fits weird, half because it's a fake and half because I just yanked it over a button-down shirt. But I love this thing.

"Hey, while I think this shit is super cool, *umm*, you should probably get it off before management sees it. They don't want you in anything Cyclones that they didn't make themselves or endorse," Bryce utters in my ear.

"Right!" My eyes go wide, and I pull my jersey off as quickly as I slipped it on and tuck it in the bag for later.

"Maybe I can wear it later," Peyton says in a low voice. She arches a brow, and suddenly all those imaginary times I touched her over the last few days come flooding to the surface of my mind.

I can't exactly steal her away without spending time with the family first, especially after Reed drove an RV . . . err . . . *tour bus* for twenty-two straight hours to get them here in time for my game. But thankfully, Reed pushes for an early dinner at one of his favorite spots in Portland, probably anxious to shut his eyes for ten hours before turning around and driving everyone back.

It's just after eight and the sun has set by the time I get Peyton alone in our apartment, and the moment I carry her across the threshold, my mouth is on her body. While the thought of her in my jersey is sexy as hell, I really don't want to wait for her to change just to get her undressed again, so I toss the plastic bag with my jersey onto the side table by the entry, then quickly go to work lifting the Cyclones T-shirt up her body and over her head.

"I wish I wasn't so frumpy for you," she says as I toss her shirt to the floor.

I nip at her neck, then drag my tongue along her jawline until my teeth graze her plump bottom lip.

"Frumpy is never a word I would equate with you."

My hand traces the curve of her shoulder, pulling her bra strap down to her bicep so I can kiss her from her collarbone to the inside of her arm.

"I'm only going to get frumpier, too," she says, still stuck on that word.

I pull back enough to press my finger to her lips and shake my head.

"Not frumpy. Beautiful."

Her bottom lip tucks between her teeth as she lowers her chin and looks up at me through her lashes.

"You still think so? My jeans don't fit anymore."

Her hands move around the sides of her body to her

tummy. Mine follow the same path until our fingers intertwine over her belly.

"The bigger this gets, the more amazing you are." I press a chaste kiss on her lips before dropping to my knees and kissing her belly. Most people wouldn't see the bump that I can see, but it's there. She's showing.

Our baby boy is growing.

"A boy," I whisper again, looking up at her with a massive smile that forces my cheeks up so high my eyes squint. Peyton's hands dive into my hair as our eyes meet.

"Our boy," she says. "I told you so."

I laugh softly and bite my bottom lip.

"You did," I say, hooking my thumbs into the cotton waistband of her leggings and slowly rolling them over her hips.

"No cameras in here, right?" Peyton jokes.

I shake my head.

"Uh huh. So I can do anything I want," I say, slipping her leggings all the way down and removing them, along with her tennies.

My palms wrap around her calves, then slide up to her ass as I move closer on my knees. I kiss between her legs, over the black satin triangle that covers her, as my fingers crawl up her curves, then hook the top of her panties and drag them down her hips. She unhooks her bra while stepping out of her undies, tossing it to the floor with the rest of her clothes, then moving her hands back into my hair.

My tongue slides into her swollen center, my mouth covering her pussy as I close my eyes and suck. She tastes like all my favorite things, and the sounds she makes when my tongue flicks against her clit makes my cock swell.

"Since I only have you until morning, I might need to fuck you all night," I say, dragging my tongue over her once more before slowly standing and removing my button-down shirt.

"I slept all the way here," she says with a devilish smile.

I lift her, and she wraps her legs around me as I carry her into the bedroom.

"And you can sleep all the way home."

I set her on the edge of the bed, and she scoots back, her legs parted, knees bent, and I take in her breathtaking body. Every curve is perfect, from her full breasts to her round hips, the muscles on her arms and legs from her unrelenting discipline to keep her body working despite the pain she often feels.

"My God," I hum, unzipping my slacks and pulling my cock out to pump while I stare at her.

"I don't think I need to touch you to come, baby. I could come right now," I say, toeing my shoes off and kicking my pants from my legs as I stroke myself.

"You better touch me. I drove a thousand miles for this," she teases, and I lick my lips as I crawl above her, settling between her legs and palming her right hip.

Her hips rise as I angle my cock and slide into her sweet, wet pussy. I go in slow but deep, holding still when she's full with me, reveling in the way she hums with pleasure and her body vibrates around me.

"You feel so fucking good," I say, sliding out of her completely to rub her clit with the tip of my dick before pushing in again.

"Oh, my God, Wyatt!" Her head tilts back as she arches her back, her hands grasping at the loose sheets on the bed, pulling them into her as I start to rock my hips at a steady rhythm.

My hands move from her hips, roaming up her ribcage until they cup her breasts, her nipples hard rocks that beg for me to pinch them. I squeeze them and pull, coaxing her to arch for me more. When I let go, she takes over, rubbing her tits with her thumbs while I brace myself on my palms and drive into her. When her body starts to quiver, she wraps her legs around me again, holding me to her and forcing me to pump my hips faster as her orgasm takes her breath away. I come with her, shocked I was able to hold on as long as I did. When we both finish, I roll us, still connected, so her body rests on mine and my cock can continue to flex inside of her until I'm ready to fuck her again.

Until then, I draw lazy lines along her spine and shoulder blades, secretly spelling boy names that I've been thinking about since we found out. She was so sure it was a boy all along, I couldn't help but believe her.

Peyton slept in my arms from four a.m. until I woke her to drive her to the Pancake House for breakfast with her family. It's hard to let her go. We won't be in Arizona until game six, and next week's final preseason game is in Detroit—nowhere near home. I'm sure Reed will come out for it. He's well-loved in that city and has a standing invitation to join the broadcast booth there anytime he wants. I'm not sure I'll be the quarterback on the field, though, and that's a tough pill to swallow.

"I'm sure we'll make it to the Vegas game, so it won't be so long," Peyton says, running her cool hand along my jawline. I close my eyes and roll the weight of my hand into her palm.

"Not so long, but still too long."

"*Mmm*, I know," she says, lifting on her toes and kissing me.

I hold her head in my hands and rest my forehead on hers, letting out a sigh.

"This is getting very real," I say. I don't just mean football, either. I mean all of it—being apart, her carrying our child, the moments I'm missing.

"What do you want to do?"

A breathy laugh slips through my nose.

"I don't know. I hate that I'm missing this," I say, dragging my palms down her arms and her hips before covering her belly with one.

"No matter what, we'll figure it out. And everything will be okay," she says, covering my hand with hers.

We stand frozen in time for a few long seconds, the demands of the day finally forcing us apart. I kiss her one last time, then hug her mom and shake Reed's hand as they all climb back into the tour bus that also looks very much like an RV. I smirk to myself with that thought as they pull away, then return to my truck to drive my tired ass to the stadium, where some hard conversations are waiting for me.

Coach Elgin asked me to come in this morning to chat. I wish we could skip this part because I'm pretty sure I know what's on the agenda. They need Chance to start next week so they can get him ample time before the first game of the regular season, which means they want him starting game one. I figured that would be the case when I got here, but damn if I didn't let my mind wander into fantasy territory for a little while. I'm good with this team. I have what it takes. But I also have an entire life away from this place that fills me completely.

I get to Coach's office ten minutes early, because I can't help myself, and I rap on his half-open door before stepping inside. His head pops up as I enter and he waves me inside to sit down.

"Wyatt, maybe you can help me with this," he says, pushing his iPad across his desk.

I pull it up to see a frozen video from our game.

"I think you just need to reboot or something. Are you pulling from the cloud?" I quirk a brow as he stares at me with a blank expression.

"Fuck if I know. That's why I ask the young guy," he laughs out.

I chuckle and nod, then press the reset button on his device to reload things for him. When the dashboard pops up again, I download the video he was looking at and tell him to give it a few minutes, then try again. It looks like he's focusing on the defense today. Whiskey's out of position in this frame. I make a mental note to give my friend a heads up. It always looks better when you call out your own errors and get to work on them.

"Thanks, Wyatt. I miss the days of video cassettes."

I laugh with him but hold my tongue. I can't imagine doing this job before modern technology. There are so many more nuances that get caught digitally, and coaches can sift through more data and information. It's made the game more complicated, but it's made it more exciting and safer, too.

"So, I called you in to let you know Chance is getting the ball Saturday," he says.

I nod.

"I figured."

My mouth pulls into a tight smile, and my skin buzzes with awkward discomfort as the two of us stare at one another. He doesn't like having this meeting as much as I don't like being here for it. I can tell by the way he keeps tapping his fingers on the desk and shrugging his shoulders.

"He's the starter . . . right?" I finally just say it.

Coach's body deflates with his exhale, his shoulders dropping as he rolls his neck. He leans forward and rests his elbows on the desk as he pinches the bridge of his nose.

"Wyatt, I'm not going to lie to you. This isn't really my call, which in all my years as a head coach . . . Well, let's just say it's always been my call. But Mickey, he sees that kid as the future. And hell, he probably is. He's young and flashy, and that's what this sport is doing right now. But I gotta tell you, there will always be a place for those quiet heroes."

My mouth curves a hint.

"Is that what I am? A quiet hero?"

I feel like an asshole.

"Wyatt, you're the kind of quarterback I dream of coaching."

I swallow the instant lump that forms. I didn't expect to be hit so hard emotionally. It's nice to hear him voice positive thoughts about me. Somehow, it makes the sting hurt less.

"I knew what this was when I said yes," I admit. I hoped I could change things, but also, I knew. *I know.*

Coach looks off to the side as he chews at his lips. He takes a deep breath, then leans back in his chair, leveling me with a hard look.

"This kid, Wyatt? He needs a mentor. And I don't have the right to ask you to step up and do it. Shit, I'm not even sure I want you to waste your time. But if you're the guy I think you are—"

"I'll do it. I can swallow my pride, believe me." I chuckle.

"Bryce said you were better than most out there when he first met with us, and I had a feeling he meant more than just the arm. He was right. You're a bigger man than I am."

Coach rocks to his feet and rounds the desk as I stand and meet him halfway. We shake, but before we pull apart, he covers the back of my hand and holds on for a beat.

"Keep competing out there, though, showing up, doing your thing. Don't just push Chance, push yourself. Because you never know . . ."

I hold his stare for a few seconds, reading into any hidden message he may be telling me. I decide he's simply making this a coachable moment, though. It's like the stuff I tell the high school kids. Be proud of the product you put on that field, every time. It's the only thing you can take with you when the game is done.

And I'm starting to think my time is coming soon.

Chapter Twenty Six

Peyton

Six weeks into the season

The Coolidge Bears cheer team is in good hands.

That thought has been on repeat ever since I asked Ms. Chester, the high school lunch lady who has been at the school since my uncle went there, to fill in for me tonight. I've waited weeks for the Arizona game, and I'm not going to miss seeing Wyatt, even if his only role is to warm up Chance Hickory and give him feedback after each set of downs. Wyatt hasn't played since preseason, but he's held up his promise to Coach Elgin. He's stood by Chance, even when that bullheaded asshole doesn't want to listen to him.

"Okay, Coach. I just got the list you sent, and I talked to the band director. They're playing the same song as last week's game, so we'll do the same routine," Alissa says from her side of our phone call.

I exhale, finally. Because the good hands I've been counting on are Alissa's. She's really stepped up as the team captain, becoming more of an assistant coach in many ways. It was her idea to bring in the dance teacher to add some contemporary choreography to our competition routine, and it's paid off a ton. This isn't the most powerful squad Coolidge has had, so tumbling isn't going to score us points. But the girls took to the hip hop we incorporated fast. We have some moves that are going to wow the judges and the crowd, which will boost our engagement points a ton.

"Thanks for handling this. You know, I meant what I said about you coming back as my assistant next season. My hands are going to be full with a newborn, and if you're going to the community college for your first two years, it's a nice paycheck."

I can't believe I'm wishing this hard to keep Alissa's mom around, but if I get Alissa in the deal, then I'm willing to put up with that vile woman a little longer. She shows up to every game, and I swear I can feel her eyes boring holes through me from the stands. She seems to love bragging about Alissa's leadership role, and it's their relationship that's more important. I couldn't give a rip what that woman thinks of me. Pregnancy is humbling that way. Your body does things for nine months that make you realize all women are superheroes, and if I can survive this, I can handle whatever Adrian Sommers has to dish out to me.

"I'll think about it," Alissa responds, the same answer she gave me last time I asked her to take the job. She has a lot of options for school, and while the community college's full ride is a good financial decision, it doesn't have the same appeal as the quarter scholarship she's been offered at Duke. She wants to be a doctor, so maybe that route is right.

"Okay. I'll lay off the full-court press," I say. "Text me some video and call if you need anything."

We end our call and I slip back into the suite, where Wyatt's mom and Jeff are still the only others in the suite. I rode with them, and Jeff regaled me with stories about young Wyatt. He brought up his dad a lot, too, and it's nice the way he loved the man like a brother.

My dad has been hanging out on the field a lot more often when he can make it to Wyatt's games. He's sort of the unofficial life coach for my husband while he drains his soul motivating Chance Hickory to succeed at the job he wanted for himself. Life is a bitter pill sometimes, but this little man swimming around my belly sure puts things into perspective.

I barely take my seat before I get up and make my fourth trip to the bathroom. Wyatt's mom laughs when I exit, and she tells me about the time she had to pull off the highway three exits in a row because of the acrobatics Wyatt was doing on her bladder. My parents finally arrive with my sister, and if it weren't for Ellie being here, I think both my mom and Wyatt's would have been happy to spend the entire first quarter terrifying me with all the crazy shit that's to come during my pregnancy.

When the teenager covers her ears and starts muttering, "La la la la," they change topics to something less . . . medical. Unfortunately for my sister, the new topic seems to be her mystery boyfriend.

"How does Mom know about him?" Ellie whispers to me when my mom finally steps away to grab a snack.

I smirk and lean in close to her.

"Moms have this massive spy network. They talk. Even to the other moms they don't like if they must, just to get the deets on their kids. Information first. Grudges later."

"Ugh," my sister groans, rolling her eyes and pushing her bangs to the side.

My sister's impromptu haircut has grown out finally, and she's learning new ways to style her hair. My mom also let her put a few green streaks in it, and the look suits her. I run my fingers through the bangs and sweep them to the side as best I can, then smile at her.

"You're really pretty, Ellie. I hope you know that."

My sister's cheeks blush as she blinks away, barely voicing, "Thanks," before turning her attention to her phone. I can tell by the way she fights against her smile, though, that my words sneak into that stubborn head of hers. I'm going to tell her she's beautiful as often as I can. It's my sisterly duty.

I'm not sure whether it's all the talk about bodily functions from before or the jug of water I've been sipping from like an anxious fiend, but I'm back to the bathroom minutes after the second quarter starts. I take my time, enjoying the quiet in the muffled room as well as the super-duty air conditioning vent blowing hairs loose from the messy braid I did during the car ride here. I let my eyes shut for a minute, resting my head against the wall to my right. The buzzing from the stadium speakers will keep me awake, so I don't worry about dozing off. If it weren't for those, however, I kind of think I could. I'm so tired all the time. And my mom keeps warning me that I'll be tired for the rest of my life.

Great.

"Peyt! Get out here!" My dad pounds on the other side of the door. I startle, my muscles tensing, but manage to get myself together quickly and back into the suite where my parents and Wyatt's mom, and Jeff are standing at the glass front, my father's fists in the air.

"What's up?" I ask Ellie who is sitting on her knees at a bar seat behind my parents.

"Wyatt's in!" she proclaims.

"He's what?" I push my way around Jeff to get a good view, and everyone scoots down to make room for me.

"Concussion protocol. Chance took a big hit, and I don't

think he's coming back in. This is it, Peyt. This is where he shows them. This is his shot," my dad says.

His focus locks onto Wyatt and doesn't let up. My father's jawline flexes as his fists tuck under his arms, which are folded over his chest. It's as if my dad is willing every move for my husband, as if he has some sort of control. It takes me a few seconds to catch up to the reality of what's happening. Wyatt is in. This is what I wanted for him for so long, for this *real* shot. *Didn't I?*

"That hit lost them eleven yards. He's taking over in a shitty field position, but he's got this," my dad says.

Running commentary when Wyatt is playing is a thing he can't help. Gramps used to do it when my father played. It's sweet. And when Wyatt's in a tight spot, or about to get nailed by the line, I can look away, knowing my dad will give it to me straight.

I hold my fists to my mouth, my Cyclones hoodie sleeves pulled over my fingers, as Wyatt sets up behind the line and counts off the play. They're only five yards out from the Arizona end zone. Not a lot of room to work with, and when Wyatt turns to his right and hands off the ball to the Cyclones running back, I stretch my fingers out to shade my eyes in anticipation.

"Not a great play call," my dad says as they lose two yards on the play.

I swallow and ball my fists again, my knees bobbing as I stand filled with nervous energy. It's only the second quarter, so there's time, but we're down ten to zip, so if we can't get out of this, it's going to be a tough climb the rest of the game.

Wyatt nods toward the sideline, probably relaying a new set of plays, then pulls his squad in for a quick huddle before breaking to take the line again.

"He needs a short dump pass here," my dad mumbles.

"I agree," Jeff says.

I don't. I know my husband and what he's capable of, and how his brain works when his back is against a wall. He's not looking at a short gain here. He's going to throw it long, and he's going to scramble to buy Jax time. In a nanosecond, I mentally play out the various outcomes as Wyatt takes the snap and spins.

He's going to get sacked.

He's going to scramble but come up short and be forced to throw it out of bounds, then they'll have to kick to get out of here.

He'll break loose somehow and run the ball himself, hopefully not getting nailed by the secondary.

None of that happens, though, because Wyatt Stone has found himself. He throws across his body as he's scrambling to his right, defenders rushing him with arms up, ready to knock his pass down. They're not even close, and Jax is all alone midfield when the ball lands in his hands mid-stride. He runs for sixty more yards to nab the Cyclones six. The kick makes it seven.

Chance Hickory may have just lost his starting job.

And I may have just lost full custody of my husband.

This is what we wanted. Right?

Chapter Twenty-Seven

Wyatt

That felt amazing.

Every single second I was on that field was euphoria. I wasn't sure I'd ever get to feel that again, but now that I have, well, it's going to make walking away even harder.

"Dude, you owned it out there today. Nice work!" Cisco pats my back as he passes me on his way out of the locker room.

"Brother!"

Whiskey steps in front of me, dressed and ready to head out. He's flying back with the team since the girls have started school in Portland so Tasha didn't come out for the trip. Their life is there now.

I hug my friend and fill with memories of what this was like years ago, when we first met, as well as our unforgettable college years.

"You gave them a lot to think about," he says, his hands fisting my shoulders.

I nod, but I can't seem to get myself over this hump of doubt.

"Hey, you killed it! If you were taking the jet home with us,

I'd be getting you shitfaced with me as soon as we land," my friend says. "You know. To celebrate."

I chuckle and pat his chest.

"Sure, to celebrate. Has nothing to do with you going home and having to watch dance recital rehearsals for the seventieth time."

"Dude, it's so bad," Whiskey grumbles. It's partly in jest, but also, Tasha is well on her way to becoming quite the passionate dance mom. Their girls have been learning jazz dance since they moved to Portland, and their first recital is coming up. Whiskey says practices have been . . . intense.

"Just wait until they start noisy tap classes," I tease.

"Oh, for fuck's sake," my friend grumbles as he walks away.

It's just me and Chance in here now. He's still sitting in the trainer's room, alone. The team had him checked out at the nearby neuro center, and the docs advised him to fly home tomorrow just in case. Concussions and flying aren't a great combo. We'll be on the same plane.

Shit.

Peyton and the family are waiting for me, but there's this heaviness to the air that I can't seem to shake. Maybe talking to Chance will help. I pull my travel bag out of the cubby and tuck my wallet and headphones inside before sliding it over my shoulder. Chance's legs are dangling from the trainer's table. He's still wearing his team shorts and the blue Nike slides he wore to the medical center in. I take a deep breath and head toward him, knocking on the door jamb to snap him out of his daze.

"Oh, hey," he says with a nod.

He looks miserable. I've been there.

"I heard they're taking it day-to-day?" I quirk a brow.

His shoulders lift with a silent laugh.

"Yeah, but you know that's just something they say. I'm probably sitting out next game, so . . . bet you're happy."

"Hey," I breathe out, my head falling to the side. "Don't do that. I'm not happy about you getting hurt. And it really might be day-to-day. You never know. Thursday comes and you check out fine, get cleared for practice, and then there you are, back in the shotgun taking Cisco's fucked up snaps."

Chance laughs out loud this time.

"He is inconsistent as fuck," he says.

We both shake our heads.

"Nice job handling that one he shot over your head, though. There were almost two of us on concussion watch," Chance adds.

"Right? That was a mess."

I flatten my hand over my head. My hair is still wet from my shower. I'm glad there isn't an enormous knot on it. The pocket closed on me fast for that play. How the hell we got out of that and ended up with a field goal beats me.

"So, hey. What are you doing for the night? You just heading back to the hotel or . . ."

It's barely three in the afternoon, and he doesn't have family in the area. Yeah, his agent stuck around, but . . . who wants to spend the afternoon with their agent? I mean, Bryce and I have found our way with one another, but I still don't want to room with the dude or hang out at the sports bar. And Chance can't even have a beer now. At least, he shouldn't.

"I guess. I don't know. I was thinking maybe I'd just sit here until they kick my ass out," he says through a soft laugh.

I nod and drop my gaze to his swinging feet. Twenty-two. Still very much a kid.

My eyes lift to meet his, and I lean my head over my shoulder a tick.

"Come with me," I say.

His face screws up, like I said something crazy. Probably because this *is* crazy, but it's the right thing to do.

"I'm good, man," he says, frowning.

"Nah. You aren't. Come with me. It's homecoming week in our town, and they do this parade thing. It's a good time. I promise."

His twisted lips have gotten tighter, his brow crease deeper, but I continue to stare at him and urge him to just give in.

"*Pfff*, fine. Fuck it," he finally says, hopping off the table and dragging his leather travel bag with him. He lets it dangle at his side, banging against his right leg as we make our way through the locker room. Everything from his gait to his posture reminds me of the high school kids when they get caught ditching class in the hallways and sent back to their rooms.

"You know, you're gonna get hurt in this sport. Probably a lot," I say as we shuffle our way through the concourse toward the lobby by the suite elevators.

"Yeah. I've been through this before. I had a good knock in high school. Probably more than one, but ya know . . . I kept my mouth shut about the others, so I didn't get pulled." His gaze shifts sideways to meet mine, and I pull my mouth in tight.

"Oh, like you never did that shit," he adds, rolling his eyes.

I let out a heavy breath.

"No, I did. I never fucked around with head injuries, though. But my shoulder? My knee? Oh, yeah. When I'm fifty, there are going to be a lot of discoveries when doctors replace joints on my body."

Simply thinking about my knee in college makes me want to limp.

I slow my pace, and when Chance realizes he's several steps ahead of me, he stops and turns to face me. I shake my head and stop moving when our eyes meet.

"I'm just saying . . . you're their guy. So don't worry about missing half of a game, or a game or two, because of a concussion. They're protecting their investment. We both know I'm just passing through. So maybe, dude . . . let me fucking help you get better."

Chance's hard swallow is a rare sight. I think it means he's considering my words for real this time, not just performatively. I've been busting my ass for a month trying to give him advice. He nods when I talk as if he's listening, but then he goes right back out and repeats the same mistakes. It's not only with me, either. It's with Phillips and Elgin, and other guys on the team, too. He doesn't listen. He's not coachable. And that is what's going to cut his career short. Not a fucking concussion.

"Before I got this shot, I was coaching with my father-in-law. You know Reed Johnson, right?"

He chuckles because, yeah, of course he does. Who doesn't.

"Well, I learned a lot from him. I'm not selfish with football shit. Let me share it with you, yeah?"

He nods slowly, and eventually says, "Yeah. I hear you. I'm down, man."

I hold out my fist, and his gaze drops to it. He bumps it with his after a second, and the two of us start walking toward the glass doors where my family is waiting.

"Sorry I've been a dick," he mutters a few steps away from the lobby.

"It's fine. I get it," I say, letting him off the hook. Because honestly? I do get it. It's what we do in this world. We're hostile, resentful beings sometimes, who feel threatened and lash out. But damn, imagine if we weren't.

I expect the surprise we're greeted with on my family members' faces. But Peyton shocks me when she moves toward Chance with open arms. I think it takes him off-guard, too, because he gives me a sideways glance that looks a lot like panic.

"How are you feeling?" Peyton asks as she hugs Chance. He towers over her, his arms awkwardly wrapping around her while he keeps his fingers flexed as if he's making sure I know he's not *fully* touching her.

"Dude, you can hug my wife."

He shakes his head and laughs.

"Yeah, I don't know. That's not how we are in my family. You hug my girlfriend and I'm kicking your ass."

I chuckle and shrug.

"That's fair."

Reed and Chance shake hands, and I introduce him to Nolan, my mom and Jeff. Chance's eyebrows lift a hint when his gaze pauses on Jeff's fire shirt, a commemorative T-shirt from the last public safety football game he played in with my dad. He doesn't remark on it, but when our eyes meet as we follow my family out into the players' lot, he gives me a quick nod.

"Reed, you mind if Chance takes the guest room tonight? He and I are both flying out tomorrow, and you know how shitty concussion protocol is when you're alone."

"Sure!" Reed says without pause.

"I don't want to put anyone out—"

"Chance . . . trust me." I grab his forearm, and he looks me in the eyes. "They've got the room."

We pile into Reed and Nolan's SUV when the valet pulls up, and my mom and Jeff hop into Jeff's truck behind us. Chance is from Texas originally, so the desert isn't exactly new to him. But Dallas isn't like Phoenix. There are still trees and lots of green where he grew up, so when we pass through Phoenix and hit the outskirts of the Native American reservation, the sudden show of saguaros, tumbleweeds, and rolling hills of rock and dried-up washes seems to mesmerize him.

The outskirts of Coolidge is in view soon after, the new builds with master planned parks like a strange oasis in the middle of the desert. The retirement homes have been out here for years, along with the golf course that could use a good rain. The grass is yellowing. The remaining dairy farms come next, then the small mile-long strip through the historic downtown, including the park square that is already filled with volunteers gearing up for tonight's festivities. The parade was this morning.

"This place looks like those Hallmark movies my mom loves," Chance jokes as we weave through the old storefronts of downtown.

"Just wait," I warn him, the best part yet to come.

When my mom and I moved out here, I remember the way the stretch of fields hit with the Coolidge stadium standing tall in the background. It's even more awe-inspiring at sunset, as is the long drive that leads into the Johnson property. It's still impressive in the bright of day, and the way Chance mutters, "Fuuuck," as we pass through the tree-lined drive to the massive barn, horse arena, and stone-covered home pretty much says it all.

"I told ya," I say, slapping his chest as I hop out of the SUV and take Peyton's waiting hand.

"This was a surprise," my wife whispers in my ear, kissing my cheek.

I meet her eyes briefly and shrug, lifting my brows.

"I couldn't leave him there alone."

She lifts on her toes and nuzzles her nose against mine.

"I know. That's why I love you."

"Chance, let me show you your room," Nolan says, guiding my teammate into the house as his head rolls from left to right to take everything in.

I hang back with Reed while Peyton joins her mom. He puts his arm around my shoulders.

"I'm so proud of you. The way you played today. The way

you're helping that jackass punk. All of it," he says the moment the front door shuts.

I shake with a quiet laugh.

"Thanks."

"What you did today. You're going to be able to write your own ticket, I hope you know that. And if you get the ball next week, and if you play like that? Wyatt, you'll—"

"I don't know if I want any of that."

The second I utter those words, Reed looks as though I've stabbed him in his gut.

"Wow, I—" He snaps his mouth shut again, speechless. I get it. I'm not sure I am ready to hear those words come out of my mouth either.

Before I can get into it with him, the crunch of familiar tires rolls along the gravel behind us, and we both turn as Bryce pulls his truck up the driveway.

"Shit," I say in a hushed voice.

"Hear him out," Reed says, patting my back and moving toward Bryce's driver's side door.

"Hey, what a game today, huh?" Bryce says with his arms outstretched.

He and Reed hug first, and when Bryce makes his way to me, Reed shakes his head from behind him and mouths, "Just listen."

"Yeah, that was unexpected. Turned out pretty good, though, huh?"

"Good? Wyatt, you were the shit. You're the only thing they're talking about on the post-shows and the pre-shows before the evening games. Your name is buzzing in a lot of rooms right now. And if Portland wants to keep you, they better call me and fast, because—"

"Bryce, I don't really think Portland is where I'm supposed to be."

His mouth hangs open, and his eyes shift to Reed for a beat, then back to me.

"Yeah, all right. I get it. Fuck Mickey. He hasn't earned you. But let's keep that to ourselves for now, see who calls. It's a better bargaining position for us if the bidders think they need to pony up big."

"Right. Bidders," I utter, scratching at my jaw. I suddenly feel like cattle.

"Babe? Do you want to eat here or wait and get something at the street fair?" Peyton hollers from the front door.

"Uh, let's wait, yeah? You like the fry bread."

Her grin stretches wide, lighting up my whole world.

"I do like the fry bread. Okay, love you!" She shuts the door, and my gaze sticks to the space she filled for an extra second or two.

"You know, I got a text from Frisco," Bryce says, pulling my focus back to him.

"Huh? Oh . . . yeah, Frisco. I . . . I don't know."

Bryce's brow pulls in.

"*Pfft*, it's Frisco. Montana. Young. Rice. Legacy. We take the call," he continues.

"Hey, I'm gonna check on Nolan and Chance. I'll see you guys inside," Reed says, his hand patting Bryce's shoulder twice before he leaves us to have this talk alone.

"Chance is here?" Bryce asks, his face puzzled.

"Yeah, we're flying out together tomorrow, and he's on concussion protocol, and I figured . . . it's shitty to be alone." I shrug, and Bryce smiles on one side of his mouth.

"You're such a goddamn nice guy. I would have been fine letting him stew and stress out about me taking his job. But not you. You want to make sure that kid is fed, has a good bed to sleep in, and gets a little love. Unbelievable."

I know Bryce is joking on some level, but he's not totally off base. I am the nice guy. I like being the nice guy. And yeah, I want to see Chance succeed. And I'm aware that means I might not get the nod from Portland when it's all said and done. It's not that I don't love to compete. I do. I fucking thrive on it. It's just that I'm not sure it's worth selling the rest of life's good stuff down the river.

"Bryce, I don't want to talk to Frisco."

His mouth snaps shut and falls into a frown, his eyes dim with confusion. He shakes his head.

"What's going on, Wy?"

I gnaw at my bottom lip as I drop my hands into my pant pockets and glance out at the wide-open space that spans the vista. This land is Peyton's family's, and it goes all the way to the edge of the mountain. It's where our kids are going to grow up exploring, learning about horses, about desert creatures, and a little bit about football too.

"I don't want to miss this," I finally breathe out.

My head pivots, and I meet his waiting gaze.

"So, you won't. You'll be home a lot. And Peyton will come to you, and maybe you guys buy a house when we land a longer contract, and—"

"This is her home, Bryce. She wants to raise our kids here. She wants more. I want more. And I don't want her giving that up for football. I don't want to miss out on the little things that happen when I'm not home. I just . . . I can't live that way."

"*Ahh*," he sighs, folding his hands behind his neck as he slowly spins in place, looking out at the same horizon I did.

"Fuck," he mutters.

"I'm so sorry, dude."

He shakes his head.

"Nah, don't be sorry. You're not wrong. And I can't argue with a damn thing you said because if I were you, I wouldn't want to give up any of that, either."

I swallow hard, glad he gets it. Doesn't take away the knot in my diaphragm, though. I feel bad leaving him in a lurch. And Whiskey—I love playing with that guy. But I love Peyton more. And I love our son. And his future brother or sister. And my mom, and Jeff. And this place.

"What if—"

Bryce stops mid-sentence, but I turn to face him and tilt my head, drawing his eyes to mine.

"Go on," I urge.

"What if I get you the perfect storm?"

I marinate on his words, not asking exactly what he means.

"It's not a money thing," I say, though if he came to me with big money, it would be hard to walk away from that. I couldn't. *We* couldn't.

"I know what it is, Wyatt. I'm asking you . . . if I get it, does that change things?"

I match his stare and fast-forward through this potential life. Football until I'm into my late thirties. A home of my own, built exactly the way Peyton and I want it, but on this land. Being able to watch my son grow up. His sister or brother grow up. My mom retire and find happiness. To stay home, where my wife's heart is and will always be.

"The perfect storm?" I ask him, our eyes locked in a silent agreement.

"Yep. All of it."

I take a deep breath and let my mouth curve up on one side. "Well, hell, Bryce. That changes everything."

Chapter Twenty Eight

Peyton

January, the last game of the season

I never thought a speech in front of my hometown school board would turn into an Etsy business, but here we are. It's more Ellie's business, but since she's still in junior high, I offered to help with the logistics. I should have anticipated the volume before I said yes.

"I think that's the last one," I holler from my mom's pantry-turned-shirt-storage room. I slide the small box I finished slapping a label on out the doorway and lean my back against the wall, blowing up at the small hairs sticking to my forehead.

"I'm printing out a new list!" My sister's voice reverberates down the stairs and into the kitchen.

I drop my head and huff out a hard laugh.

A new list. Awesome.

My sister has shipped four-hundred and sixty DO BETTER shirts in the last month. The volume is up for the holidays, which is understandable, but the orders are still going strong now, after New Year's, and there's no sign of things letting up anytime soon.

"How are you holding up?"

My mom pops her head into the pantry, twisting the fan I fashioned to the door jamb to keep things cool in here. It might be winter, but I'm the size of a theme park character, so hot is my baseline.

"She's going to outgrow the pantry at this rate," I laugh out.

My mom picks up one of the yellow long-sleeved shirts my sister made and holds it up to view.

"I like this one," she says, turning it around and laying it over her chest. It's the same slogan with flowers.

"You should keep it. I know the owner," I joke.

My mom's eyes crinkle with her smile, and she slings the shirt over her shoulder.

"I think I will."

My sister's act of protest turned into a movement among her peers, and the message spread to more youth and then their parents, and now basically everyone who has a phone or TV in their home and has seen the stories. While I don't love that the photo of me and Wyatt keeps coming up when people talk about how my sister's business started, I do admire what Ellie decided to do with the attention. She's donating half of everything she makes to a shelter in Southern Arizona that helps women leaving domestic violence circumstances to find work, housing, and healthcare. My mom is making her put the rest in a savings account. Ellie protested a little, but I reminded her that I was a pancake waitress for two summers to "build character."

"Dad's got the game on. Kick-off is in a few minutes if you want to take a break. I can help her finish this up," my mom says, holding out a hand to help me up from the ottoman I pushed into the small room to avoid sitting on the floor.

"Thanks," I say, gripping my mom's hand tightly as I work my way to a stand. Before I take a single step, though, my abdomen spasms and a lightning rod of pain shoots down the backs of my legs and up into my spine.

"Oh, shit," I groan, doubling over.

My mom scrambles to brace me as I find my way back to the ottoman, sitting down but keeping my legs out in front of me to stretch out my body.

"Mom," I gasp, a new wave shooting through me. I cringe and crumple at the same time.

"Reed! Call nine-one-one!" my mom shouts, her hand clutching mine as I hold on to her so I don't pass out. My dad rushes in then starts dialing the moment he sees me doubled over in pain.

"It's okay. You might be in labor, Peyt. But it's okay. You're okay."

My mom's calm voice is normally helpful, but I'm barely thirty-two weeks along. This isn't the right time. Wyatt is supposed to be home for this. Instead, he's on a sideline, in Portland. My face burns, and tears blur my vision.

"It hurts, Mom. It hur—*ahhhh!*" I tuck my chin and squeeze my eyes shut, holding my breath as every beat of my heart throbs inside of me.

"Honey, we need to get you out of this room. Not far. But let's get you out of this room."

"I can't," I plead, shaking my head violently.

"Peyt? What's wrong?" My sister slips past my mom to my side.

"She's in labor, El. Help me move the ottoman. The fire department is coming," my mom says.

"Don't move me. I can't move. Don't . . ." I run out of breath and wince with a new sharp pain. My mom and sister take advantage of this small window and slide the stool, me along with it, out into the kitchen.

"El, get a cool washcloth. Pull one out of the bottom drawer and run it under cold water for a few seconds," my mom orders.

My sister dashes the long way around the island twice, and the whole scene makes me laugh.

"It's not funny. I'm scared," my sister wails, tears running down her cheeks.

I laugh harder, then abruptly stop when fresh pain hits, turning my chuckle into a deep moan.

"Me, too, El. I'm scared too," I pant out.

"Here," Ellie says, slapping the wet cloth on my head.

My mom purses her lips and glares at my sister, who holds up her palms.

"What? I got the rag!"

I laugh again, and my mom's mouth ticks up on one side.

"You guys, this isn't funny," Ellie cries. She stomps away but doesn't go far.

"You promise this is going to be okay?" I say, looking my mom in the eyes, blinking away tears as I gulp breaths of air.

She blots my forehead and cheeks with the cool cloth, and it does feel amazing.

"It's going to be okay," she says.

And I believe her, because any other option is madness.

Within minutes, our kitchen is filled with firemen. I would enjoy this more if I weren't turning inside out with every contraction that hits me. One of the paramedics wraps my arm to take my blood pressure while another begins to prep me for an IV. My dad's voice comes from the background, and I do my best to call out for him, but it's getting harder to yell.

"Reed!" I finally bellow out, and he steps into view, his cell phone plastered to the side of his head.

"I'm calling the team now. They'll get him. He'll get here. It's going to be—"

"Do not say okay!" I shout before roaring with another contraction.

I don't even remember being moved to the stretcher, but I suddenly find myself being rolled through the house, through the double patio doors in the dining room that are never fully opened, and through the back gate where my dad stores the garbage cans.

Could I seriously not fit through the door?

My mom climbs into the ambulance with me, waving off protests from the medics. My dad has a lot of friends, and when he drops their chief's name, they relent. I'm glad, because I'm freaking out. I need someone with me who has done this before, and the two male firefighters don't count.

"Did he get Wyatt?" I ask my mom as they pull the doors shut.

"I don't know, but I'm sure he will. Your dad is relentless for his little girl." Her eyes glisten as she runs her hand through my hair.

I glance up as far as I can and realize how awful I must look. I haven't worn makeup for three days because I haven't left the house, and this sweatshirt has a spaghetti stain on the front. Plus, the washcloth hair is not doing me any favors.

"I'm hideous," I whine, and my mom chuckles at my expense.

"You're beautiful. And you got this."

I respond with a tiny nod, then focus on the whirl of blue sky and clouds, and the occasional street pole I can see out the back window. We get to the hospital in minutes, and I'm taken to a private room and hooked up to what feels like a thousand monitors the minute they roll me in.

Nothing feels the way the blogs and podcasts suggested it

would, but that's probably because I'm early. Dr. Mazel enters the room as a new cramp takes over my body, and she rests her palm on my swollen belly while I breathe my way through it.

"Looks like someone decided to get to the party early," she says, and the ease in her tone makes me relax for a moment.

"He wasn't invited today. Not yet," I answer while she maneuvers a tray of tools into position and guides one of the nurses to bend a light as she settles on a rolling stool at the base of my bed.

"Lesson number one, Peyton. Your kids don't care what your plans are," she says, guiding my feet to the footrests at the end of the bed. The nurse helps me scoot down, and my mom holds my hand up top while my doctor looks at the business downstairs.

"Everything looks good. Peyton, let me know how this feels," she says, putting pressure on one side of my insides. I grunt from the force, but it isn't painful.

"Good, and this," she says, repeating with the same result.

She stands from her seat and holds her gloved hands together.

"I'd like to slow this labor down. I don't think it would be wise to stop it, but we can normalize things a little, give the baby more time to get fully into position, and maybe give you some time to mentally prepare. How does that sound?"

I glance to my right, where my mom is standing at my side.

She nods.

"Yeah, I would like to do that. Thank you," I say.

"Okay," she says, turning to her nurse and the medical assistant and rattling off a series of drug names that I assume are about to pickle me.

A few more waves pass, and my mom holds my hand through them. Things finally ease when one of the nurses pushes something through my IV, and when five whole minutes pass without excruciating pain, I release my death grip on my mom's hand.

"I'll find Dad and Ellie. Would you like them to come in?"

I glance down at my body, covered under a blue sheet and a very unflattering open-front gown. I waggle my head but decide I'm modest enough.

"Sure."

My mom leans over to kiss my head, then heads out of the room, leaving me alone with the nurse who gave me my miracle drugs.

"It's nice that your family is here," she says.

"*Mmm*, it is. My husband is in Portland. He's a quarterback for the Cyclones, and it's game day, so—"

"Oh, my God, are you dating Chance Hickory?" she squeals.

My expression freezes in place, my brow pinched, and my mouth soured, but I am on the verge of incredulous laughter.

"No. The other guy."

"Ah," she says, placating me with a soft smile before moving on to write my stats on the whiteboard on the wall.

"You know, my husband was the one who taught Chance how to roll out of the pocket and throw side-armed," I say, for some reason feeling a deep need to defend Wyatt's pro experience.

"Cool," she says, but in a flippant way.

"It is cool. Wyatt's still better at it, but Chance is getting there."

She nods over her shoulder and smiles. I should stop talking.

"He only has a one-year contract, so . . . you know. We're not sure what next year holds. We have our hands full with this little guy, of course. Anyhow . . ." I sigh, realizing how crazy I sound.

The nurse leaves without another word, and frankly, I wouldn't be shocked if she begs someone to trade patients.

My dad and sister are a welcome sight. I hold out my hand for Ellie, and she clambers up close, snuggling against my side so I can hug her.

"You were so helpful, Ellie. Thank you."

She's still freaked out. I can tell by the way her mouth is shut tight and her gaze darts around the room. The last time she was in a hospital with me was when I was recovering from my spinal surgery. That was a scary time, and she was young.

"Wyatt's on his way to the airport right now. They got him on a four-thirty flight. Jason is going to pick him up in Tucson. We'll get him here," my dad reassures.

I nod, then breathe out nice and slow as a contraction takes hold. I'm grateful not to be feeling the rush of pain like before, but this shit still hurts.

Over the next six hours, in shrinking increments of minutes, I manage to breathe my way through labor and hold off long enough for Wyatt to arrive. I cry the second I see him, and he swoops right into position, running his hand through my hair and kissing my forehead.

"I'm sorry I'm late. You're doing great," he says. I grip his shirt in my fist as a new wave hits, and he glances across me to my mom.

"Is this normal?" he asks.

"Quite," my mom responds.

Dr. Mazel comes, and I introduce her to Wyatt. The Chance Hickory fangirl keeps eyeing him, too, but I don't introduce them. She might think my husband is hot, but she missed her chance of me letting her into our bubble. She can hope she gets to deliver Chance's baby someday. *Pfff!*

The doctor walks Wyatt and me through everything that's about to happen. Because I'm early, I need a C-section. And because of my condition and the risk of messing with my spine, I'm going under general anesthesia. I'm scared. It's something I've *been* scared about, worried about.

"Are you ready to meet your baby?" Dr. Mazel asks.

My gaze flashes to Wyatt's, and rather than reflecting the panic I know is contorting every angle of my face, he's the epitome of calm. He's ready.

"We can't wait," he says through his warm smile.

He leans over and presses a soft kiss to my lips, then wraps my left hand in both of his. I hold on tightly for as long as I can, until he must leave and I'm taken down a long hallway for surgery. I count the lights on the ceiling on the way. Fourteen. That's how far away I am from Wyatt. Fourteen lights.

Thirteen.

Twelve.

Elev—

"**H**i, Mommy," Wyatt whispers.

His voice sounds miles away, and I cling to the peaceful dream I'm in. The ocean is lapping at my toes, foam tickling the tops of my feet. The water is cold, but the sun feels warm. I'd like to stay here.

"Want to meet our son?" Wyatt says.

He's closer now, and I remember why I'm here. I blink a few more times, and Wyatt comes into view.

"Hi," I say in a sleepy voice.

I'm becoming more aware by the minute, and the more my surroundings make sense, the faster the beeping sound is next to me.

"It's the heart monitor," a nurse explains. I hope that's not the Hickory fan. I want a Wyatt fan. *I may be a little fuzzy.*

The beeping slows and eventually stops. A small bassinet, completely covered in clear hard plastic, is wheeled right to my bedside.

"Let me help you," Wyatt says, guiding my hand through a sleeved opening so I can reach in and touch my son in his portable incubator.

My head rolls to the side, and my eyes finally focus, and there he is. My perfect little human. The most amazing creature to ever bless this earth. A piece of me and Wyatt, our families, our world.

"He's perfect," I say, my fingertips soft as I caress his tiny warm body.

"You can hold him soon. He's very strong. He just needs to put on a little weight," a new doctor explains. I don't recognize her, but I'm guessing she's our baby's.

Our baby.

Our boy.

"He needs a name," I say, turning back to Wyatt in a flash. "We can't just keep calling him Baby, like *Dirty Dancing*."

My husband chuckles.

"I like the one you picked. I think we should go with that," I say.

Wyatt's eyes soften, and his smile subdues.

"Are you sure?" he says.

"Positive."

World, get ready to meet Warner Todd Stone. All four pounds and three ounces of him.

Chapter Twenty-Nine

Wyatt

Peyton hasn't slept this late since Warner was born four months ago. I never thought the day would come when seven in the morning feels like sleeping in, but here we are.

She must have fallen asleep feeding him in bed last night. It was a welcome surprise for me to wake up to his eyes wide open, staring at me. I've been letting him hold my pinky finger for the past ten minutes, studying how his little mind works. Everything he touches and sees is so new, and it makes everything new in my eyes.

"Hey, what time is it?" Peyton rubs a fist in her right eye, and her voice is groggy.

"It's seven. Go back to sleep. I got him," I say, rolling in close enough to kiss the tip of her nose before scooping up my son and carrying him into the living room.

I pop him in the fuzzy green slingback chair that buzzes and makes fish bubbling sounds while I warm up a bottle. He's getting so big, and I swear it's not because we're overfeeding him. The kid can eat like a champ, though. He was sixteen pounds at our last doctor's visit a week ago, and I'd swear he's put on a couple more since.

He starts to fuss, so I crouch next to him while I wait for the bottle. He likes it when I count his toes, so I start at the pinky and tap my way to the big one on his right foot, then do it again for the left. His mouth pushes into the cutest smile, and the spit bubble only makes it cuter.

"Who wants breakfast?" I whisper, rushing to get his bottle. I test the temperature on the inside of my wrist, then lift him out of the magic nap chair to carry him to my favorite recliner. I prop him in the crook of my elbow and touch the bottle's nipple to his mouth. He opens wide and begins to guzzle, so I guide his hands to the bottle while he's drinking. He's close to figuring out how to hold it.

I left my phone on the nightstand, so I snag the remote and turn the television on at a low volume. It's been ages since I've watched it, between the baby and helping Reed with spring ball. I'm exhausted when I hit the pillow at eight, and Peyton is basically exhausted all the time.

I buzz through the channels, stopping on cable sports news, and I click the volume up just enough to catch most of the words. It's baseball season, and this household doesn't compute anything that isn't football, so pretty much every story is news to me. One of the Diamondbacks hit for the cycle last night while I was sleeping, so that's cool. And the Dodgers' new fireball thrower needs Tommy John surgery.

I'm surprised there isn't more of that happening with young quarterbacks, honestly. There's this insane pressure to overperform, and it starts in college. It took me an entire season to get Chance to take his arm care seriously. Hell, it took me two-thirds of the season to get him to trust me. I'm still not totally sure the kid likes me, but he did send me a nice card along with a ton of wine from some vineyard he invested in.

He wanted to thank me for mentoring him. Peyton joked that he was really thanking me for giving him the job. I didn't give it to him, though. It was always his, never mine. Like I said, I was simply passing through.

It stung when Portland didn't sign me again, even though I saw it coming. I gave that team my heart, even when I wasn't at the helm. It never felt like home, though. It felt like a test. Who knows if I passed or failed, but at least I wasn't the only face to go.

Granted, Coach Elgin left on his terms. He was the one who requested a one-year contract. I don't think Phillips is ready to step into the role, but Mickey seems to, and that's the guy they're going with.

Warner's eyes grow heavy as he drains his bottle, and when he lets it fall from his lips, I set it to the side and hold him against my chest while I rub his back. The little guy snores. Peyton says he's just breathing, but I swear there's a faint whistle sound in there. My dad used to do that, and I bet there's something about the way Warner's nose was formed that's just like my dad's.

He's fast asleep in my arms in minutes, so I settle in for the long haul and turn the volume up one more tick so I can at least hear the program. They move from baseball to tennis, and then a commercial break for a new shake flavor at the DQ. My stomach rumbles, but I don't dare get out of this chair while the house is this quiet.

I'm about to power the TV off when the next story catches my attention.

"Jerry Caswell . . . remember him?"

I sit up a little, but glance down to make sure Warner is still fast asleep. He is.

"Yeah, he was one of my favorite players for the Lions back in the day," the co-anchor says.

"You and a lot of folks. Well, Jerry Caswell went in with Michael Payne on the Portland Cyclones expansion team, if you remember."

"I do."

My pulse is speeding up thanks to their banter. They're dragging this out, and the ticker at the bottom of the screen isn't giving any clues as to what this is all about. *Get to the point, fellas!*

"Well, reports came out today that Caswell sold his interest in the team. Now, I'm not sure whether he was unhappy with the business investment or unhappy with Payne, whom I have heard—"

"Can be a *pain*, yeah. I've heard that, too."

I chuckle at their joke. Also, why did I never think of that?

"It will be interesting to see if Jerry Caswell surfaces somewhere else, maybe with another team. Or, who knows, perhaps he'll be joining us on the desk come fall."

Huh.

"In other news, a young Olympic hopeful set a new record for twelve-year-olds in the swimming pool . . ."

I turn the volume down again and mull over everything I just heard. I wonder if Reed has heard anything. He and Jerry were getting close again during the season. I'm not sure they talked business, though. I can't say I blame Jerry for cutting ties with Mickey. Portland has the potential to be a good team if Mickey would just let the good people he hires do their jobs.

I consider sending Jerry a text, but by the time Peyton wakes up and takes over Warner duty from me, I forget.

We tag-team a few chores around the house, finally putting our own laundry away and starting another load of onesies. I swear, our infant has more costume changes than a Taylor Swift concert. I fix Peyton her favorite sandwich for lunch, a toasted hoagie roll piled high with salami and prosciutto and those little yellow peppers she likes.

I try to remember to give her the little things, to remind her that I love her more than anything on this planet other than Warner. My dad always made sure he did the little things for my mom, like always making sure her gas tank was full or that she had a clean towel waiting for her after a shower. Peyton does them right back for me, too. I may be nearing thirty, but I still love pancakes decorated with chocolate chips. Peyton makes them for me, just like they do at Jack's, then draws me a funny face in semi-sweet morsels every time.

"You should get to practice. I think we're going to take a nap together," she says, kissing Warner's forehead as he sleeps in her arms.

"Maybe I skip today, take that nap with you," I say, truly tempted.

Peyton playfully pushes my chest, though, coaxing me toward the door.

"I'm kind of looking forward to hogging the bed to myself. And you won't fit in the bassinet with Warner, so . . ."

I chuckle.

"I got it. Okay, fine. I'll be home in a couple of hours."

I kiss her goodbye, then slip out the side door, gently closing it so I don't make a loud sound.

The ground is beginning to take shape on the back acre of the property. I can see it from the guest house's kitchen window, but the view is extremely clear from the driveway. Peyton and I decided to start building our place slowly. Her dad, of course, offered to help, but it's enough that they gave us the land. We want to do this ourselves. And the money from my one-year deal is going to get us mostly there. From where I stand, the foundation looks good.

I climb into my truck and make my way to the high school. I

pull in next to Reed's truck, and the old Lions sticker he still has on his back window reminds me of the news I learned regarding Jerry.

Reed's sitting on the first row of bleachers when I head out to the field, so I follow his gaze and see the group of freshmen and sophomores running the long route around the school's perimeter.

"Someone show up late?" *I'm late. I hope he doesn't think I'm running too.*

"Someone showed up with weed. The entire fucking locker room stinks. They *wish* they were late."

I squint as I look across the field, honestly proud that they're not half-assing things. They aren't jogging this.

"Is this one of those 'if you won't tell me who did it, then you're all being punished' moments?"

Reed nods.

"Sure is."

I take a seat next to him and reminisce about the time he and Coach Watts made us run bleachers in the middle of the night.

"Bunch of assholes, you guys were," he mumbles.

I cackle out loud. He cracks me up when he's ornery.

"Yeah, I've heard your stories from Buck, so don't think you're better than me," I push back.

"Shit, I know I'm not. You don't know half the crap we pulled." He gets up to walk away after dropping that bomb, and I simply stare at his back. I tag along when I realize he's heading to the field.

"Hey, you talk to Jerry lately? You hear the news?" I ask.

"I haven't talked to him, but I saw on the news that he sold his shares. Good for him. That Mickey Payne character is bad for football. Jerry can do better. He's got too much to give the game."

I nod and pull my pack of gum from my pocket, unwrapping a piece and popping it in my mouth. I offer Reed one, and he takes two.

"Thanks. Coffee makes my breath stink."

I consider how many cups I had to get myself moving today and decide I should add another dose of mint, too.

The upperclassmen trickle out to the field, and a few of them remark about the stench in the locker room. When one of them dares to make a joke, Reed sends him on a lap around the school. And when he asks if Reed is joking, he doubles his assignment. Nobody cracks a joke after that.

Once the underclassmen make their way back to the middle of the field and finish throwing up or guzzling water, Reed orders the guys to all take a knee. That's when I spot the familiar silver truck parked next to Reed's and mine through the scaffolding of the bleachers. Bryce steps out of the driver's side a second later.

"Hey, I'm gonna go catch up," I say, nodding toward my one-time agent and semi-friend. Our relationship is weird, but I'd be lying if I said it wasn't a relationship. Somehow, I feel close to the guy.

"Go ahead. We're gonna be here talking for a while," Reed says, his sunglasses blocking the expression in his eyes. He's pissed. He hates the way pot smells. Always has. When Buck smokes for his pain management, he makes his father go outside, *way* outside. That's why the man usually sticks with the gummies.

I jog over to Bryce as he folds his arms along the fence between the bleachers and the track.

"Hey, man. It's been a minute," I say, holding out my hand. He grips it and we hug over the fence, slapping each other's backs.

"I know. Things have gotten busy at the firm. I wanted to stop by a month ago to see the baby. I bet he's getting big."

My grin is automatic.

"Little guy is doubling every few weeks, I swear. He makes the cutest noises all damn day, and he's a sleeper, thank God!"

Bryce laughs softly.

"That's good. I bet Peyton's happy about that, too. I can't wait to see him. Maybe next weekend. I'll be in town longer, I hope."

I fight the urge to break out my phone and inundate him with photos of everything my son has done over the last ten days. I get the grandparent move now, the way they constantly want to brag and show off their grandkids. I would put Warner on a billboard and change it out every day just to show him off to the world.

"What's got you in town today? You driving to Tucson for a Wildcat?" There's a running back down there who set a ton of records last year. He's only a junior, but I've heard he's thinking of declaring for the draft.

"Maybe, if I've got time. I came here to see you."

It takes my brain a second or two to catch up to my ears. Eventually, I shake myself out of the instant stupor and scrunch my brow. My stomach is tight suddenly, and I wish like hell Bryce would take his sunglasses off so I can read his eyes.

"I told you, I don't want to be Chance Hickory's babysitter." I figure if Portland were to come back with any type of offer, that would be it.

Bryce shakes his head.

"Nah, that ain't it." He pulls his glasses off finally, tucking them in the collar of his polo shirt. His mouth rests in this faint smirk, like he's got a secret, and his eyes lock onto mine with an intimidating level of focus.

And it hits me.

Fucker did it.

"Arizona," I blurt out.

He nods.

"How long?"

"Three years, with the option for five."

Fuck.

I squint one eye and brace myself, my pulse racing so fast I can feel it in my fingertips.

"Money?"

He chuckles and leans in, like there might be ears listening nearby.

"One-sixty guaranteed. We negotiate if they pick up for five. And they'll pick up for five."

My mouth drops open, and I blink slowly.

"Perfect fucking storm, man. You said that would change everything. Well?"

I turn around and look out at Reed, his finger waggling as he heats up with his lecture. Unable to help myself, I let out a howl and hold up my fists when my father-in-law's head pops up to look at me.

"He fucking did it! I'm playing for Arizona! At home!"

It takes Reed a few seconds to react vocally, but when he does, it's with a very loud, "Fuck yeah!"

I turn back to Bryce and launch myself over the fence to hug him like a brother.

"Dude, you did it!" I pat his back hard, and he lifts me off my feet.

"*You* did it. I'm just the negotiator," he says. I'd rather throw the ball than do his work any day. He has earned his cut.

"There's more," he says, when we pull apart.

My heart is beating so fast, I can hear it. The thumps are deafening, and I feel like I could either fly or pass out. I fold my hands over my head and rock in place.

"Give it to me. What's more?"

"Well, you probably saw the news about Jerry," he begins.

I nod intensely.

"You can't own a percentage of another team if you're going to coach. It's a bad look," he says.

"So that's fucking why—" I don't even finish before I leap at him again, throwing my arms around him and shaking him before hurdling my way back over the fence and rushing out to Reed. I nearly tackle my father-in-law, but he snags my arm and keeps us both upright while I get my mouth to form words.

"Arizona! Jerry's the new head coach. Three years with an option for five. A hundred and sixty mil. Dad! I did it!"

Reed wraps his arms around me and grips the back of my shirt, and the tears hit both of us in an instant. I called him Dad —because he is. And Jeff is like my dad, too. And my real dad would want them to step into that role. Especially now, when I've hit the pinnacle of so much hard work. When playing by the rules paid off. When I waited for the right thing to come along, Bryce delivered.

"I'm so proud of you, son. So unbelievably proud." Reed relaxes his arms and steps back from our embrace, pinching the bridge of his nose to mask his tears. He turns to face the guys, most of them still kneeling.

"Practice is cancelled today. My son-in-law is going back to the NFL. Here! For us!"

The spring squad roars, and I'm not sure whether they're cheering for me or because they somehow got out of a major ass-chewing and get to go home. I don't care why they cheer. I wouldn't care if they booed, I'm running on such a high right now.

"I gotta tell Peyt," I say, spinning in circles while I flail around my body for my phone.

I pull it from my pocket as Bryce walks up and gives Reed a

hug. I let the two of them talk as I wander down the field toward the other end zone. She was looking forward to this nap, but this news might fall under the category of "really good reasons to wake Peyton up."

She answers on the third ring.

"Is something wrong?" Her voice is sleepy, and I want to contain myself and not blast her with energy through the phone. But I'm about to burst.

"Peyt, Bryce did it. He's here. We just talked. He did it. I'm playing for Arizona."

She gasps, and a sniffle follows a few seconds later.

"Baby . . . you did it," she says, her voice soft so she doesn't wake our son.

"We did it. You. Me. Warner. And football . . . forever."

Chapter Thirty

Peyton

Final Game of Regular Season with Arizona

"You know I like the black jerseys best." I tug the fabric at the center of Wyatt's chest, the bold, red number eighteen puckering as I pull him toward me.

"So . . . my black jersey is your red dress? Is that what you're saying?" He tips my chin upward and kisses my lips, ignoring the cameras to our right that capture every moment. Wyatt just finished doing pre-game media. We're heading to the playoffs as a wildcard. It's a big deal for his and Jerry's first year. The attention has been *extra*.

"That jersey is *very much* like my red dress." I let the coy smirk linger on my lips.

Wyatt blows out a hard breath that shifts the hair lying across his forehead, then shakes his head.

"Woman. Not the time to get me started," he teases, dropping his hands into the pockets of his athletic shorts as he walks backward slowly.

"Remember the terms of our bet," I remind him.

He holds up four fingers, wiggling them, then kisses his palm and tosses me a kiss. I catch it and leave my closed fist in the air as he heads down the concourse toward the team elevator.

Wyatt has been ready for another baby for a while. Heck, I think he was ready to go about five days after Warner was born. I needed a little more time to recover and get used to this new insane sleep schedule that comes with parenthood. But I'm ready to grow our family now, and when Wyatt suggested a little bet—he throws for four touchdowns today, we try to make a baby tonight—I couldn't resist. The trying is the fun part, after all.

Fatherhood suits him. I knew it would. There are so many of his father's lessons woven through his fabric, so much of his mother's strength and goodness. It would have been impossible for him not to rise to the occasion of parenthood. But he's gone beyond.

As perfect as the storm was that Bryce brought to our doorstep, I was still wary of being at home with a baby while Wyatt hit the road for another pro football season. Even playing at home meant he was away every other weekend. And I don't know that I'll ever fully stop worrying about him taking a wrong hit. That's something I know to expect, at least. I grew up with that fear always lingering over our house.

But this team has taken such good care of him. The ownership wants to look at his five-year option as soon as playoffs are done. My husband exceeded expectations, which I always knew he would. He simply needed the right team and the right ownership behind him.

Jerry was the unexpected gift, though. Turns out he's a brilliant coach. My father isn't surprised. He says Jerry was always the guy who could see the big picture on the field, even from the sidelines. The players really respect him, too. For Wyatt, he's like one more father figure.

I make my way to our family's suite a few hundred feet from the player elevator. Wyatt's mom and mine have been on Warner duty for me so I could watch Wyatt's interviews. I'm sure they're both anxious for me to return. They love being grandparents, but our son started walking a few weeks ago, and I feel like he's ready to run. Chasing him can be exhausting.

I step into the suite in time to rescue my mom from having to sit under the buffet table with Warner. He's gotten into forts and camping lately, something he picked up from Whiskey and Tasha's girls over the holidays.

"I think someone is ready to take a nap," I say, swooping Warner from the floor as he crawls out from under the other side of the table.

My mom gets up from her knees and mouths, "Thank you," before joining Wyatt's mom at the pub table for a well-earned beer.

My son is a little fussy, but once I get him settled into the seat next to me at the front of our box, his eyes get heavy, and by the time the kick-off is ten minutes out, he's fast asleep. My sister, who is deep into her teenage angst years, is asleep next to him. Her ear buds haven't left her ears since she got here; they've become her shield from the adults. She was out late last night, though, for a sleepover party—one where boys were present—so I'm not surprised she conked out. I'm also not shocked she's avoiding our questions about the party. The key part of the night, again, is that boys were present. And lately, Ellie has been getting and paying *a lot* of attention to boys.

I sit back in my seat and take in the debate Jeff and my father are having over whether Wyatt should play today. The team will face the same game against the same opponent, New York, win or lose today. But Wyatt is on the verge of a few interesting numbers for Arizona, and if he hits those four touchdowns that we put on the table for our bet, he'll win more than me in the red dress. He'll also tie a record for single-season touchdowns set eighteen years ago on this very field.

Now, if he throws five? Well, he still gets me and the red dress. But we'll get home a little later, because there will be a lot more media folks waiting around to talk to him post-game.

"Hey, check this out, Peyt. Whisk managed to score a touchdown," my dad says, handing his phone over my shoulder with a video queued up. I press play and zoom in with my fingers on the tiny screen, and sure enough—he not only scooped up a fumble, that big man ran for thirty yards and made it to the end zone.

"Tasha is going to turn this into a Christmas card," I joke, sort of, as I hand my dad his phone.

"Hell, I might," he tosses in.

I can't wait to share that news with Wyatt. He misses playing with Whiskey, but Portland gave him a good deal to stay. Those two might find their way onto the same team again down the road, though, at least one more time before they hang it up for good.

But do any of them every really hang it up for good?

We fly through the opening program for the game, the national anthem performed by a local trumpet player who is a bit of a lucky charm for our hometown teams. We won't have a single playoff game at home, so this is our last chance to squeeze him in.

Wyatt's tossing the ball on the sideline, warming up his arm while the in-house talent introduces the winners of a youth sportsmanship contest at the center of the field. I glance to my right, where my son is out for the count in a makeshift napping spot fashioned out of puffer jackets and a stadium seat. I like to think he'll win an award like that someday—one for being the stand-up kid who doesn't care so much if he wins or loses, but cares about his team.

He's still got Johnson blood, so . . . he'll care a little. If he wins.

A lot.

Hell, we'll all care; who am I kidding?

But he'll be a good sport about it—the winning.

"Here we go!" Jeff says, stirring me from my thoughts as he holds up a beer to toast. My dad clinks glasses with him, and I grab my water bottle from the cupholder so I can participate.

"That counts, right?" I laugh out.

"I mean . . . if he throws an interception, that's on you," Jeff teases, and I chuckle until my back is turned to him again. Then, my lips settle into a knowing smirk.

Wyatt lines up behind the offense as I twist the cap from my bottle and take a sip of water. The first play is a shuffle pass that gains seven yards. A good start, and the crowd praises the team for it with a hefty roar. But there's a lot more in that tank of his, and when Wyatt's next pass is for thirty yards, I let myself mentally prepare for the long night ahead. Not just the celebration, the black jersey, and the red dress, but also the news I get to deliver when he's done talking to the press about breaking more records.

Wyatt doesn't know it yet, but we're pregnant again.

And this one? She's a girl. I just know it.

Buck Johnson

Three years later

I'm an old man.

To say I've been around or seen it all is only the tip of the damn iceberg. Hell, there's some stuff I've damn near invented at this point. But this family . . . it's my legacy. And I love every new member of it.

Eighty years is a long time to be on earth. I've lived most of those years hard, sometimes wild. My wife, Rose, sometimes calls me Kitten. My son teases me about it because I guess it sounds sexy or something. But I know the real reason she calls me that. It's because of the nine lives I've got. I know I've burned through eight of them, though, so this last one—I'm going to take extra good care of it.

I've been so blessed. I've loved two women, deeply. My first wife would tell you I loved more than two, but all that dating between my marriages wasn't love. It was a stupid man getting older and trying to stop time by surrounding himself with beautiful young women. I hope every single one of them found someone a lot better than me after we parted ways. I'm sure they did. It isn't hard.

How I convinced Rose to stay by my side beats me. She knew all the ugly parts of the Buck Johnson story—the bad ticker, and the obsession with a game and this town. She still decided to give this thing with me a try. Thirty-five years later and here we are, going strong. Seems our love story is inspiring.

I guess that's why Peyton and her husband want me to do this minister thing for Wyatt's mom and that fella she's marrying. He seems like a real good guy. Retired firefighter who worked with her late husband. He seems honorable, and that's important.

To get ordained so I could oversee her mother-in-law's wedding, Peyton hooked me up on some website to fill out a questionnaire. But the minute she left, I had Rose drive me down to the town clerk's office, and she set me up with the paperwork. Notarized it right there and everything. No clickety-clicking necessary.

"We're almost ready, Grampa. Can I take you down the aisle?"

Peyton's gentle touch is her superpower. I cover her hand as it rests on my arm and glance up at her for a moment to admire how she looks when the desert sunlight kisses her hair.

"You're so much of your mom, you know that? All the pretty parts. Now, that temper? That's your dad."

She laughs with me, leaning down to kiss my cheek before guiding my wheelchair to the end of the brick pathway that cuts through the middle of the town square. It's a nice setting to make some vows.

Peyton wheels me up the small ramp to the platform in front of the rows of white chairs while guests filter to their seats, the soft hum of a violin playing behind me. My granddaughter gives my hand a squeeze, then skips down the ramp to join the other bridesmaids who are gathering in the back. Her mother-in-law made her the matron of honor. And I guess Wyatt has the honor of giving his mother away. Seems to me they're doing this whole thing pretty damn right, especially for a second time.

I clear my throat and flip through the cards in my hand, my speech peppered with my famous jokes. *Hey, they knew what they were getting.* The music shifts, and soon, my great-grandson Warner meanders down the aisle, his little sister, Serena, tugging on his arm and asking him to stop every few steps. She's gone and flipped her dress up over her head by the time they make it halfway down the aisle, so Peyton rushes in and scoops her up, leading her and Warner to the first row, where Nolan and my son are waiting to keep those two tethered for the next twenty minutes.

Peyton rushes to the back rows again in time to re-walk the aisle along with Jeff, the groom. I don't know the next two couples who join the party, but I'm sure by the end of the night, we'll all be friends. When Wyatt and his mom step into view, I find myself getting caught up in . . . *what is it Peyton says?* The feels? I get teary is all, something about this whole day reminding me of my wedding to Rose. And the times when both of my boys made this trip to promise their hearts to great women. My other granddaughter will be doing this one day, but she swears her wedding will be in London. She spent a year there for college, so it's her entire world right now. The world is big, though, just like life. And by the time she's ready, she may decide she wants something else entirely. I just know I'm gonna do my damnedest to be here to see it.

Wyatt kisses his mom's cheek and brings her hand to Jeff's. The big fella wipes away a few tears of his own, so I chuckle and swat at his thigh, teasingly. We share a smile as I hand him a handkerchief.

"And we're off to the races," I begin.

Our guests laugh and take their seats.

I begin with the traditional stuff, sharing my perspective on love as the town elder. But it's when I talk about second chances that everyone gets quiet.

"You both had great loves. It's so easy at the beginning to imagine that the road is going to go one way, but that's not how adventures work. Love and life aren't simply a trip. They're a journey. And we must be willing to ebb and flow, to bend with the curves and hit the brakes or go full throttle when the road calls for that. When life slowed down, both of you hit your brakes at the same time, and it brought you to an intersection. You had a choice. Wave the other through or turn and follow them home. I think it's safe to say you both made the right choice to throw out the maps and follow your instincts—and each other."

I pause for the sniffles in the crowd, as well as the ones from the bride and groom.

"I didn't expect to make *so* many people cry with that bit, but I guess I've gotten pretty good at speeches over the years."

There's a soft, collective chuckle among the crowd. I give everyone a moment to find their tissues, then begin with the vows. In all, the entire ceremony lasts maybe fifteen minutes, but it's this next bit that kicks off the long part of the night—the party.

"Ladies and gentlemen, may I present Mr. and Mrs. Jeff O'Neill."

The whistles are piercing, but they've got nothing on the bagpipes that kick in as the newly wedded couple makes their way down the aisle under a shower of birdseed and bubbles. Firefighters love that crap, but I don't know—those things are *loud*. Peyton and Nolan both insist it's romantic, though, so what do I know?

It's almost homecoming in Coolidge, so the downtown has been decorated for a while. We called in a few favors to have the lights in the park trees flicker on with the sunset, and they're just now filling in the shadows.

"Do you want me to make you a plate?" Rose asks as she hugs me from behind. I tilt my head and kiss her cheek.

"Please. And maybe not one-hundred-percent strict to my diet?" I give her the puppy-dog eyes, but she's iron-clad tough when it comes to me and the ticker. She winks, and that means I may just get a little butter for my roll. She's probably right, but damn if that buffet with the fresh-cut prime rib doesn't look amazing.

Once the music kicks in and people hit the dance floor that Reed constructed under the canopy of lights, I ease back and indulge in the single glass of wine I'm allowed to have. I sip it slowly, appreciating the notes. I used to think all that wine crap was a bunch of malarkey, but when a man can no longer have his usual beer or whiskey, he appreciates the little things that make up every sip of what he is allowed to have. If I had it to do over, I may have invested in a vineyard instead of cars.

I raise my glass as Nolan makes a toast, and again when Wyatt speaks about his mom and his new stepfather. I toast my wife quietly at our table, draining the last sip from my glass a second before my grandkids dart around our table, taking a few of the plates with them. We're in the grass, so the dishes bounce on the ground, and the plates are mostly cleaned, but Peyton rushes over to catch up with her kids anyway. She's trying her best to keep those two calm and quiet, but it's a special day, past their bedtimes, and they've had cake. She's doomed.

But I have a secret weapon.

"*Psst!* Peyt, come here," I say, waving my granddaughter over.

She marches my way with a kid tucked under each arm,

and I lean toward Rose, asking her to get the bag from under our table.

"What's this?" Peyton gestures toward the bright yellow gift bag.

I shrug and hand it to Warner, who dives into it like it's Christmas morning, tossing tissue paper in every direction. He pulls out a football, then a box with a throwing target inside.

"Gramps, you didn't have to do that," she says.

"Kid needs to go up a size. That little kid ball isn't cutting it. Plus, maybe he can teach his sister how to throw?" I quirk a brow, and my great-grandson nods excitedly.

Warner's barely four, but he's got quite the arm. What can I say? I have to nurture these things.

"What's this?" Wyatt asks as he steps up.

"I brought a little distraction. Weddings are a hard thing for kids to make it through unscathed," I explain.

Wyatt's eyes light up, and he takes the plastic target in his hands. He rips through the box and snaps it together easily, and my granddaughter gets a moment to sit down and breathe as he leads his kids away from the dance floor and the tables so they can burn some energy for a little while.

The three of us watch as Wyatt instructs Warner on where to put his hand on the ball. It's a little big yet, but he'll grow into it. And when he manages to unleash a tight spiral that almost makes it through the plastic circle, we all clap.

"This is how it begins," Reed says as he joins us, taking a seat next to his daughter.

Within minutes, the entire family is together watching Wyatt chase down pass after pass as his son switches from wanting to be quarterback to kicker and back again. Serena spends the entire time chasing them both, and when she gets knocked over amid the roughhousing, she simply dusts off her dress and gets right back up.

"I heard that's what you all do," Jeff says.

"What's that?" I ask.

He meets my gaze and chuckles.

"You make damn good football players."

"Ah, yes. We do," I respond with a nod.

I settle in and watch a few more passes, each one getting a little closer, the spiral tighter. And when one bounces off the ground and somehow finds its way into Serena's hands, she rushes to the other side of the park with Wyatt and her brother trailing behind her.

Yeah. We make football players around here, all right. But we make fighters, too. And that's how the Johnsons and the Lennoxes and the Stones always win. Because this life will knock you on your ass, but if you're ready, it's worth all the trouble.

THE END

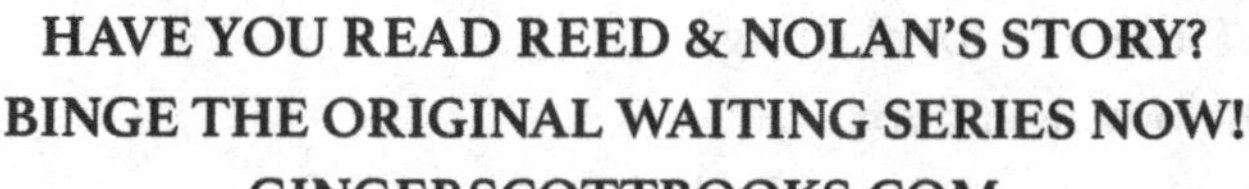

HAVE YOU READ REED & NOLAN'S STORY?
BINGE THE ORIGINAL WAITING SERIES NOW!
GINGERSCOTTBOOKS.COM

Ginger Scott

. . .

IF YOU ENJOYED THIS SERIES, YOU MIGHT LIKE:

The Varsity Series
A New Adult Sports Romance Series

Begin Your Binge with Varsity Heartbreaker
https://books2read.com/VarsityHeartbreaker

Lucas Fuller is a lot of things.
He's the boy next door.
He's the first crush I ever had.
He was my first kiss.
He's also the only person who has ever broken my heart.
For two years, I've wondered what happened to the us I used to know.
We were best friends, and then suddenly...we weren't.
I tried to run away from it. I even changed schools just to make the hurt disappear.
But no matter how hard I tried to not think about Lucas, I just

couldn't stay away from the high school quarterback with perfect blue eyes and so many secrets.

I'm back. We're seniors now. We've grown—all of us. And Lucas Fuller might be different, but I'm different too.

This is my time to take risks, to experience life and to fall in love for real.

I want Lucas Fuller to be a part of my story, but I know for that to happen, I need to know the truth about our past.

Acknowledgments

And here we are.

I'm not foolish enough to say I'll never visit this place again. I thought that more than once. This world was only going to be one book and look how that turned out.

The truth is this series—this family and the place they live and the games they play—changed my life. Of everything I've created, this collection of books is the most me. It's everything I love rolled into a warm, Arizona heart. And I cannot thank you all enough for embracing it as you have.

The usual thanks are in order.

Autumn, you keep me and my fire going. And you don't let the flame burn out. Your guidance and patience and friendship is everything.

Mom, you know I would never have had that courage in the start if it weren't for you.

My boys—you believe in me far more than I'll ever believe in myself. I am so lucky to have you.

To Brenda, the best editor in the word, thank you for championing me through the hard stuff.

And to Arizona, hot small towns, desert parties, high school football games, young love, and a land that shouldn't grow anything but seems to grow so much—thanks for the lifetime of inspiration.

Maybe we'll all stop in again sometime. I know better than to call this done.

About the Author

Ginger Scott is a *USA Today, Wall Street Journal* and Amazon-bestselling author from Peoria, Arizona. She has also been nominated for the Goodreads Choice and RWA Rita Awards. She is the author of several young and new adult romances, including bestsellers Waiting on the Sidelines, The Hard Count, A Boy Like You, This Is Falling and Wild Reckless.

A sucker for a good romance, Ginger's other passion is sports, and she often blends the two in her stories. When she's not writing, the odds are high that she's somewhere near a baseball diamond, either watching her son swing for the fences or cheering on her favorite baseball team, the Arizona Diamondbacks. Ginger lives in Arizona and is married to her college sweetheart whom she met at ASU (fork 'em, Devils).

FIND GINGER ONLINE: www.gingerscottbooks.com

facebook.com/GingerScottAuthor

instagram.com/authorgingerscott

tiktok.com/@authorgingerscott

Also By Ginger Scott

Final Score Series

The Tomboy & The Captain

The Wallflower & The Running Back

The Best Friend & The Short Stop

The Boys of Welles

Loner

Rebel

Habit

The Fuel Series

Shift

Wreck

Burn

The Varsity Series

Varsity Heartbreaker

Varsity Tiebreaker

Varsity Rule breaker

Varsity Captain

The Waiting Series

Waiting on the Sidelines

Going Long

The Hail Mary

The Waiting Series - Next Generation

Home Game

Game Face

Final Down

Like Us Duet

A Boy Like You

A Girl Like Me

The Falling Series

This Is Falling

You And Everything After

The Girl I Was Before

In Your Dreams

The Harper Boys

Wild Reckless

Wicked Restless

Standalone Reads

The Moon and Back

Southpaw

Candy Colored Sky

Cowboy Villain Damsel Duel

Drummer Girl

BRED

The Hard Count

Memphis

Hold My Breath

Blindness

How We Deal With Gravity